T0130162

Praise for Sharon Pape and her novels

"Pape has a sure-handed balance of humor and action."
—**Julie Hyzy**, *New York Times* bestselling author

This Magick Marmot

"Magical, mystical and marvelous fun! *This Magick Marmot* is a delightful whodunit with just the right touch of magic to keep the pages turning."
—**Debra H. Goldstein**, Anthony and Agatha nominated author of the Sarah Blair mystery series

"Sharon Pape's *This Magick Marmot* will keep you spellbound [...] *This Magick Marmot* kept me reading well past the magickal hour of midnight. With spells, charms, and ghosts, Sharon Pape has conjured up another enchanting mystery."
—**Kym Roberts**, author of the Book Barn Mysteries

"Another magickal romp with Kailyn Wilde, her aunt, their ancestor Merlin and Merlin's marmot as they investigate the murders connected to a ten-year-old drowning. A pure cozy delight!"
—**Marilyn Levinson** aka **Allison Brook**, Agatha nominee and author of the Haunted Library mystery series

Magick & Mayhem

"Magic, Merlin, and murder are a great mix for this debut cozy. Up to her ears in problems, both magickal and mortal, Kailyn's a fun and adventuresome heroine. Crafting a spell, summoning a familiar, and solving a murder shouldn't be this hard—or this fun."
—**Lynn Cahoon**, *New York Times* and *USA Today* best-selling author

"Sharon Pape's *Magick & Mayhem* is spellbinding, with magical prose, a wizardly plot, and a charming sleuth who, while attempting to protect a cast of sometimes difficult and always surprising characters, has a penchant for accidentally revealing her own powers and secrets to exactly the wrong people."

Other Books by Sharon Pape

Magickal Mystery Lore*
Magick Run Amok*
That Olde White Magick*
Magick & Mayhem*
Sketcher in the Rye
Alibis and Amethysts
Sketch a Falling Star
To Sketch a Thief
Sketch Me if You Can

*Available from Lyrical Press, an imprint of Kensington Publishing Corp.

This Magick Marmot

An Abracadabra Mysery

Sharon Pape

LYRICAL UNDERGROUND
Kensington Publishing Corp.
www.kensingtonbooks.com

LYRICAL UNDERGROUND BOOKS are published by

Kensington Publishing Corp.
119 West 40th Street
New York, NY 10018

All Kensington titles, imprints, and distributed lines are available at special quantity discounts for bulk purchases for sales promotion, premiums, fund-raising, educational, or institutional use.

Special book excerpts or customized printings can also be created to fit specific needs. For details, write or phone the office of the Kensington Sales Manager: Kensington Publishing Corp., 119 West 40th Street, New York, NY 10018. Attn. Sales Department. Phone: 1-800-221-2647.

Lyrical Underground and Lyrical Underground logo Reg. US Pat. & TM Off.

First Electronic Edition: April 2020
ISBN-13: 978-1-5161-0874-9 (ebook)
ISBN-10: 1-5161-0874-4 (ebook)

First Print Edition: April 2020
ISBN-13: 978-1-5161-0875-6
ISBN-10: 1-5161-0875-2

Printed in the United States of America

To Loki—welcome to your furever home.

Chapter 1

Tilly stood in the doorway, surveying my bedroom. Dresses covered the bed, shoes littered the floor. I was standing in the middle of the mess in my bra and panties, no closer to a decision than I had been thirty minutes earlier. Sashkatu, who had no interest in fashion or human dilemmas, had fallen asleep on the high ground of my pillow, safely beyond the tide of clothing. The five younger cats had run for their hidey-holes when the second dress hit the bed.

"I expected to see you all decked out by this time." My aunt sounded disappointed. "If you don't get moving, you'll miss the whole cocktail hour."

"You just want to hear the reunion gossip," I teased her.

She lifted her chin in mock indignation. "I'll have you know that I merely wish to learn how everyone is doing in their chosen field of endeavor, who married whom and how many little ones they have." In her defense, I couldn't think of a single time she'd relished hearing ugly gossip, with the exception of gossip about our nemesis, Beverly. But I couldn't fault her there.

She moved a few of the dresses aside and sat on the edge of my bed. "It's not like you to be this indecisive. Any one of these would look smashing on you. But that isn't the real problem, is it?" She arched one eyebrow at me.

She was right of course. From the day back in January when I received the first email about my ten year high school reunion, I'd been dealing with a mixture of nostalgia, curiosity and dread. Now that the Welcome Back Dinner was upon me, *dread* had claimed top billing. It thrummed in my veins like the background music in a thriller. I'd considered skipping the entire weekend, but that wasn't a practical solution in a town the size of

New Camel. If I didn't show up for the reunion, the reunion would come and find me.

I plucked a red and white flowered sundress off the bed and shimmied into it. I would look festive even if I didn't feel that way. "This reunion is going to be like reliving the night of the prom."

"Come here so I can zip you," Tilly said. I went over to her and scrunched down so she could pull the zipper to the top. "Ten years is a long time. I guarantee you that most of the kids won't bring it up or even think about it."

I sat down beside her. "Scott and I were friends for as long as I can remember, Aunt Tilly. He was never a risk taker. His voice was always the voice of caution. And poor Genna was traumatized because she was in the water too and doesn't remember anything."

Tilly took my hands in hers. "Scott is at peace. You must find a way to let it go dear girl. Now," she continued in a more Tilly-like tone, "that dress is simply begging for your fabulous red patent leather peep toe sling backs. If I didn't have arthritis and bunions, I'd be strutting around in them every day." An image of her *strutting around* in one of her muumuus with my shiny red heels on her feet made me smile. I kissed her cheek.

"That's more like it. My work here is done." She consulted her watch and sprang to her feet so quickly that I heard her knees pop and creak. She winced, but didn't complain. "I'd best get home before Merlin runs out of patience waiting for dinner and orders a dozen pizzas." She wasn't using hyperbole. We'd been down that particular road before.

Half an hour later, I slapped on what felt like a serviceable smile and walked into the lobby of the Waverly Hotel, which had opened less than two months earlier. All the finishes were high-end, so dazzling and bright they made me a little dizzy, even though I'd already been there with Travis for dinner. Maybe the malaise had more to do with the reunion itself than the lights ricocheting off the shiny surfaces. I sank into one of the elegant armchairs, until I felt properly anchored to the ground again. Once I felt better, I had no problem finding the room where the cocktail hour was being held. I just followed the noise.

The reunion invitation had specified that the Friday night dinner was strictly for alums. It was described as a time to catch up with old friends without boring our spouses and significant others. Saturday night would include everyone. Travis had beamed with relief when I told him he wasn't expected to attend the Friday night *shindig*—his word.

The cocktail hour was in full swing. A highly polished bar ran the length of the room, shelving on the wall behind it filled with gleaming glassware and liquor bottles of every shape and color. Small tables were scattered around the rest of the space, but no one was seated. There was too much catching up to do.

Before I could take another step into the room, two of my closest friends from kindergarten through high school, spotted me and shrieked like adolescents at a boy band concert. They rushed over to me, trying not to spill their cocktails on the way. Seeing them brought back a rush of good memories that made me glad I'd come.

We were as different as three girls could be. Charlotte was always ready for a party, always over the top in everything she did. She took words like *no* or *can't* as suggestions and went full tilt for whatever her heart demanded. Genna liked a good time too, but she also had a serious side. Her ability to argue any point made her queen of the debate club and put off many a young man. I was the most conservative and circumspect of the group, because I had to be.

They'd both gone off to college in California, and the west coast weather and vibe had wooed them into staying out there. At first we tried to keep our relationships going by email, phone and an occasional visit, but it became clear to me early on that life was pulling us in different directions. The threads that had drawn us together as kids, unraveled as we spread our wings.

Genna caught me around the shoulders. "The third musketeer!" Her mother had dubbed us the three musketeers back in elementary school and taught us the famous phrase that came from the story about them. We used it whenever possible, to the chagrin of many a teacher.

"One for all and all for one!" Charlotte sang out, stumbling in her stilettos and plowing into me. Instead of pressing her cheek to mine, she came in hard and we smacked cheekbones. She grabbed onto Genna for balance, their drinks splashing everywhere. We all would have gone down in a heap, if not for the silent spell I remembered from childhood:

> We stand up tall; we do not fall,
> I know we have the wherewithal.

The spell stopped us on our downward spiral, suspending us in midair for a split second before reversing our course. As soon as we approached vertical, our equilibrium kicked back in. It all happened so fast, I was probably the only one who noticed the blip. If someone *had* seen it, they were apt to blame their alcohol intake.

When we didn't hit the floor, my pals dissolved into giddy laughter and I joined in. Genna was breathless. "I was sure we were going down."

"It's the alcohol," I said, "it messes with your inner ear and how you perceive things." They were both inebriated enough to take my word for it.

"Are you okay?" Charlotte gingerly touched the spot on my cheek. I pulled back, surprised by the pain. "We have to get this girl some anesthetic," she said threading her arm through mine and steering me toward the bar.

Genna ordered me a club soda and lime. "That's not going to make her feel better," Charlotte protested. Genna reminded her discretely that I couldn't drink. As far as anyone knew, I abstained due to stomach issues. I hated to lie, especially to close friends, but I was forbidden from telling anyone about the ins and outs of our magick. "It's for our safety," my grandmother Bronwen had explained, when I'd railed against the restriction. Since it only took a little alcohol to loosen Charlotte's lips, I realized my family had been right to enforce the rule.

Genna asked for another Dirty Martini.

"Sorry, I forgot," Charlotte murmured. "Sorry about your cheek too." Her tone was so pitiful and out of character, it bought us another round of laughter.

"Hey, I'd know that laugh anywhere."

The voice came from behind us. I turned around to find Adam Hart grinning at me. His face was fuller, his forehead higher as his hairline started to recede. He was my first boyfriend in high school. I recalled a movie date, a dinner date, a few study dates, and a couple of kisses I had to initiate. He was that shy. No hearts were broken when it was over—perfect first boyfriend material.

Genna and Charlotte excused themselves and left us to chat. When I asked Adam how he was doing, he held up his left hand with its band of gold and pulled up a picture on his phone of his two young daughters wearing tutus and ballet slippers.

"They're adorable. Looks like you got started right out of the gate."

He returned the phone to his shirt pocket. "Stacy and I met at freshman orientation and we married the summer after graduation. Those were the longest four years of my life. How about you?" he asked, glancing down at my hands. "Hasn't anyone swept you off your feet yet?"

"There's someone hard at work on it. You'll meet him tomorrow night. Will I get to meet the woman who's made you so happy?"

"She'll be there. You're going to love her."

A guy whose name eluded me clapped Adam on the back. "Look at you," he said with a short bark of a laugh, "gaining weight and losing hair ahead of schedule."

Adam turned to him with a wide grin. "Says the guy who had to attend summer school so he wouldn't get left back."

"Hey man, I was all about priorities—studying women instead of chemistry and math."

I left them to their put-downs. I've never understood the way men insult and ridicule each other. If we women did that with our friends, we'd be friendless in no time. I went looking for a place to discard my glass. Between the air conditioning that was cranked up to frigid and the cold drink, my fingers were getting numb. A moment later, a busboy came by carrying a tray of discarded drinks as if I'd cast a spell to make him appear. Could I have subconsciously summoned him? I'd have to look into it. According to Morgana, any skills I left untried, by the time I reached thirty, would lie dormant for the rest of my life. I chafed at having a deadline, but it had made me more alert to possible new talents I should take out for a spin.

I spotted a knot of women across the room—the three other founding members of the Green Love Circle we started as juniors. The club arranged for people in the environmental field to address the student body several times a year. It also raised money and awareness to shut down puppy mills and promote no-kill animal shelters. I was headed in their direction when Ashley Rennet stepped into my path.

My heart clenched. She and Scott had been voted most likely to wed. I hadn't seen her since his funeral. According to the grapevine, she'd gone off to college in Maine as planned, but dropped out after the first semester. I felt bad about not reaching out to her back then to see how she was doing, but I'd lost Scott too and I didn't know how to comfort either one of us.

In my mind, I had imagined Ashley losing weight, her face wan, dark circles beneath her eyes. I was relieved to see I was wrong. She looked exactly as I remembered her. However heartbroken she may have been, she'd made it back to herself. That was before I noticed Scott's class ring on its silver chain around her neck, the way it had been all senior year – engaged to be engaged. It was possible she'd just put it on for the reunion, but it was more likely she'd never taken it off.

She had to know it would deter men from asking her out. And if a man did approach her, when he asked about the ring, her explanation would surely have sent him running. The ring was like a silver cross worn to keep vampires away. In Ashley's case, she wore it to keep her life from moving on.

Anticipating this encounter, I'd come up with a few neutral things to say that wouldn't be likely to upset her. But when I opened my mouth, they all gushed out at once. "It's so good to see you. You look wonderful. How are you? Where do you call home these days?"

Sidestepping my embarrassing attempt at conversation, she answered the last question. "I'm still in Maine. It's quiet – folks there mind their own business." She spoke softly, slowly, as if the whole cadence of her being had been transformed by the pace of her life there. "Turned out college wasn't for me. I went to baking school instead and found my niche. Now I have my own little bakeshop." There was satisfaction in her tone. Who's to say that didn't qualify as happiness? "Are you still here in New Camel?" she asked.

I nodded. "Still working in Abracadabra." I decided not to mention that Morgana and Bronwen had died. I didn't want our conversation to be about death.

"I used to love browsing in your shop," she said wistfully. "All the great natural cures and the best makeup. I've never found products anywhere else that measured up. Plus yours didn't cost a fortune. I have to make time to stop into Abracadabra before I head home."

"Great. I'll show you all our new merchandise." We smiled at each other. I tried to think of something else to say, but came up empty. Our smiles were wilting and the silence was growing awkward. Ashley finally rescued us both.

"So tell me, what do you do when you're not running the shop?"

I could tell her about Travis, but that might be like rubbing salt into a wound, albeit a ten year old wound. Besides, she'd meet him on Saturday night. "Well, I've been hunting down killers in my spare time." And just like that I shoved my foot in my mouth and halfway down my throat—what my grandmother used to call *hoof in mouth disease.* When I made a social blunder, I didn't do it by half measure.

I heard Ashley's breath catch in her throat. "Seriously? Are you good at it?"

"I've done okay, but I've only tackled a few cases." I knew what was coming next. I'd set myself up for it. Was my brain back home snoozing with Sashkatu?

"Have you looked any further into Scott's death?" Like me, she believed there was more to his passing than the official version.

"I haven't," I admitted. "I doubt I could find anything after all this time. And Duggan, he's the head detective now, he would never give me access to the old files. We're not exactly on good terms. In fact he'd like nothing better than an opportunity to lock me up and throw away the key."

"Would you try—as a favor to me?" Ashley's voice wobbled. "No, forget me. Do it for Scott and what his friendship meant to you."

I don't like being manipulated. Attempts to *handle* me that way are usually doomed to failure. But I told her I'd do what I could, because there was a chance that with more information she might finally be able to put Scott's death behind her. And maybe I could too.

The lights flickered a few times and as the room quieted, the maitre d' invited us into the adjacent room for dinner. There were no cards telling us where to sit. The reunion committee had wanted it to be more organic, letting the alums decide on the spot with whom they wished to eat and reminisce. As a result, there were several chaotic minutes that resembled the Oklahoma Land Rush. Since the tables only held six, many of the alums had to settle for seats wherever they could find them. There was almost a skirmish between a group of cheerleaders and a group of computer nerds for possession of one table. The maitre d' came to the rescue by setting up an additional table before things got out of hand. The reunion committee would have been wise to take note, if they had any intention of presiding over another milestone event in the coming years.

I headed straight for the table Green Love had staked out. They were holding the last seat for me. I made my way around the table saying a proper *hello* to all the members, since I didn't have the opportunity earlier. I'd worked so closely with them on issues that were often emotional in nature that the bonds we formed were easily reclaimed.

The evening flew by too fast. We were all groaning about overeating and simultaneously wondering what was for dessert. Charlotte stopped at my table to hug my neck on her way to the bathroom. "I love you. You're like the sister I never had."

"You have two sisters," I reminded her.

"Wow, you're right—I do! How about that?!"

I grabbed her hand before she could walk away. "Charlotte, promise me you won't drink any more tonight."

"I promise. Just coffee. *Strong* coffee." She kissed my cheek and teetered off to find the restroom. Less than a minute later, a horrific scream ripped through the air. I knew that scream—it was Charlotte. I jumped out of my seat and ran through the lobby toward the sound of her cries. When I reached the restroom, I had to elbow my way through the growing crowd outside.

I'm sure I got a lot of nasty looks, but I wasn't paying attention. I burst through the door into the ladies room.

"Get out! Get away," Charlotte yelled before she realized it was me. She was sitting on the porcelain tile, shaking. Beside her Genna lay face up, her head in a dark pool of blood. I sank to the floor.

"I think she's dead," Charlotte sobbed. A siren screamed in the distance. Whoever was manning the New Camel police substation was already on his way. The paramedics and detective Duggan wouldn't be far behind. I steeled myself to take a better look at Genna. Foam oozed from her mouth and down her chin. Her dark eyes stared back at me as if she too were wondering what on earth had happened.

Chapter 2

After leaving the hotel, I called Travis so he could scoop the other networks with news of another possible murder in New Camel. It was a vague report at best. Although I gave him the victim's name, he couldn't divulge it until we were sure her family had been notified. And he couldn't say it was definitely murder, until the Medical Examiner came to that conclusion. He kept asking me if I was all right. By the fifth time, I threatened to hang up on him. He said he was anchoring the morning news, but he'd come by in the afternoon for background on Genna and my take from inside the reunion on the way things went down.

When the phone rang at five thirty in the morning, I wasn't surprised to hear my aunt's pained question. "Did you lose my number?"

"I didn't forget to call you, Aunt Tilly. I was so shell-shocked last night, I thought you'd understand if I waited till morning." Playing on her sympathies had worked back in my childhood, but she didn't seem to be in a forgiving mood.

"I should have heard what happened from you, not from Beverly, who called and woke me at five fifteen. She was absolutely gloating, because you hadn't told me."

"I am so sorry you had to deal with her. I can't believe she called you that early. It's my fault—I should have told you last night. I really am sorry."

"You're forgiven," she relented. "At least Beverly didn't know the victim's name or the cause of death. She wanted me to let her know if I learned anything more – do you believe the audacity? She'd better not hold her breath."

I told Tilly everything I knew—the deceased was Genna Harlowe. Tilly had known her for as long as I had.

"We're going to catch whoever did this!" she vowed with tears in her voice.

My aunt had helped out with my earlier investigations, sometimes inadvertently, sometimes on purpose. I did my best to keep her out of danger, but I wasn't always successful. At that moment, she needed to be part of the case, so I didn't try to dissuade her. She was always the sweet, funny one in the family, deferring to the stronger personalities of her mother and sister. But during the years since their untimely deaths, she'd come into her own.

After we hung up, I was too wide-awake to fall back to sleep. Besides I expected company before too long. I jumped in the shower, brushed my hair and teeth, put on a touch of makeup, and was dressed, with two cups of coffee on board, before the doorbell rang.

When I made the decision to leave the Waverly before detective Duggan arrived, I was fully aware that he would not look kindly on my absence, or on Charlotte's. I took her with me when I bailed. She was far too drunk and hysterical to have been interrogated or left on her own. I'd shoulder the blame for both of us. There was no doubt in my mind that Duggan would be coming by early for his pound of flesh.

I opened the door, surprised to see who was on the other side. Instead of Duggan's ruddy face and narrowed eyes, I was met by Paul Curtis's good-natured, but solemn, expression. A woman in her thirties, dressed in a gray pantsuit, stood next to him. She wore what my aunt would call *sensible heels*, had her badge clipped onto her belt and her gun holstered beneath her jacket. Her brown hair was pulled back into a bun at the nape of her neck. Her eyes were a steely gray blue. She looked every inch the professional.

"Morning, Miss Wilde," Curtis said in police business mode. "I want to introduce you to detective Mary Gillespie. She's filling in while detective Duggan is on vacation." *Duggan was away?* I would have broken into a dance if the circumstances weren't so grim.

Gillespie acknowledged the introduction with a nod. "We want to speak to you regarding the death of Genna Harlowe. May we come in?"

"Of course." I held the door open and led the way to the living room. Once they were settled in two armchairs, I sat on the couch across from them.

Gillespie withdrew a small notepad and pen from an inside pocket of her jacket. "Do you happen to know the whereabouts of Ms. Charlotte Greene? She checked into the New Camel Motel yesterday, but was not in her room this morning. No one there has seen her."

Before I could answer the question, Charlotte came into view, making her way slowly down the stairs as if each footfall was reverberating in her head. She was wearing a pair of my pajamas that were essentially shorts and a T-shirt. Her hair looked like it was styled by Medusa. Her eyes were streaked with red, lids puffy from crying. Shock, grief, and a bad hangover made one nasty combination. I'd had the benefit of Morgana's elixir to make me look all right even though I also spent most of the night awake and crying. I'd give Charlotte our hangover decoction after the police left. For now the worse she looked, the more innocent she would seem.

She didn't notice us until she came off the stairs. "Kailyn?" she said, squinting in the daylight. She sounded like a lost little girl. I went over to her.

"The police are here to talk to us about Genna," I told her.

She shook her head. "I can't...not now. My head is screaming and my stomach is doing flips." She sounded like she was about to dissolve into tears again.

I put my hands on her shoulders. "Charlotte, I know you want them to find out what happened to Genna. If she was murdered, every minute that goes by gives the killer more time to slip away forever. We can't let that happen." She didn't say anything, but she followed me into the living room and sat beside me on the couch like a dutiful child. I introduced her to the detective and Curtis.

Gillespie started with me. "Why did you leave the Waverly last night before speaking to a detective?"

"Charlotte and I both spoke to officer Curtis," I said.

"Didn't officer Curtis instruct you to wait for me?"

"He did, but I should explain that Charlotte, Genna and I have been close friends since we were little kids. We're practically family. After Charlotte found Genna, she was hysterical and she'd had a lot to drink. All I could think about was getting her out of there before she got sick or passed out. She wasn't in any shape to answer questions. You can see for yourself she's barely with it today."

"My condolences to both of you," Gillespie said without emotion. "I didn't know the extent of your relationship. As long as you cooperate with us, I won't charge either of you with leaving the scene."

"Sorry about your loss," Curtis murmured.

"Ms. Greene," the detective continued, "please take us through the moments before and after you came upon your friend in the bathroom."

Charlotte looked at me as if for permission to speak.

"Go ahead," I urged her.

"Like Kailyn said, I'd been drinking, which meant I had to go to the bathroom a lot. The last time was when I stumbled over Genna. I went down hard on my knees and just missed landing on top of her."

I caught Gillespie looking down at Charlotte's knees that were both bruised.

"So as far as you recall, you didn't touch her except with your shoes?"

"No."

The detective looked up from her notepad. "You did touch her?"

Charlotte frowned. "No, I didn't touch her." She turned to me. "Isn't that what I said?" I gave her a little nod.

"What did you do after stumbling over the victim, Ms. Greene?"

"I called her name and shook her like I thought that would wake her up."

Gillespie held up her hand. "Excuse me. I thought you didn't touch her."

Charlotte bit her lip. "Oh—I guess I did, but only on her clothes."

The detective crossed out a part of what she'd written and sighed. I was beginning to wish Duggan were there. I didn't like him, but I knew his buttons and which ones to avoid.

Gillespie looked up. "Please continue."

Charlotte took a moment to remember where she left off. "Okay…so when I saw the foam on her mouth and chin, I knew she was gone—I've seen movies where poison makes that happen—but I didn't want to believe it." Her eyes filled with tears again at the memory. I handed her a tissue from the box on the end table.

"We'll leave the cause of death for the ME to decide," the detective said crisply. "Did you see anyone else in the bathroom?" Charlotte shook her head. "Did anyone come in while you were there?"

She shook her head again. "When people tried to come in, I told them to leave. Except for Kailyn."

"Do you ever experience blackouts when you've had a lot to drink?" I knew where Gillespie was going with that question, and I wasn't going to let her turn things around to make Charlotte appear guilty.

"She doesn't have blackouts," I answered for her, though we hadn't lived in the same town for a decade.

"I didn't ask you, I asked Ms. Greene."

Charlotte backed me up. "I've never had a blackout."

"Can you think of anyone who would have wanted to kill Genna Harlowe?" The detective looked from Charlotte to me.

"*No…no,*" we replied, slightly out of sync.

"Did Genna confide in you that she was worried about her safety?"

"*No...no.*" We were beginning to sound like lousy backup singers in a musical performance. I hadn't had two words alone with her before she was killed. I kept that explanation to myself. Anything extra I volunteered might come back to bite me—a lesson Travis had drummed into my head.

The sound of a key turning in the front door lock made us all look toward the foyer. "Are you expecting anyone?" Gillespie asked.

"Well sometimes my aunt—" the door flew open and Merlin went sprawling on the hardwood as if he'd been leaning his full weight against the door. The detective was on her feet in a split second, her hand hovering near her shoulder holster.

"Do you know this person?" she demanded without taking her eyes off him. Charlotte was looking at me with alarm too, but Curtis and I were finding it hard not to laugh. Leave it to Merlin to provide some much needed comic relief.

"He's my English cousin," I said as I went to help him up.

"He's a harmless old man," Curtis assured the detective, whose hand was still poised over her gun.

By the time I reached the wizard, he was up on his knees. I put my arm under his and helped him stand. I was never more grateful that Tilly had finally tossed out the threadbare garments he'd been wearing since the day he crashed into my storeroom over a year ago. At least he didn't look homeless or crazy in his new clothes, with his beard trimmed and his long white hair tethered by a leather thong, the one item she let him keep. Of course a simple conversation with him could easily undo a person's belief that he was sane. The word *eccentric* often came in handy when we had to explain his appearance or behavior.

"Your aunt is on the warpath," Merlin grumbled as I steered him into the living room.

"What did you do?"

"Me? Why do you always take her side of—who are these people you're entertaining at such an early hour? Ah, Officer Curtis, I'm glad to see that you're here to safeguard my niece in whatever foolishness is happening."

"Merlin," I said, turning him toward the detective. "I'd like you to meet detective Gillespie." She held out her hand and the wizard took it and brought it to his lips. "A beautiful lady such as yourself should always be clad in dresses and finery. I will never understand the mixed up notions of this modern age."

"Nice to meet you too." The detective withdrew her hand, looking as if she wished there was hand sanitizer available.

When I introduced him to Charlotte, he was clearly taken aback. "What horror has befallen you? Tell me the name of the blackguard who dared assault you in such a fashion and I will see that he pays dearly!"

"It's okay, Merlin, I'll explain later. Why don't you go watch TV up in my bedroom until we're finished here?"

"Call if you need my help and I will be at your side in a jiffy."

He made his way up the stairs just before the front door flew open again and Tilly came raging in. "Where is he? He can't get away with this. It's past time to draw a line in the sand!" Her red hair was in rollers and she was wearing one of her faded old muumuus and the stretched out slippers that accommodated her bunions and arthritic toes. When she saw the four of us in the living room, she looked mortified, but too curious and concerned to run back out.

"What's going on here? Oh—Officer Curtis—hello."

"Another family member?" Gillespie inquired.

"Matilda Wilde, my aunt." I turned to Tilly. "Everything is under control here. If you're looking for Merlin, you'll find him upstairs." It wasn't like I'd betrayed him. There were a limited number of places where he might have fled, since we'd impressed upon him that without identification he could be picked up and sent to a psychiatric ward from which it would be difficult to spring him.

"My apologies for barging in," Tilly said to the detective. "As a rule, I don't leave my house until I look presentable. Charlotte? Charlotte, is that you?" Tilly opened her arms and Charlotte allowed herself to be smothered in layers of faded blue muumuu.

"Merlin?" I reminded her.

"I'm on it. I'm on it." She kissed Charlotte's cheek and headed for the stairs.

"Should we expect any other visitors, Ms. Wilde?" the detective asked as we all resumed our seats.

"No, Tilly and Merlin are all the family I have left."

"Well they do a fine job of seeming like more." She must have realized she'd overstepped the bounds of polite discourse, because she immediately apologized. "A murder investigation stresses everyone," she added. Nice way to spread her guilt around to all of us. Curtis must have seen the anger flare in my eyes, because he gave me a subtle shake of his head—a warning to let it go.

"Maybe this is a good place to stop for today, Detective?" he said. "We can always come back if we have more questions." For a moment, I thought she was going to lambast him for interfering in her investigation, but she must have thought better of it.

"Maybe so," she said getting to her feet. She stowed the pad and pen and withdrew a business card she handed to me. "If you think of anything that might help us find Ms. Harlowe's killer, please give me a call."

After they left, I made Charlotte the hangover tea we sold in the shop. It was a blend of Creeping Thyme, Rose Bay Willow, Meadowsweet, Roseroot, Self-heal, White Willow, Stinging Nettle, and Dandelion. By itself it was marginally effective, but with the infusion of Morgana's spell it was pure magick.

Charlotte took my advice and went back upstairs to sleep for a few more hours. I wished I could have done the same, but I had to see if Merlin needed saving from Tilly's wrath.

Chapter 3

"He does what he wants without giving a thought to how it might impact the rest of us," Tilly said. We were sitting around the kitchen table nibbling on the spare coffee cake I'd taken out of the freezer and reheated. Some families kept emergency kits at the ready. My family kept emergency cookies and cake.

"I have every right to summon a familiar of my own," Merlin said, dribbling crumbs into his beard as he spoke. "I believe a familiar will have a beneficial effect on my magick. It may even restore it to full function and capacity, which should boost your abilities as well."

I plucked a walnut off the top of the cake and popped it into my mouth. "That's fine, but you need to be cautious. Your unexpected journey here should be proof of how out of whack things can get."

"I still contend that it was not your doing alone that snatched me from my home and century. I was casting a spell to find my favorite mushrooms for dinner at the selfsame moment *you* were summoning a familiar. Our magick clashed in the ether and the resulting shock waves sent me spinning through time and space to wind up here."

Tilly cut another sliver of the cake. "There is another issue to take into account. You are no longer a young wizard and your memory is not what it was."

He turned to me, spewing crumbs in my direction. "Do you hear that, Kailyn?" Maybe we needed to rethink the type of cake we kept for emergencies. "She resorts to insults to make her point!"

"If the truth is an insult, you'd better grow a thicker skin," she replied before I could jump in to referee. "Need I remind you about that little duck problem you had?"

"A mistaken word or two proves nothing," Merlin sputtered.

"Aunt Tilly," I said in the best diplomatic tone I could muster, "we gave Merlin carte blanche to cast spells as long as he was discreet about—"

"Aha! You see!" he pounced on my words, claiming victory too fast. "And you, Merlin, promised to keep us in the loop at all times."

"I don't remember your *lordship* mentioning that you wanted to summon a familiar," Tilly said, clearly enjoying his comeuppance. The wizard grabbed the cake and pulled off a big chunk of it with his hand. Tilly took the opportunity to remind him that he was no longer living in the barely civilized Middle Ages. "In this century, we use utensils when we eat."

"Okay," I said, raising my voice over theirs. "Tilly, you and I will consider ourselves informed that Merlin wants to summon a familiar. Merlin, you will keep us abreast of your attempts so that one or both of us can be present if we wish to be." They both grumbled their acceptance. My grandmother Bronwen had taught me that a good compromise left both parties somewhat disgruntled—job done. I carried my teacup and plate to the sink, feeling pretty good about the way I handled the problem. "Now," I said, turning to them, "you can stay here or not, but I have a shop to open."

"But what about the elephant in the room?" Tilly asked.

"Excuse me? What elephant?" Was there some important subject I failed to address? I looked from her to Merlin, who was focused on eating every last crumb on his plate.

Tilly sighed. "The one in my living room."

"Are you talking about a metaphorical elephant or an actual one?" I dreaded the answer.

"A very real elephant who is presently dining on an infinite supply of peanuts Merlin conjured up to keep him busy."

"Don't you think you should have led with the elephant headline?"

"Now that you mention it, I suppose I should have," my aunt allowed, "but what concerns me the most is what happens when all those peanuts reach the end of the beast's digestive tract."

"We have to get back there before he destroys your house." Why was I the only frantic one? I herded them out the door, and we piled into Tilly's car that was behind mine in the driveway. Her house was only a couple of blocks away, but at five miles per hour it felt like we'd never reach there in my lifetime.

Although I'd been told about the elephant, it was still astonishing to see the huge creature standing in the living room where his head skimmed the vaulted ceiling. He was calmly eating the peanuts Merlin had left for him. Uneaten and crushed peanuts were everywhere, and the air was heavy with the pungent aroma of elephant. When he saw us, he raised and lowered his trunk a few times as if he were waving *hello*.

I looked around for my aunt's Maine Coon and found him on the top shelf of the bookcase, his go-to when he felt threatened. He appeared none the worse for the circus going on below him. I turned to Tilly. "Did you try to reverse the spell?"

"We each tried and then we tried together," she said. "Needless to say, it didn't work."

"An animal of this size may require more magickal thrust," Merlin said, scratching the elephant's chin.

"There's no time to waste," I said. "Let's join hands and repeat the reversal spell at the same time. And pray it works."

"A spell was cast
Now make it past
Remove it here
And everywhere."

To play it safe, we recited the reversal ten times. The magickal power the three of us generated was substantial. It crackled like a live electrical wire, rampaging through our ring of hands. It was becoming increasingly difficult to hold onto each other. I tried to stay positive and banish any thoughts of failure. After a couple of torturous minutes, during which doubts laid siege to my good intentions, the elephant started to fade back into the ether from which he'd come. The large bubble of anxiety that had set up shop in my chest diminished with the pachyderm.

When it was over we were all drained and wobbly as Jell-O. My aunt gathered me into a weak embrace, her arms limp from her efforts. Merlin rubbed his eyes like an overtired child and announced he was going to take a nap.

Tilly held up her hand. "Oh no you don't. You're going to open all the windows in this house to clear out the smell of elephant, then you're going to pick up every last bit of the crushed peanuts. And try to be quiet about it, because *I'm* going to take a nap."

I must be a coward at heart, because I double-timed it out of there before they could draw me into their drama.

I stopped at home to check on Charlotte, who was still asleep, and to pick up Sashkatu. When I tried to kiss the top of his velvety head, he turned his face away from me, punishment for allowing the earlier commotion in his home. In spite of his snit, he followed me to the shop. I wasn't surprised.

One of his greatest pleasures was napping on his tufted window ledge where the sun warmed his ancient bones.

By the time I opened for business it was ten thirty. Not bad, given all that had transpired that morning. Several locals came in for refills of products and to poke around for gossip. They expressed their sympathies over the death at the reunion and their hopes that I wasn't close to the young woman who perished. They wanted to know if I thought she was poisoned, and they wondered what she could possibly have done to deserve such a death.

I kept my answers vague, which was easy. I didn't know any more than they'd already heard through New Camel's grapevine. It was a good thing they loved my products, because they didn't leave with any new information.

Lolly popped over at noon, when the shop was empty. We hugged, no words needed. "How are you holding up?" she asked, taking stock of me with sharp grandmotherly eyes. "I know this one hit pretty close to home."

"You'd think I'd get used to death, or numb to it, but it's wrenching in a different way every time."

Lolly rummaged in the pocket of her candy making apron and handed me a piece of wax paper holding an oversized dark chocolate caramel—my favorite. "Eat it when you're alone so you can savor each bite. Chocolate has its own magick."

I thanked her and leaned over the counter to put it on my desk. Lolly was my unofficial investigative assistant; the fudge shop was her headquarters. People in the throes of chocolate ecstasy had been known to have loose lips. "I haven't spoken to Travis yet today. Have the police issued any statements?"

"All I heard was that the rest of the reunion festivities were canceled, but the police want everyone registered for it to remain through the weekend." It made sense. Once they left for home, follow-up interviews would be a whole lot more difficult to conduct. "The official police statement is that they won't be talking to the media, until the ME issues his report." Nothing surprising there.

"Beverly came in bright and early," Lolly added. "She told me Genna will be laid to rest in California. I guess that makes sense, since it's where she lived and where her husband and children are. But given the source, you might want to verify it." If Beverly ever moved away, the entire New Camel grapevine would probably collapse. "I'd best be getting back to my shop," she said. "With all the folks here for the reunion, I'm busier than ever."

I picked up the candy she'd brought me and sank into the chair I kept near the counter for weary shoppers or bored spouses. I had hoped to say goodbye to Genna here in New Camel where we spent our childhood together. It was selfish on my part. I would concentrate on finding her killer—my farewell gift to her. I bit into the chocolate and was working my way slowly through it when the phone rang.

In answer to my *hello,* the voice on the other end said, "Scott Desmond isn't dead." It was a man's voice, one I didn't recognize.

My heart was pounding. "Of course he is." I saw him at the wake. I went to the burial.

"Well I saw him two days ago looking very much alive."

There was a click and the line went dead. I sat there staring at the phone as if I could will the man to call back and provide details. I tried every white magick spell I knew to encourage him to call, with no success. More powerful spells that forced someone to act against their will were generally in the realm of black magick—forbidden territory. I was still sitting there when Travis walked in.

Chapter 4

"It could have been a prank," Travis said.

We were sitting at a two-top in The Soda Jerk, discussing the strange phone call. Since I'd opened my shop late, I'd intended to work through lunch. But when Travis turned up on my doorstep, starved for food and my company, how could I resist? Charlotte had finally slept off her hangover in my guest room, but she declined an invitation to join us. Instead she asked to be dropped off at her hotel. She said she needed to have a good, sober cry for our lost musketeer and she preferred to do it in private.

The restaurant was always busy during the tourist season, but that weekend was crazier than ever with all the reunion people stuck in the New Camel area with nothing to do until Sunday at noon, the time detective Gillespie was lifting the travel ban.

As soon as Margie had spied Travis and me in the crowded waiting area, she grabbed my hand and propelled us over to the small table that was being cleared from its last occupants.

"Sorry it couldn't be a booth," she whispered.

"You didn't have to do this," I said. "If someone complains, you could wind up in trouble."

"The way I see it, our regular customers deserve preferential treatment like quick seating and extra whipped cream. Besides, the owners need me too much to let me go. I'm the oil that keeps this machine purring. Do you need menus or do you know what you want?"

"Same menus as always?" Travis asked.

"Let me put it this way—the only things that ever change on the menu are the prices."

"In that case I'll have a cheeseburger medium and fries."

"A small salad and a chocolate ice cream soda for me." A well-balanced meal in my opinion. After hearing me, Travis tacked a strawberry ice cream soda onto his order.

"Coming up." Margie stopped at the next table to drop a check before heading to the kitchen. A lanky teenage boy came by with water that slopped over the rims of the glasses when he put them down. He didn't apologize or bother to clean it up. In recent years, the summer staff of teenagers seemed less interested in doing a good job, as if the work was beneath them. Or was I just looking down my adult nose at them?

"Do you really think someone would pull a prank like that?" I asked, getting back to the phone call once we were alone again.

"There are plenty of creeps out there who love messing with people, especially if they can be anonymous."

"You mean like a kid making a phony phone call?" I shook my head, answering my own question. "This guy was no kid, and what he said didn't sound like a joke."

"Okay, but why would he claim Scott was alive, when it's common knowledge that he not only died, but was autopsied? I'm telling you, the caller was a nut job."

"Maybe what he saw was Scott's ghost." Travis seemed about to roll his eyes. "Come on," I said, preempting him, "you may not like it, but you do know ghosts exist, courtesy of my mom and grandmother."

"Your family has magickal DNA, and yet Bronwen and Morgana only appear as energy clouds. I'm not convinced regular people can appear as ghosts – much less ghosts who look exactly like they did when they were alive."

He had a point. But why was I having such a hard time shrugging off the call? I ran my finger through the spilled water, making spirals and infinity loops like a kid finger painting.

Travis reached across the table and took my hand in his. "You're still reeling from last night. It's no wonder that phone call spooked you. Maybe we should wait a few days before starting the investigation."

"No, we have to start now. I'll do better having the case to focus on."

"All right—suspects, motives, and opportunity!" he snapped like a sergeant drilling a group of green recruits. I knew he was trying to nudge me into a lighter mood, but I was too knotted with emotions to relax.

"I wish I'd had a chance to really reconnect and catch up with Genna at the dinner. We might have had a better starting point."

"I doubt it would have helped. Reunions are all about the way things were. That's why I never went to any of mine. You can't recapture the past."

You get all hyped up over this momentous event and it's always a letdown, because you've all moved on. You're not the same people you were."

"Why didn't you say any of that to me before I went to my reunion?"

"Some things you've got to find out for yourself."

The lanky teen returned and plunked our lunches down in front of us, dropping half a dozen fries in Travis's lap when he angled the plate too sharply. Margie followed with our sodas.

"Sorry about the fries. That's why *I'm* carrying the sodas. Yell if you want a free order of them," she called over her shoulder as she headed back to the kitchen.

Travis dug into his burger like he hadn't eaten in three days. "Do Genna's parents still live around here?" he asked when he came up for air.

I was lost in ice cream bliss for a moment. Music may soothe the savage beast, but my drug of choice has always been ice cream. "No, they followed Genna out west when she decided not to come back here after college. Her dad died of a heart attack a few years ago. I don't want to intrude on the family's privacy for now. If we can't make any headway with the investigation, I'll reach out to her mother down the road. Our first priority has to be talking to people here for the reunion—they'll be leaving tomorrow."

"Right—Gillespie's freeze on leaving town. I heard some griping about it outside. From her viewpoint, the people here for the reunion had planned on staying until Sunday anyway."

"The griping might have something to do with her attitude," I said. "After spending an hour with her, I wished Duggan would hurry back."

Travis winced. "Since we can't possibly talk to all the attendees in the next twenty-four hours, we're going to have to narrow it down."

I drew up the last mouthful of ice creamy seltzer. My salad remained untouched—what can you do? Stress demands comfort food. "In the reunion packet, there was a list of email addresses for the whole class so we could keep in touch. I thought I'd send out an email blast asking if anyone saw or heard anything suspicious with regard to Genna's death. That could give us some leads. And I think I'll tack on another question—did anyone see anything unusual lately."

"Like a dead man wandering around." Travis polished off the last of his burger. "Flag down Margie for the check and let's get this show on the road."

Five minutes later, we were back in my shop and I was installed at my computer, composing the email. Sashkatu woke from his nap, stretched languidly, and came down his custom steps to wind around and through Travis's legs.

"Hey, when did I start to count?" he whispered to me as if trying not to spoil the moment.

"Sashki is a pensive and wise cat. He doesn't love every person who comes through the door. It takes him a while to develop an affinity for someone." Unless of course you happened to be Merlin. "He's never once made the mistake of trusting an unworthy soul."

In my email to the alums, I mentioned our success as investigators and leaned on the emotional aspect of losing one of our own, taken down in the prime of her life, never to see her young children grow up. I showed it to Travis.

"A bit over the top emotionally?"

"This is our one chance to beg for information."

"You're right. Go for it."

"I've got one last thing to add—a spell to open their hearts and coax them into helping us. But first I have to weave it."

The door chimes jingled, announcing a group of customers. I knew the two guys from school, although we'd never run in the same circles. Tony had been a big deal on the football field. His popularity bought him the title of senior class president. Between the two, he had his pick of colleges. The guy with him was Chris, his constant sidekick and wingman.

I didn't know the women—no doubt wives or girlfriends. I turned to Travis. "Greet them and show them around a little—I just need a minute to finish this." Fortunately my brain was clicking along from my sugary lunch. The spell practically wove itself:

> Sharpest eye and ear recall
> All you saw and all you heard—
> Furtive act or troubling word.
> Help us find who took away
> One of ours just yesterday.

I repeated it silently three times and hit *send*. Time to rescue Travis, who was answering every question with, "Sorry, I don't know. Kailyn will be with you in a minute." He was a newsman, accustomed to asking tough questions, not floundering without answers.

I found him with the group in the first aisle, trying to figure out what the various products were used for. When he saw me, he excused himself and beat a hasty retreat to my desk.

"Never visited your shop before," said the guy I knew as Tony, "but my mom has always come here for natural stuff."

"Do you have natural cosmetics too?" asked the girl who seemed to be with him. She held out her hand. "Sorry, I'm Courtney, Tony's wife and this is Tessa, Chris's better half. If we wait for the guys to introduce us, we'll be beyond the help of makeup."

I laughed. "Some things never change. What you're looking for is in the second aisle." I led the women there and the men trailed after us as if they were wearing lead boots. They were thoroughly bored. I knew the signs. "Why don't you guys go say *hi* to Lolly and get some fudge?"

"The fudge shop!" they cried in unison and made a beeline for the door as if I'd magickally regressed them to the age of five.

"Thanks," Courtney said, "it's impossible to shop for things when the guys are practically groaning out loud." We spent a half hour filling their baskets with products.

"Do you have a website we can reorder from?" Tessa asked. We were at the counter, where I was ringing them up.

"Sorry, I haven't taken that leap yet." I watched their faces fall. I'd been getting so many requests lately, was I a fool not to look into it? "I promise to give it some serious thought," I told them. Travis was still at my desk behind me. Out of the corner of my eye, I caught him wagging his head. Whenever I'd brought up the possibility, he asked if I wanted to run a big company or if I wanted my life to continue as it was. *"Because you can't have both."* Any decision would have to wait until we'd put Genna's death to rest.

I packed their purchases into two tote bags imprinted with the shop's name. The guys returned at that moment with bags of Lolly's fudge and chocolates, instantly elevating the mood. They offered Travis and me candy, but we declined. With easy access to Lolly's goodies, we had to pace ourselves.

Courtney was eating a pecan turtle and trying to speak at the same time. "This is too amazing."

"I hope you can enjoy the rest of your time here," I said. "And if you think of anything that might help us, please call or email." They all promised they would. By the time they reached the door, the girls had taken possession of the candy and the guys were left holding the tote bags.

Chapter 5

I checked in with Charlotte after I closed the shop for the day. She sounded much better, except for a hitch in her voice. She thanked me for taking care of her and apologized for drinking too much. I couldn't be angry with her. To be Charlotte's friend was to accept her for who she was. For as long as I'd known her, she'd been the life of every party she attended, whether it was a princess themed birthday in third grade, spin the bottle in middle school, or a homecoming dance in high school. She loved a good time.

"I'm sure you're ready to go home," I said, trying to sound upbeat despite a pang in my chest that felt a lot like homesickness. I ached for a time that was gone and friends who belonged to that time. Genna was lost to me forever and in a few hours Charlotte would be three thousand miles away again. Travis was right. I would have been better off without the reunion. All three of us would have been.

"I don't know," Charlotte said. "One minute I can't wait to leave and the next I feel a tug to stay here."

"Your life is in Portland. Your interior design company, your gorgeous condo, and your Andrew."

She laughed. "*My Andrew* would be insulted that you left him for last." She grew serious again. "I know you're right. I'll be fine. It's just a little nostalgia for what was my home once upon a time."

"You can always come back for a visit." How many times had I said those words to her and Genna over the years? And how many times had they invited me out to see them?

"I intend to." She sounded determined, as if she'd given it some serious thought overnight. "And I'll bring Andrew. We go back to *his* hometown every year for Thanksgiving, Christmas and Easter. It's about time he came to see *mine*."

I was still a little teary when I sat down next to Travis who was watching the evening news anchored by one of his junior associates. "You okay?" He put his arm around my shoulder and cuddled me closer to him. I nodded, my head resting under his chin.

"Better now." He kissed the top of my head. We sat quietly listening to the news that didn't seem to have any relevance to my life.

"What do you think of this guy?" Travis asked. "It's his first time anchoring."

"I don't know. He lacks gravitas. Maybe it's his baby face. I'd probably switch to a different network if he was the permanent evening anchor."

He drew his head back so he could look at me. "You're brutal."

"I'm honest."

"The two are not mutually exclusive, you know." He rested his cheek against my forehead.

"We should figure out what to have for dinner," I said, although my appetite was MIA.

Travis laughed. "You're just trying to change the subject. As it happens, food is the one subject that works for me. How about gyros? You call in the order and I'll go for it."

When he left for the Greek Taverna, I went to make the cats their dinner. I was a little late. My brood had no patience for human excuses. When I walked into the kitchen they were pacing back and forth. Sashkatu was watching from the counter like a general reviewing his troops.

I set their bowls on the floor and carried Sashki's to the powder room. As he'd advanced in years and slowed down, he preferred to dine alone, beyond the greedy reach of the younger cats. He usually followed me and his dinner, but when I put down the bowl and turned around, he wasn't there.

I found him still atop the kitchen counter. Although he'd managed to jump up there unaided, he seemed to have serious concerns about getting down that way. He leaned over the edge as though wondering why his steps weren't where he needed them to be. He looked up at me, clearly assigning blame. One set of his steps was in the bedroom, the other in the living room near the couch. I chose the easier option. I scooped him up and deposited him in the powder room. He tucked into his dinner with a fervor reminiscent of his younger days, lifting my heart.

I made a pitcher of iced tea and had the table set by the time Travis returned. The gyros smelled great, but even with generous amounts of tzatziki sauce, I could only pick at mine. "I can't get Genna out of my head," I said. "The fact that she was killed on the tenth anniversary of Scott's death, makes me feel there's a connection."

Travis finished a mouthful and washed it down with iced tea. "You think Genna was killed as revenge for what happened to Scott?"

"It's not that far-fetched. He died right before graduation. Now she's been killed at the first class reunion. And what about that guy who called and said he saw Scott? Maybe the killer is dressing up to look like Scott to push the connection. My gut is telling me it's not just a weird coincidence."

"But *why* would the killer think Genna was responsible for what happened to Scott? You saw the police and ME reports on his death. It was an accident—a tragic accident. They didn't say anything that singled out Genna, or anyone else for blame."

"That summer after graduation there was talk," I said. "You know, small town gossip. People whispered that Genna went into the lake at the same time as Scott. But even if she did—what would that prove? I shut down anyone who was stupid enough to say it to me."

Travis put down the last half of his gyro. "How did Genna answer the accusations?"

"She didn't. She knew there was no point arguing with malicious gossip. She avoided going out in public as much as possible, until she left for college. Of course the gossips said that proved she was guilty. It was an awful situation. My heart broke for her."

"Don't take this the wrong way, but being close to someone can skew your perspective, your objectivity."

I took a deep breath. I didn't want our discussion to turn into an argument. Travis was just trying to make me consider all the angles. "What if her killer chose her as a scapegoat, because they needed someone to blame for losing Scott? If you've been grieving for ten years, you may be far enough down the rabbit hole to convince yourself of pretty much anything, especially if you believe it will ease your pain."

Travis studied me. "If anyone other than you or your aunt talked to me about *feelings*, I would laugh them out the door."

"Meaning you won't dismiss my theory?"

"Meaning for now your theory is the only one around and since it's based on *your* gut feelings, I'm willing to look into it." He polished off the sandwich in two more bites. "I don't know if it occurred to you, but we have an advantage in this case that we don't always have."

"What's that?" I asked, thinking I could use some good news.

"There's a good chance you know the killer." He let that sink in for a minute before explaining. "You know whose lives were changed forever when Scott died. They're the most likely suspects in a case of revenge." He was right—that should be an advantage. On the downside, I wasn't thrilled to count another killer among my acquaintances.

"How long a list of suspects are we looking at?"

"Scott's mother, his older brother Charlie, and his fiancée Ashley."

"Do they all still live around here?"

"His mother Lillian does. I bump into her at least once a week running errands. And lately she's been in and out of the knitting shop down the street. Charlie has a wife and a toddler. Last I heard, they bought a place somewhere in Pennsylvania. Ashley lives in Maine, so we should try to talk to her before she heads back there tomorrow afternoon."

I had no trouble tracking her down. She was staying at the Newcomb B&B in New Camel, a beautifully maintained Victorian with three guest suites. She agreed to meet us in the parlor at ten o'clock Sunday morning.

I'd never been inside the house and had no idea how thoroughly the owner, Shirley Newcomb, subscribed to all things Victorian. Heavy velvet upholstery and drapes, thick, flocked wallpaper, fringes on the lampshades and bric-a-brac on every possible surface all contributed to making the room feel airless. Travis, who never paid much attention to interior design, looked like a lion who was just introduced to its cage. He wanted out of there. When Ashley suggested we sit outside, he jumped at the opportunity and led the way out the door.

The porch wrapped around three quarters of the house. We arranged ourselves in a circle of rocking chairs off to one side so as not to be disturbed. It was the most relaxed I'd ever been conducting a murder interview. I imagined Travis and me dragging three of the cumbersome rockers along to every interview. I ordered my mind to behave.

"How are you doing, Ashley?" I asked once we were settled.

"I'm fine, but I'm more than ready to get back to Maine and the life of a small town baker."

"I can imagine. It wasn't the reunion anyone was expecting."

"How well did you know Genna?" Travis asked, the reporter in him going straight to the heart of the matter. He wasn't a fan of small talk, of lulling the subject into a feeling of comfort and trust. His direct approach served him well in his day job, but I'd seen it work against him when we interviewed skittish suspects.

Ashley's body stiffened slightly and she reached up to touch Scott's ring on its chain around her neck. "I didn't know Genna that well. We never really hung out together. Not that I had anything against her," she rushed to add, as if she was worried about giving us the wrong impression—one that could flag her as a person of interest. She didn't seem to realize she already was one.

I smiled. "It's not possible to be close friends with everyone in school. It would be a full time job and you'd never have time for homework." I wanted her to let her guard down, feel like she was talking to friends. She'd be more helpful if she wasn't a bundle of nerves. Travis didn't get what I was doing. He looked at me as though I was speaking a foreign language. I glared back at him. Our nonverbal communication skills were a work in progress.

"I've always been an introvert," Ashley said. "I've never had a big group of friends. Scott was the opposite. He was one of the most popular guys in school. I guess opposites do attract."

"I bet it wasn't easy dating someone like that," Travis said. "Other girls must have tried to take him away. Sometimes just to see if they could."

Her eyes narrowed. She knew what he was getting at and she didn't like it. "Some tried, but no one succeeded." Her tone had a snap to it.

"Were you at the lake with Scott and the others the night he drowned?" I asked. I knew she wasn't, almost everything about that night was imprinted in my head, but I needed to say something to keep them from butting heads.

She turned to me and her voice softened. "I was exhausted and I had a migraine. He dropped me off at home on his way there."

I nodded. "I didn't go either. It was so late by that time, the thought of sleeping trumped everything else." A little commiseration goes a long way. I felt the tension between us begin to ebb.

"We need to figure out who was at the lake that night," Travis said. "The police didn't release any names except Scott's. Most of the others were minors at the time."

"I can tell you that Genna was in Scott's car when he dropped me off," Ashley volunteered. "She was in the backseat with Todd and Alan."

It must have occurred to Ashley that she was still holding onto the ring, because she let go of it and intertwined her hands in her lap as if to prevent them from finding their way back up to it. After ten years the habit was deeply ingrained.

"I don't think the police ever had an accurate list," she continued. "From what I heard, some kids left after a little while, others came later. Nobody was taking attendance. For a long time, I drove myself crazy trying to figure out who was there, until my mom sat me down and said, 'Scott's death was a stupid, tragic accident. What does it matter who was there? What would knowing change?'"

The three of us were silent for a minute, our rockers stilled out of respect for the truth and the pain it couldn't alleviate. When I'd spoken to Genna the day after the prom, she had no clear memory of what went down at the lake. She'd had a lot to drink and only knew for sure that she was in the water at the same time as Scott.

Travis found his voice first. "Do you have any theories about why Genna was killed?"

"I gave up on having theories," Ashley replied. "I spend my time baking. It's much more rewarding. When someone leaves my shop they're always smiling. The only thing that keeps me up at night now is whether or not I remembered to reorder everything from the wholesaler."

"I have one more question, if that's okay?" It had bothered me since I saw her at the dinner. Ashley shrugged, and I took it as permission. "Why did you come back for the reunion?"

Her words were measured, her expression untroubled. "To prove to myself and everyone else that I was healed, whole again. That I could lose the love of my life and continue to live and be happy. For a long time after Scott died, I didn't think it would ever be possible."

Travis got to his feet and thanked Ashley for her time and her candor. I added my thanks and wished her continued success with her bakery. We were setting the rocking chairs back where they belonged, when a black SUV with dark tinted windows flew up over the curb and plowed into a group of people who were standing on the grass in front of the B&B.

Chapter 6

The driver immediately slammed the SUV into reverse and when the tires bit into the pavement and found traction, he tore off down the block. Travis, Ashley and I ran across the lawn to see if anyone was hurt. A man was on the ground, two of the others were kneeling beside him. A woman was standing, calling 911. As I got closer, I realized these were the two couples who had been in my shop the day before. The guy on the ground was Tony. Courtney and Chris were the ones at his side. Tessa was on the phone, her voice shaking. "I…I don't remember the address. W–wait a second…" I held out my hand, and she passed the phone to me. I gave the 911 operator the address of the Newcomb B&B and told her to hurry.

Shirley Newcomb came out of her house to see what all the commotion was about. "Oh my, oh dear," she mumbled as she took in the scene. "Is that poor man alive? There's a lot of blood." Sweat was beading on her upper lip and she was starting to hyperventilate. I told her the police and ambulance were on their way, and as if on cue, their sirens ripped through the air.

I wound my arm around hers in case she became faint. "You'll see, everything will be fine." It wasn't a lie, at least not yet. I walked her back inside, promising to keep her informed. She could have used Tilly's calming tea. I ought to carry a packet of the leaves in my purse.

With Mrs. Newcomb seated in the house, I rejoined the others who were sitting or standing around Tony. I hunkered down beside him to check for a pulse, but when I touched his neck, he opened his eyes. That had to be a good sign. I smiled at him. He needed to believe he'd be okay.

"You were always an attention hog in school," I teased him. "Apparently you haven't changed a bit." He was one of those kids who made teachers tear their hair out, yet he was bright and good-natured—likeable in spite of himself. He tried to smile back at me, but he only managed a grimace. There had to be something I could do to help him. I could try a healing spell. They worked up to a point. They couldn't bring people back from the brink of death. To save a life that was beyond prayer and medical help, you had to turn to black magick. My mother and grandmother had taught me, in no uncertain terms, that if they were ever in such dire straits, I was to let them go. As it happened, the accident that took their lives killed them instantly. But a simple healing spell is white magick at its best. It draws and focuses the positive energy in the universe to help an individual human or beast. With all the people around me, I had to cast the spell silently:

> White light gather round this man,
> Darkness keep at bay.
> Ease his pain and give him heart
> For whate'er comes today.

I completed the third repetition as the police car arrived with Hobart at the wheel. He swung the car around to block the street to traffic at one end and raced over to us. He dropped to his knees next to me. I told him the little we knew and introduced him to Courtney who was on the other side of her husband, trying to hold it together.

The ambulance was a minute behind Hobart. It pulled to the curb with a screech of its brakes. One of the EMTs jumped out of the cab with a medical bag. The other offloaded a gurney from the rear. In minutes they had Tony hooked up to an IV and loaded into the ambulance for the ride to the hospital in Watkins Glen. Courtney went with them. Travis and I followed in our car as did Tessa and Chris in theirs. Ashley stayed back with Shirley Newcomb to try to keep her calm.

"That was no accident," I said once Travis and I were underway. "I'll bet Tony was at the lake that night just like Genna." Ahead of us, the ambulance raced through an intersection on a red light.

"Only a fool would bet against you. If Gillespie has half a brain, she'll order the rest of the reunion attendees to get out of town before this place turns into a killing field." He reached for my hand and squeezed it hard. "I'm glad you weren't at the lake."

"Me too." Without me, my aunt Tilly would be adrift in the world with no family—unless you counted Merlin. But Merlin was a lot of work and that would only worsen with the years. *What was I thinking?* I shut down that train of thought. It fed on negativity, and for Tony's sake we all needed to focus on the positive. I sent another email from my phone, warning the alums to take extra precautions.

When we reached the hospital, Tony was being wheeled into the operating room. Courtney filled us in. She seemed to be coping better now that he was under medical care. According to the doctors, he'd suffered a ruptured spleen, some bruising to other organs, several broken ribs, and a broken leg. He was lucky, they'd said. A matter of inches one way or the other and he would not have survived.

We stayed with Courtney and her friends until the surgeon came into the waiting room. This was the part I hated. The seconds before the doctor opened his mouth, the seconds during which the future hangs in the balance.

"He should make a full recovery," he said. The relief in the room was palpable, the heaviness in the air dissipating like fog in the sunlight. "We'll keep him here a couple of days for observation." Courtney would be able to see him when he came out of recovery.

Travis and I caught up with the surgeon in the hall. Travis introduced himself, so the man wouldn't think we were two crackpots suffering from paranoia. Luckily he'd seen Travis on the news. We explained what was going on and suggested he request police protection for Tony during his hospital stay.

Back in the waiting room, we asked Chris if he was at the lake on prom night. He was happy to say he was down with a stomach bug and missed the whole weekend. What had seemed like miserable luck back then, was now cause for relief. Time changes everything.

Travis had been planning to go home with me, until he received a text from his boss to anchor the news that night and run with the details of a possible serial killer. He couldn't say *no.* The words *serial killer* had the potential to rocket the story across the country. The fact that there was a possible link to a high school prom made it all the more troubling, fascinating, frightening and relevant.

I had to get back to New Camel and open my shop for at least a few hours. I needed a dose of normal, or what passed for normal in my life. Besides, working would be cathartic, and money was always helpful when the bills came in. Rather than have Travis drive back and forth, wasting an hour and a half on the road, I decided to try the new car service that had finally come to the Glen.

Since I'd left Sashkatu at home when we went to interview Ashley, I had the driver drop me off there. I went looking for my crotchety old fellow, but he was nowhere to be found—common enough when he was in a snit. I'd committed the unforgiveable sin of leaving him home with the riffraff.

"I'm going to the shop," I called with my hand on the doorknob. I counted to ten and opened the door. "Bye." I was pulling it closed when he slinked through the narrowing space. "Nice of you to join me," I said as we crossed the porch. "One day you'll lose the tip of that tail if you cut it any closer." Inside Abracadabra he climbed his stairs to the window ledge in the sun and dozed off. I flipped the *closed* sign to *open* and sat down at my computer to wait for customers. My original email blast asking for information about Genna's murder had garnered a few dozen responses. I'd already skimmed through them on my phone in the hospital. There wasn't any substantive information from any of the alums, but they all wished me luck in finding the killer. Either no one had information or no one wanted to get involved.

The email I'd sent that morning, elicited even more replies. No surprise—I'd upped the ante with a killer on the rampage, who appeared to be targeting reunion attendees. They wanted all the information *I* could supply. They probably didn't see the irony of it.

I pushed back from my desk and was coming around the counter to do a little dusting, when Morgana's energy cloud popped out of the ether, inches from my nose. I jumped back a good two feet. I loved my mother, but I drew the line at inhaling her.

"There you are," Morgana said, seemingly unfazed by our close call. Maybe she knew such a thing wasn't possible. Bronwen appeared beside her. Both their clouds were white and fluffy—no heavy agenda on their minds.

"It's been hard to pin you down," my grandmother said. "We wanted to assure ourselves that you were all right." I did a slow three sixty so they could see for themselves that I was intact. "We heard what happened to Genna."

Not for the first time, I wondered if there was a celestial news crawl or a grapevine that carried alerts from Earth. But I knew better than to ask. They'd made it clear from their first visits that they were forbidden to discuss their circumstances with those still hooked up to flesh and bone.

"Another alum was nearly killed today," I said in case that news hadn't yet reached them.

"You see," my mother said, "aren't you glad I didn't let you go to the lake after the prom?"

"You didn't even know about the lake, until the next day when Scott's death was on the news. I made that decision myself."

"She's right," Bronwen said. "You still try to take credit for things you didn't do. Even after that intensive course on the value of being humble."

"You're just as bad as I am," Morgana bristled, streaks of garnet spinning through her cloud.

"When did I claim a deed that wasn't mine?"

"Ladies," I said. "I haven't seen you in weeks. Can you fight on your own time?" I'd thought they were doing better at not sniping as much, or maybe it just seemed that way since I hadn't seen much of them lately.

"You're right," my mother said and my grandmother's cloud bobbed in what I took to be a nod. "We wanted you to know that we don't drop by as often, because it's not as easy as it once was." She lowered her voice and looked around like a spy worried about being overheard. "It seems we've been taking too long to move on to the next—." She was gone in mid sentence. It wasn't the gentle way she usually winked out. It was like she was yanked away by an unseen hand or the crook at an old vaudeville show. Bronwen's cloud had turned a squeamish green.

"What just happened?" I asked.

Bronwen's voice trembled. "I'm afraid she crossed the line. I warned her before we came. I should leave before I'm charged with aiding and abetting." She disappeared, her last words still hanging in the air.

My insides were tumbling around as if they'd come untethered. My mother had just been trying to explain their absence. Maybe she would have to take remedial courses or start at the beginning again, like being left back a grade. The chimes over the door erupted, startling me.

Mimsy Wethers sashayed in, wearing a low-cut sundress with a pushup bra that was one wrong bounce away from a wardrobe malfunction. Some things never change. We weren't friends in high school, we hung out in different circles, our orbits hardly ever intersecting. I'd noticed her at the dinner the other night, but managed to avoid her.

She gave my shop a quick once-over and headed straight toward me. We did the kissy cheek thing and I was nearly knocked out by the heavy perfume she must have bathed in. "Nice to see you Mimsy," I said. "Is there something I can help you with?"

"I have to talk to you," she said in the throaty whisper she once reserved for the boys. I offered her the chair and I leaned against the counter. "Can I trust you to be discreet?" she asked. I assured her she could, expecting her to request a spell to make someone fall in love with her, or to get rid of another woman, or to turn somebody into a frog. I was stunned when she blurted out, "I'm being haunted."

"Why do you think you're being haunted?"

"Because I keep seeing Scott Desmond."

"In your dreams?"

"No," she snapped. "I can tell the difference between a dream and reality. I wouldn't have bothered to come in here if it was just a dream." She took a deep breath and slowly let it out. "Sorry, I'm a bit on edge."

"When did this start?" My mind had instantly gone to the anonymous man who claimed to have seen Scott.

"A few days before I came down for the reunion."

"Down from where?" Did she think I was psychic? Maybe she was mixing me up with my aunt.

"Rochester. It's like two hours from here. Why?"

"If I hear similar stories from other alums, I'll be able to look for a pattern." That wasn't quite why I wanted to know, but it should serve to answer Mimsy's question. "Have you seen Scott since you've been in New Camel?"

"This morning. That's why I'm here. I really can't take it anymore." Her voice was high and shrill, on the edge of hysteria. "He's not only haunting me, now he's stalking me."

"Where did you see him this morning?"

"I was in the hotel lobby and I saw him getting into the elevator."

"Did you follow him?"

"Are you out of your mind? Of course not. Lord only knows what he might have done to me."

"I understand how frightening it must be to see someone who's dead," I said, "but it's been ten years since Scott died. Is it possible the person you've been seeing is just someone who looks like Scott?"

"No, uh uh," she said. "I had a huge crush on Scott for years. The person I saw was definitely Scott Desmond!"

"It is a bit strange for a ghost to suddenly start haunting a person or a place so long after their death." Not that I was an expert on ghosts. Morgana and Bronwen were my first and they didn't look anything like themselves. I wondered if departed souls could choose to look like they did in life, instead of like energy clouds.

"Well then how do you explain what I saw!" Mimsy challenged me.

"I don't know. Did he try to communicate with you?"

"No, but he had this smile—like the cat that ate the canary. I think he enjoys freaking me out."

"Did he appear or vanish while you were watching him?"

She took a moment to think about it, then shook her head. "Look, I didn't come here to play twenty questions with you. I just need a spell or something to make him go away."

"I can give you a spell, but it won't work unless you fully believe it can."

"I'll believe whatever I need to believe. Can we please get on with it?" I found her a pad and pencil. "*I* have to write it down?" she said as if I'd asked her to clean the bathroom.

"Only if you want it to work."

"Fine!"

I recited the spell slowly enough for her to take it down without errors.

Between this plane and the next,
Close the door and don't permit
Passage of a soul unkind
Come to steal my peace of mind.

"Repeat it three times," I said. "If it doesn't work, you can try repeating it a total of ten times."

She looked up from writing. "And if that doesn't work?"

"Then it's not going to."

She gasped. "I've got to have a plan B."

"You said he seems to enjoy scaring you. Use that to your advantage. When you see him, don't display any emotion. Better yet, pretend you don't see him. Hopefully he'll give up."

"Thanks, but I could have figured that out for myself." She slipped the spell into her purse and rose from the chair.

I jumped down from the counter to ring up her purchase.

Mimsy balked when she saw the price. "You can't be serious. You want fifty bucks for a few words that may not work?"

"I'll tell you what," I said. "I'll meet the price you're given at any other magick shop."

"Where on earth am I going to find another magick shop?" she demanded.

"Precisely."

Chapter 7

"You've had a busy day," Elise said after I told her about Tony's close call with the SUV, the anonymous caller, and Mimsy's claim she was being haunted. Elise had popped into my shop with a free half hour before she had to pick up her younger son Noah from a track meet. I usually kept her abreast of things by quick phone calls. We both led busy lives. When I was a kid, she was my babysitter, and as a teen, I babysat her two boys. Once I reached adulthood, we reconnected and quickly became best friends.

"I don't suppose I can help in any way?" she asked with a hopeful gleam in her eyes. "Maybe a bit part in one of your investigative adventures?" She'd helped me with cases in the past and been instantly hooked. But she was a single mother, so I drew the line at involving her in anything dangerous.

"I'll keep you in mind," I said, "but it has to be something with no chance of blowback."

"I get it and I agree. I'm a mom first and foremost. I wouldn't have it any other way. But I wouldn't mind a mystery to tweak my brain and a little adrenalin rush to blast me out of my rut."

"I thought that was why you were dating Jerry. Or are things cooling off between you two?"

"No, no cooling. If anything the boys have adopted him, which makes him even hotter to me. But there are different kinds of rushes. If you're going to be talking to Scott's family, I might be able to help. I babysat for him too, back in the day."

I clutched my chest. "You just destroyed my long held childhood belief that I was your one and only."

She laughed. "Sorry to disappoint, poor dear, you had such a dull and uninspired childhood."

My childhood had been so wildly the opposite that we both dissolved into laughter, tears streaming down our faces until we were doubled over with bellyaches. We were catching our breath and still grinning like idiots when we felt the first rumblings. The counter vibrated like a coin-operated bed in a seedy motel. We jumped down, thinking it was finally collapsing after all our years of sitting on it. But the floor was no steadier than the counter.

"Is this an earthquake?" Elise gasped. Neither of us had any experience to draw upon.

"Outside! We need to get out!" I dashed around the counter to pluck Sashkatu from his ledge. He opened one critical eye, no doubt wondering why I was making everything shake. The rumbling had segued into swaying that was making it hard to stay upright. Glass jars flew off the shelves and crashed on the floor, splattering their contents. Display tables fell onto their sides. I headed for the door, a skier on a slalom course, barely able to stay on my feet. I whispered to Sashki, "we'll be fine, we'll be fine," repeating it like a mantra so I wouldn't think about other things like whether or not the magick shop would crumble to the ground. It was sturdy, but also centuries older than any other building in New Camel, including Tilly's shop.

As I joined Elise outside, she was clicking off her phone with a shaky sigh of relief. "Are the boys all right?" I asked.

"That was Jake. He already spoke to Noah. They're good." She shook her head. "Jake sounded like this was some kind of exciting adventure. He said Noah was scared, but that he reassured him. I want to drive over to the school this minute and get him."

"Way too dangerous until we know this is over," I said, trying to hold onto Sashkatu who only liked this much closeness when it was his idea.

"What about Tilly?" Elise asked. "Her sign says *closed,* but I know she sometimes does her baking there."

"Not today." But my aunt and I lived so close to our shops, our houses had to be in the quake zone. I pulled my phone out of my jeans pocket and called her. She answered out of breath and in a prickly tone. She and Merlin had just made it outside, after capturing Isenbale, who'd fled to the top of a kitchen cabinet.

Down the length of Main Street, shopkeepers and would-be shoppers clustered out on the macadam. None of the structures in New Camel were quakeproof, since there'd never been any reason to design them that way. If they fell, even the sidewalks would be dangerous. We'd all adopted the stance of seagoing men, with our feet apart for balance, while the earth pitched and rolled beneath us.

Drivers had stopped in the middle of the street and jumped out of their cars. Sirens screamed as police cars, fire engines and ambulances took to the roads. I realized Lolly wasn't outside. I thrust Sashki into Elise's arms and went to find her. At that moment, she appeared in her doorway as pale as the white chocolate she sold.

"Since when are there fault lines here?" she muttered, making her way to me like she too was walking the deck of a ship in high seas. She listed sharply to the left as if she might go down with the next rumble, but I got to her in time, taking her arm and using my body to keep her upright. We had just made it back to Elise, when the earth heaved a deep groan and the temblors subsided as suddenly as they began. Sashki meowed to get my attention and leapt back into my arms. If he had to be in someone's clutches, he clearly preferred to be in mine.

We humans exchanged wary glances and stayed where we were for several minutes. We all knew about aftershocks from the news coverage of earthquakes in other places, never thinking they could possibly happen here. Blizzards were our thing, and they were enough.

"Is it over?" Elise asked me.

"I don't know. Can't aftershocks happen days and weeks after a quake?"

"I can't wait. I'm going to get Noah now," Elise said already headed for her car. "Talk to you later."

When everything remained quiet and motionless for another ten minutes, we all became impatient and went back into our shops to assess the damage.

Cleaning the mess in my shop and restocking would have to wait their turn. I locked up and went straight home to check on the rest of my cats. They came running at the sound of the door opening. They'd all fared well, but wouldn't leave Sashkatu's side, until I set out their dinners.

Chairs, lamps and other lightweight furniture had fallen over. Knickknacks were on the floor, some in pieces. I'd see what could be salvaged after I checked on my aunt, Merlin and Isenbale. I pulled into her driveway and did a quick survey of the outside of her house. Some of the roofing tiles were missing and there were cracks in her driveway, but that seemed to be the extent of any outside damage.

She opened the door with a sour expression that dissolved into a smile of relief when she saw me. "Thank goodness you're okay," she said, grabbing me to her muumuu-clad bosom.

"How is Merlin?" I asked.

"You've heard the expression, *saved by the bell?* Well when you rang the bell, you saved his harebrained life. Come, come inside where we can talk."

She bundled me into the house and gave a quick look up and down the street, like a crook on the lam, before shutting and locking the door.

Inside the house, there was the same kind of mess I'd found at home. Merlin was sitting at the kitchen table looking grim. When I walked in, he perked up a bit. "You are, as ever, a ray of sunshine," he said, rising and bowing just enough to kiss my hand. He'd foregone much of his gallantry for the more informal ways of our times. Although I missed the old-fashioned niceties, I never said anything. He had every right to adopt our less rigid standards.

"I'll make some tea to soothe our nerves," Tilly said, "while his majesty there tells you about his latest misadventure."

Merlin's smile collapsed with resignation. "After my attempt to summon a familiar went awry and deposited an elephant in the living room, your dear aunt was concerned about what might happen if I gave it another try." Tilly glared at him over her shoulder. "And with good reason," he hastened to add. "Although to be fair, the elephant was quite charming. We hit it off from the moment he arrived and—."

"Skip the asides and get to the point," Tilly said, setting three cups on the counter.

"Yes, yes. Well the only logical thing to do was to fix the underlying problem we have all been experiencing with our magick."

I held up my hand to stop him. "Wait—you tried to restore the ley lines to their original positions?" We'd all commiserated about the situation, but he'd never said one word about having a solution. "How?"

"With a singular magick spell I've kept tucked away in my brain against a time that I might need it."

"You didn't cross the line into black magick, did you?" A frisson shimmied up my spine at the thought.

"He came mighty close," Tilly grumbled. She poured the hot water and added the tea infusers.

"Not by a long shot," he snapped, having regained some of his vinegar. "It was gray magick—dark gray, but gray nonetheless. The spell is meant to restore the norm. A reset button of sorts. It does, however, require the utmost focus on the exact thing you wish to reset and therein lies the problem."

I could imagine any number of missteps with such powerful magick. "I take it the spell caused the earthquake, but did it at least restore the ley lines to their original positions?"

Merlin's shoulders slumped. "I don't know."

Tilly brought the mugs and fixings to the table and took her seat. "To test it, he wants to try summoning another familiar."

I added a spoon of honey to my tea and took a sip. "Are you okay with that?"

"It wouldn't be a proper test if he tried too simple a spell," she said, "so I suppose I will have to be." My aunt had more steel to her than was obvious with the naked eye. Until my mother and grandmother were taken from us, I hadn't seen it myself.

I tried to keep my mouth shut even though *I* wasn't okay with Merlin testing a major spell so soon after the earthquake, but the words shot out in spite of my best intentions. "That earthquake wreaked havoc in my shop and probably in all the shops. In my case, it will take weeks to replace the merchandise I've lost. And without merchandise, I have nothing to sell and no way to pay my bills." I was getting myself all worked up. I took a deep breath and sipped more of the tea.

"Merlin intends to work for you until you're caught up," Tilly said. The wizard's eyebrows told me this was news to him, but he knew better than to cross my aunt under the circumstances. "And I will gladly cover your bills," she continued, "until your shop is at one hundred percent again. I only wish I had the wherewithal to do as much for the other shopkeepers." When I started to decline her help, she stopped me. "I have lived a quiet, unpretentious life all these years and to what end, if not to help the one who is like my very own daughter?"

"Thank you, but—."

"No buts about it. That's my final say on the matter. I should also tell you that I made the tea double strength." That explained how fast my body was relaxing. The tea was like liquid silk, smoothing the ragged edges of my nerves. I put my cup down. If I drank any more of it, I'd relax right into a coma.

"When will you try to summon your familiar?" I asked as they walked me to the door.

"Soon," Merlin said, "I just wish to be sure there are no more aftershocks."

"You need time to go through the whole cleansing ritual anyway," I said.

He chuckled. "Fadoodle. I come from a time when it was believed that bathing left one open to all manner of bad humors, including the plague. You people take cleanliness too far. The tiniest odor and you're spraying and scrubbing everything and *everyone* in sight." He gave Tilly a sideways glance as he said the last.

"I can't help it if I have an acute sense of smell," she muttered.

"Do you know what kind of familiar you want?" I asked to change the subject.

"I have one in mind, but I prefer to keep it a surprise."

Chapter 8

"I only called Lillian once after Scott's funeral," I said to Elise. "I feel awful about it now." We were on our way to visit her.

Elise took her eyes off the road for a moment to glance at me. "You were graduating, getting ready for college. It was a major milestone in your life and you had a million things on your mind. Knowing Lillian I'm sure she doesn't hold it against you."

"No no, I don't want a free pass on this one. I was wrong. I've known her nearly all my life. The least I could have done was check on her from time to time. Something more than a wave on the run when I see her out and about."

"True," Elise said as her tone turned hard as stone. "What you did was despicable. You buried the poor woman along with her son, wiped her out of your mind. For you, she ceased to exist."

"That's more like it," I said, a giggle escaping in spite of myself. Elise had a way with hyperbole that made it difficult to wallow in self-pity or pointless guilt.

"I seem to remember that Bronwen, Morgana and Tilly took her under their substantial wings," she pointed out.

"Yes they did, and Tilly baked her so many goodies, she grew two dress sizes and took up exercising at the Y, which brought her blood pressure down. But that doesn't excuse my absence in her life."

"You've broken me," Elise said. "I officially give up." She turned onto Lillian's block and pulled to the curb in front of a house that defied easy classification. Lillian called it *a cottage with delusions of grandeur.* At some point in its history, an earlier owner had added a second story and years later another owner extended the roof line to create a front porch with spindly columns that looked like they would snap one day like toothpicks. The house would have benefitted from a coat of paint and the bushes needed trimming back, but the windows sparkled in the sunlight and the porch was swept clean. A woman living alone couldn't be expected to do everything, especially if she didn't have a working knowledge of magick or the DNA with which to implement it.

"I wish this was just a social call," I said, "but we do need to see if she could possibly have been looking for revenge." I shook my head. "I feel terrible for even saying that."

"I think we can do it without showing our hands or upsetting her." I was glad Elise was there with me.

Lillian was expecting us. She opened the door when we stepped onto the porch. She looked smaller than I remembered, her dark hair threaded with silver. She gathered me into her arms and held me tight, reminding me what an intense hugger she was. She released me only to grab onto Elise. I glanced around the living room, surprised by the piles of crocheted blankets folded neatly on the couches. There were solid ones and others in multicolored hues that covered the color spectrum.

"You have enough blankets to open your own shop," I said, following her and Elise into the kitchen.

"I find it's wonderful therapy for my arthritic fingers. And if I crochet while I watch TV, it keeps me from snacking too much."

"I bet some of the shops would be happy to carry your blankets on consignment."

She smiled. "I'm a few steps ahead of you. Two shops here and one in the Glen are already displaying them, and they're selling so well, I can hardly keep up with demand."

"Look at you, reinventing yourself," Elise said.

"To be honest, the extra money comes in handy."

We sat at the kitchen table, where I'd lunched on many a tuna sandwich. Lillian hadn't changed a thing in the room, which made it hard for me to focus on the reason for our visit. I had to keep pushing aside the memories that crowded my mind like cobwebs.

"Kailyn," Elise said in a tone she used when she wasn't close enough to poke her elbow into my ribs, "Lillian asked if you'd like some lemonade."

"I'm sorry—yes, I'd love some." After she filled my glass, she brought a plate of donuts to the table.

"These are from the new donut shop on the way to the Glen. Promise you won't tell Tilly or she'll whip up a few dozen of her own to bring me." She passed me the plate, and I went straight for the maple-frosted one. Lillian winked at me as she handed me a napkin. It had always been my favorite. She sat down beside me. "It's so nice to see you girls. What's new?"

"I'm sure you heard about Genna Harlowe," Elise said, choosing a jelly donut.

Lillian set the plate down between Elise and me. "Terrible thing. First my Scott and now Genna. It's almost like your graduating class was cursed. Not that I think anything else is going to happen," she hurried to add. "Please forgive me—my censors are asleep on the job these days. I can hardly believe what comes out of my mouth at times." She'd given me the opening to segue into Scott's death.

"I never asked what you thought of the ME's report on Scott," I said, nibbling on the donut in an effort to make the question appear casual rather than probing.

"I believe it was accurate as far as it went. It's entirely possible that Scott consumed alcohol that night, although to the best of my knowledge he was never particularly fond of the stuff." She gave a little shrug. "Then again how much do parents really know about their teens? It's clear that he went swimming and that for some reason, or combination of reasons, he drowned, regardless of the fact that he was a pretty decent swimmer."

She looked at me. "I remember taking you and Scott to swimming lessons when you were only four years old." I had vague memories of the lessons. "You do whatever you can to protect your kids," she said. "You teach them to swim, so they won't drown, but it doesn't always save them." Tears welled in her eyes. She tried to blink them away, but a few spilled onto her cheeks. She wiped them away with a napkin.

Elise and I concentrated on our donuts to give her a chance to compose herself.

"Anyway," she continued after a minute, "I don't think we know the whole story of what happened at the lake. It's been ten long years and I still feel like I'm missing an important piece of the puzzle."

"Wasn't Scott involved with a girl at the time…Ashley, I think?" I knew the answer, but it would be worth hearing what Lillian thought of her.

"Yes, Ashley Rennet, a nice girl. I liked her, and Scott was serious about her. I remember when he told me he was going to give her his class ring." She smiled wistfully. "Teenagers always think their first love will last forever. Who knows, maybe it would have."

I finished my lemonade and declined a refill. "About that missing piece of the puzzle," I said, "do you think it involved another person?"

"Well I don't know. If I had suspected someone, I would have gone to the police about it, and if they ignored me, I would have hired a private investigator." I'd given her the opportunity to point a finger, but she wasn't taking it. "All things considered," she said, "it might have been easier for me if there had been a person to focus my anger on. Being angry with fate and circumstances has been a lot harder." She nodded, as if acknowledging the truth of her own words. "Now," she said with a soft smile, "I want to hear what the two of you have been up to."

We gave her brief synopses of our lives. She laughed at the funny stories about Noah and Jake, and wanted to know how serious Travis and I were. It seemed Tilly had been feeding her tidbits about our relationship. "Your aunt would love to see you married," Lillian said, eyebrows raised, clearly angling for a scoop.

Elise came to my rescue. "I guess we'll all have to wait and see. Your turn. Tell us how you spend your time when you're not crocheting."

"I read and watch my programs on TV. Would you be scandalized to know I watch the Bachelor?" We all laughed. "On Wednesdays I meet my sister for lunch. She lives over in the Glen. I have a book club meeting once a month. A group of us started it years ago when Oprah was still doing her show."

"How is Charlie doing?" I asked. He was Scott's older brother by two years.

"He's well, thanks. Married a girl from Pennsylvania. They have a three-year-old little girl," she added beaming. "My one and only grandchild. They come to see me when they can. That old Irish saying is true, at least in my case: 'A son is a son till he takes him a wife, but a daughter's a daughter for the rest of her life.'" She shrugged. "We don't get to choose."

We thanked Lillian, declining her offer to take donuts home with us. "If Tilly catches us with contraband baked goods there will be hell to pay," I said.

Lillian chuckled as she walked us to the door. "Tilly is a force to be reckoned with."

Elise and I were silent on the way back to my shop, deep in our own thoughts. "What do you think?" she asked after parking at the curb.

"She's trying to live her life the best she can under the circumstances. Would she like to see someone pay for Scott's death? I'm sure she would."

Elise nodded. "I'm going to invite her over for dinner from time to time. She might enjoy seeing the boys."

I unhooked my seat belt and opened the door. "Tilly and I will have to do that too. She might get a kick out of Merlin."

"Thanks for the ride-along," Elise said. "I think that's what cops call it when they take a civilian out with them."

"What's the phrase for when an amateur detective takes another amateur along?"

She grinned. "Poking their noses where they don't belong?"

Sashkatu gave me a bleary-eyed glance when the door closed behind me, grumbled like the old man he was, and fell back to sleep. "Thrilled to see you too," I said. I stowed my purse behind the counter and put the *Open* sign in the window. Two minutes later someone rapped on the door. People knocked on the door of a house, not on the door of a shop, especially if said shop had an *open* sign clearly displayed. I was more bewildered when I realized it was Lolly. She never stood on ceremony. Then I saw the carton in her arms. She was leaning it against the door to free one hand for knocking.

As I turned the doorknob, she called out for me to wait. She shifted the carton off the door and took its full weight back into her hands and gave me the *okay*. She toddled over the threshold, where I took the carton from her and set it down gently on the hardwood. The address on the return label told me it was my rushed shipment of jars to replace the ones that crashed and shattered during Merlin's earthquake.

"I'm sorry they delivered this to you by mistake," I said. "If it happens again, just call and I'll come right over. You shouldn't be lifting such heavy things."

Lolly took a minute to catch her breath, her face flushed with exertion. "No, they did deliver it to you, but you weren't here to take it inside. I didn't want to leave it out there. I heard on the news about thieves who follow delivery trucks so they can steal the packages when no one's home."

"Here in New Camel?" We'd had an uncanny number of murders lately, but no theft, unless you counted Beverly's claim that the three pounds of Swiss chocolate she ordered online must have been stolen, because she never received the package. The company made good on the order, but those of us who knew Beverly, knew she wasn't above a lie or two where expensive chocolate was concerned.

"They were talking about New York City," Lolly admitted, "but there's no telling when criminals around here decide to give it a try."

After she left, I unpacked the carton and set the jars on the shelving unit in my supply room. Now all I had to do was mix the components of every product I'd lost to the earthquake and add the magick spells that elevated them far above the more pedestrian products available in regular stores. My aunt had said Merlin was indentured to me until that work was completed, so I went down the short hall to the interior door that connected our shops. As I opened the door and was about to walk in, Merlin shouted for me to close it. Before I could react, a brown furred creature bounded past me and down the hall toward my shop. Merlin, with another one of the creatures in his arms, rushed after it as fast as his old bones could carry him. A third one scooted through the open door behind him, followed by Tilly, who looked like she'd seen better days.

Chapter 9

I could tell by the determined look in my aunt's eyes that she was not going to stop to answer questions, so I followed the crazy train of humans and critters back to my shop. With any luck, no customers would come along until we had things sorted out.

Merlin was pursuing the two animals that looked like huge squirrels up and down the aisles of the shop, raising the possibility that any glass still intact after the quake would now meet its end. The animal in his arms leaped down to join the game. They were having a dandy time. They moved like squirrels in bounding leaps, then sat up on their hindquarters to get their bearings before taking off again. Although they appeared brown at first glance, now that I was close enough to study them, they were a motley combination of brown, gray and a yellowish white that must have provided camouflage in their natural habitat.

We needed some strategy if we were going to capture them. Merlin and I took up positions at each end of the last aisle. Tilly was to shoo the creatures into that aisle, after which we'd use the old squeeze play and each grab one. I made a dive for the biggest one. It was two feet long and had to weigh at least ten pounds. Merlin scooped up another one, but the third one broke free from Tilly's grasp.

"The only way we're going to round up these…" I looked at Merlin, "what the heck are they anyway?"

"Marmots," he said. "I've always had a fondness for them."

"Yes, lovely, but we have to send them back from wherever you summoned them."

"I'm keeping one as my familiar," he said in a tone that brooked no debate.

"Oh dear, I hope it will get along with Isenbale," Tilly murmured. "He's used to ruling the roost, you know."

"One issue at a time, please." The marmot in my arms was struggling to free himself and since there was no longer any point in holding onto him, I set him down. "Which one do you want to keep?"

"I rather like the little lady I'm holding."

"How did you wind up with three of them?" I was afraid I already knew the answer.

Merlin looked up at the ceiling, then down at the floor, from marmot to marmot, to undeniable marmot, to his fingernails bitten to the quick. "It would seem my magick wasn't quite up to par," he mumbled finally.

My heart sank. "In other words, your attempt to reset the ley lines failed." All the inventory I'd lost as a result of the earthquake had been lost in vain. My frustration was building to a scream, but since that wouldn't change anything, I talked myself out of it. However, the marmots chose that moment to let loose with a trio of high-pitched, whistle screams that pierced our heads like metal skewers. We clamped our hands down over our ears, about to run for the door and relief. But the marmots' synchronized shrieks ended as suddenly as they'd begun. They looked at each other, their little buckteeth chattering in what was clearly satisfaction for a job well done.

"I guess that's why they're also called whistlepigs," Merlin said. "Nasty sound. I don't know what set them off, but I intend to figure it out so it never happens again." I had my own idea about it, but I wasn't ready to go public yet. Tilly didn't look like she could take any more.

"We need to resolve this now," I said, locking eyes with the wizard who was being nuzzled by his marmot. "Do you think the *undo spell* will work to send the other two back?"

He hesitated. "There is the chance that we overused it too recently on the elephant. Perhaps you can create a new spell. Your ability in that regard is quite amazing."

"Flattery won't make up for the disaster of the earthquake. Now please get the marmots out of here so I can concentrate on creating a new spell," I said through clenched teeth.

Merlin giggled. "She could be a ventriloquist like that fellow we saw on TV. All she lacks is a dummy."

"I happen to know one she could use," Tilly said as they herded the marmots out of my shop.

In spite of everything, I had to admit that the creatures were cute, even charming, like big old ground squirrels on steroids. I sat down in the chair near the counter and tried to settle my mind enough to weave a spell. The door chimes announced a customer before I made any headway. Beverly, the person I liked least in all of New Camel. Aunt Tilly shared that opinion, as had my mother and grandmother. With excess marmots weighing heavily on my mind, I didn't have the patience to deal with her.

"Why Kailyn, from what I've heard, you have far too much work to be sitting there like a bump on a log. What would Morgana and Bronwen have to say about that?"

I pulled myself out of the chair. "I'm fine, Beverly, thanks for asking."

"No need for attitude," she said indignantly. "You're not the only one who suffered damage in the earthquake."

"What can I do for you?" I asked in a sugared tone while counting to ten and then to twenty in my mind.

"Well that's more like it. I came by to see if you were having a sale on items that sustained minor damage. That's what most of the other shopkeepers are doing." I found it curious that she'd stopped in to most of the shops, yet she wasn't carrying any shopping bags. She must have realized the hole in her con, because she was quick to add that she'd dropped off her other purchases in her car.

"Everything that was damaged here was beyond use," I said, which was true.

"You don't mind if I browse on the off chance of discovering something you might have missed?" she asked heading for the first aisle.

"Be my guest." Ten minutes later, Beverly was back with a few items. She set them on the counter. At first glance, I didn't see anything wrong with the bottles. When I said as much, she pointed out that the lid of one had a slight dent in it. A second one had a label with a corner torn off, but the third item, a neck firming cream she favored, was pristine.

"That one's okay," she said, when I asked where it was damaged. "I just thought you might throw it in for half price, seeing as how I'm taking the other damaged merchandise off your hands."

There were so many things I wanted to say, but Beverly's salon counted among its clients most of New Camel's female population and a good percentage of the women in greater Watkins Glen. She could have a serious impact on any business with a few well chosen lies. I sometimes let her think she'd gotten the better of me, because I had other ways of settling the score. I didn't even need gray magick to accomplish it. All it required was a simple weakening of the magick in the products she bought.

I rang up her purchase, silently casting the spell of dilution over the items as I packed them in a tote.

Reduce the magick in these jars,
Water down their charm
Enough to get her wondering
What's wrong, yet cause no harm.

If she mentioned the drop in efficacy to anyone who used the same products, they'd think she was crazy. And she couldn't blame me for what she'd bought, because she had picked out the bottles herself. I handed her the tote and wished her a good day with a smile that was genuine since she was leaving.

She was halfway to the door when she turned back. "I almost forgot," she said, returning to the counter. My smile drooped. "I have an odd bit of news to pass on to you. It may be useful in your investigation of that young woman's death." If it was, she would expect some kind of remuneration. With Beverly you had to pay to play.

She set her tote and purse on the counter. "One of my clients graduated the same year as you and that young man who died the night of the prom." She had my attention. "She moved back home to New Camel with her little boy a few months ago, after her philandering husband left her. But that's neither here nor there."

"Trudy Campion?" I asked. Tilly had mentioned she was back living with her parents, until she figured out her life. I hadn't paid much attention at the time.

"Well yes, she did go back to her maiden name after her divorce. Look –if you keep in touch with her, there's no point wasting my time telling you what you already know." Beverly sounded put out, as if I'd purposely covered up a relationship with Trudy.

"We don't keep in touch. We weren't even close in school."

Beverly seemed placated. "Okay then." She shifted her shoulders and gave her head a little toss as if she was changing positions at a photo shoot. "Trudy was very agitated when she came in to have her cut and blow out this week. I asked if she was all right, and she started crying. I took her into the room where we do waxing to give her some privacy. I'm all about protecting my clients from the gossip mill." Beverly *was* the gossip mill, but I bit my tongue to keep from pointing that out. "That's when she told me about the ghost."

"Whose ghost?" As the words left my mouth, I realized my mistake.

Beverly narrowed her eyes at me. "You don't seem very surprised. Most people who hear the word *ghost* are at least taken aback, if not completely rattled. *Whose ghost* is not the first thing they say."

"Of course I'm surprised, but everyone reacts differently to these things." I had no intentions of telling her that I'd already heard this particular ghost story from two other people.

"I suppose," said Beverly, who'd never come across a situation that didn't require a dramatic response. "In any case, Trudy claimed this ghost was the spitting image of Scott Desmond."

I widened my eyes and sucked in my breath for effect. "You're kidding!" Once again I wondered why the two ghosts who visited me were simple energy clouds. But why would Beverly make it up? I'd have to ask Bronwen and Morgana about it the next time they dropped in, unless that was restricted knowledge too. I didn't want to get them in more trouble.

"Did the ghost speak to her or threaten her?" I asked.

"All she said was that she saw him twice and almost had a heart attack each time."

I clapped my hand over my heart. "Well who can blame her! Did she say where she saw this ghost?"

"No and I wouldn't pump her for more information. Poor thing is afraid she's losing her mind as it is and she doesn't know where to turn for help."

"I should talk to her—for the sake of the investigation, I mean. Do you have her phone number?"

"I'll ask her to call you. Privacy and all. You understand."

If someone else had said those words, I would have understood. But Beverly had just betrayed Trudy's confidence. How could she have qualms about giving me her number? Did the woman ever listen to herself? A moment later, I realized what Beverly had in mind. After she arranged for Trudy to call me, she'd expect a little *thank you* in the form of a freebie from my shop. She probably wanted to leave it for another time, because I'd already given her more than she deserved for one day.

My aunt called as Beverly was walking out the door. "Do you have the spell yet?" she screeched. If her voice rose any higher, only dogs would be able to hear her.

"Not yet. Beverly was here so I couldn't work on it. How are you doing in there?"

"I don't mean to rush you, but two more marmots have fallen out of the ether and they're all hungry. I fed them the leftover scones and now they're gnawing on the table legs." *Perfect, a little more pressure to get my creative juices flowing.*

Chapter 10

I put the *closed* sign in the window and sat down in the comfy chair at my desk. I tried to clear my mind. Not easy when your life is being overrun by marmots. If the table legs didn't agree with their digestion, I'd have to take them to a vet. How many marmots qualified someone for the label *crazy marmot lady?* And what if the beasts kept falling out of thin air in the vet's office? By sheer force of will, I shut out every thought except the spell I had to write. Fifteen minutes later I had a basic one. Time to take it out for a spin.

I opened the connecting door and stepped into Tilly's shop, hoping the marmot deluge had finally stopped. It was strangely quiet, which kicked my anxiety level up a few notches. Neither my aunt nor Merlin was ever low-key in a crisis. I had a horrible thought—could a pack of hungry marmots attack a human? Would they? I was afraid to peer around the corner into the main part of the shop.

At that moment, Tilly cried out, "I'll have to turn this place into a Japanese restaurant where you sit on the floor." A remark like that would normally make me run in the other direction, rather than become caught up in their drama. But this time was different. This time her complaint brought with it a wave of relief. At least she and Merlin were still among the living. When she saw me, she let loose with a *hallelujah.* "Do you have the spell?" she asked. "If not I'm leaving home and never coming back."

Merlin didn't react. After a year of living with Tilly he'd learned that she was just venting and the less he said the better. He was sitting on the floor, rubbing the tummy of his new familiar. The other marmots, seven by my count, were feasting on table and chair legs.

"I do have a spell," I said. "Let's hope it works." I told Merlin to wait in my shop with his marmot. I didn't want to chance sending his familiar away with the others or we'd be back where we started. When he was gone, I took up a position from which I could see all the marmots and began.

All the marmots I can see,
Go back from whence you came.
The words that summoned you were flawed,
Though you bear no blame.
I close the door to anymore,
For here you can't remain.

One by one the marmots winked away. Tilly applauded, collapsing with relief into a chair with uneven legs that toppled over, spilling her onto the floor. The good news was that the chair was so low she didn't have far to fall. She sat there in layers of billowing chiffon muumuu, laughing at herself. I couldn't help but join in. Hearing the merriment, Merlin returned with his marmot and we spent another five minutes laughing until my belly hurt—a much-needed antidote to Beverly and the marmot brigade.

I helped my aunt off the floor, since Merlin was too occupied by the new lady in his life to come to her rescue. Tilly dusted herself off and headed to her computer to order new furniture. I suggested some kind of composite that was less likely to appeal to a marmot, in case the spell didn't work at full capacity.

I made it back into my shop in time to welcome a group of four women in their sixties, whose company my family had always enjoyed. They'd been making the pilgrimage down from Albany twice a year for the past seven years to stock up on health and beauty aids. The trip had also become a much needed mini vacation away from their spouses. This time they were staying the night in the new Waverly Hotel.

When they saw how bare the shelves were, they were taken aback. I explained about the earthquake and promised to ship them whatever wasn't in stock as soon as possible. They insisted on paying in full upfront.

"In all the years we've been coming here, your family has never taken advantage of us," the most outspoken of the women said, "and your products have always worked better than advertised. We trust you implicitly, so say no more on the subject."

The others echoed her sentiments. They stayed a while to chat and when they left, they each hugged me *goodbye* with such warmth that I was almost brought to tears.

By the time I dragged myself home, I was exhausted. Sashkatu, who'd slept through the ups and downs of the day, including the exploding marmot population, was so groggy I was afraid he'd walk smack into a tree. To be safe, I carried him. I wondered how he would take to the new member of our family. He never suffered change well, but age had ground his aggressive tendencies down to mere grumpiness. And as long as Merlin's marmot didn't try to usurp his favorite snoozing spots, peace might be possible.

I fed my wildlife and tried to interest myself in an egg sandwich, but it didn't go well. I decided to call Travis and fill him in on Beverly's visit. Maybe I'd be hungrier and more favorably disposed to the egg by the time we hung up.

He answered the phone with a jaunty, "Hey!"

"You're in a fun mood. Good day at work?"

"No—awful."

"I'm confused."

"Hold on"

I was still waiting for him to get back on the line when the doorbell rang. I opened the door ready to send any solicitor away. "Travis?" My heart broke into its happy dance while my brain was busy playing catch-up.

"You're not sure?" He caught me around the waist with one arm and pulled me close to kiss me. He smelled delicious, like he'd doused himself in *eau d'* Chinese food. When he let go of me to shut the door, I finally saw the shopping bag in his other hand. "I come bearing gifts. Hope you haven't eaten yet."

"I was going to have an egg, but I'd much rather have an egg roll." I followed him into the kitchen. "Why didn't you tell me you were coming?"

He set the bag on the counter. "I like surprising you."

"Why?" I understood surprise parties, but surprise Chinese food? "What if I wasn't home? You would have driven all the way here for nothing."

"You're not going to let this go, are you?" I shook my head. He focused on taking the containers out of the bag as if he didn't want to look at me. "When you're surprised to see me, there's this flash of happiness in your eyes. The day it's not there, I'll know it's over." His tone was solemn, weighty, like when he was anchoring on a bad news day.

"Have I given you any reason to think that way?"

"No, but it's happened to me more than once, and I'm tired of being blindsided."

I wrapped my arms around his neck and pressed my cheek to his, the stubble of his beard as rough as sandpaper. I couldn't think of any words that would comfort him. I could swear my feelings for him would never change, but the women who preceded me had probably sworn similar vows. Even wedding vows were no guarantee of lasting love. The proof he wanted depended on the test of time.

"I can't imagine I will ever want to leave you," I said, stepping back so I could look in his eyes. "But no one can know for sure. Not even my aunt Tilly. My grandmother used to say that everything in life involves risk. With each choice we make we have to ask ourselves if the risk is worth the reward. I think that's the best anyone can do."

A smile tugged at his lips. "Where you're concerned, that's an easy one for me."

"For me too." I lay my head against his chest and we held onto each other until my stomach gurgled loudly and made us both laugh.

"I think we'd better get some food into you," Travis said, the heaviness gone from his voice. He set the table while I made a pitcher of iced tea. Between mouthfuls he told me about his day, in which everything that could go wrong did just that. From wearing mismatched socks to faulty equipment in the newsroom to a profanity laced tirade of a state senator that was broadcast live.

I told him about Trudy seeing Scott's ghost. "I think you were right from the start," he said, helping himself to sesame chicken. "This ghost is someone dressing up to look like Scott, trying to scare the people he blames for Scott's death. After ten years, memory fades. Odds are this ghost doesn't even look that much like Scott."

"It would explain why the *ghost* isn't an energy cloud like my dearly departed. But why wait this many years to go after people you hold responsible?"

"Maybe he was waiting for the class reunion so everyone would be together again and it would become clear the killings and ghostly appearances are payback. But I don't see how pretending to be Scott's ghost does more than give them a scare."

"Oh I do," I said, nibbling on a sparerib. "Seeing the ghost of someone you helped to kill would freak out most people. And if you knew the ghost was on a revenge-fueled rampage, you might be scared enough to confess and beg for mercy."

"But there haven't been any attempts on the lives of the people who've seen the ghost," Travis pointed out. "Not yet anyway."

"Maybe the *ghost* isn't sure about their guilt." I tried to twirl some pork lo mein into a neat, bite-sized forkful, but failed miserably. I took my knife to it and cut the slippery strands into more manageable portions. "You're still with me on revenge being the most likely motive Genna was murdered, right?" Travis nodded. "And our most likely suspects are Lillian Desmond, Charlie Desmond, and Ashley Rennet." He nodded again. "After seeing Lillian today, I think we can drop her to the bottom of the list."

Travis downed his glass of iced tea in one breath. "Tell me why."

"I didn't see the fire of revenge in her eyes or in anything she said. She's coping. It's a work in progress."

"But you're not saying she can't possibly be our killer."

"No, I can't go that far."

"What's next on your to do list?"

"First I want to speak to Trudy Campion, seer of ghosts, followed by Charlie Desmond. He was two years ahead of Scott and me in school. What I recall most about him is that he loved to tease us and play pranks on Scott, like frenching his bed. But now I probably couldn't pick him out in a lineup."

Chapter 11

The dishes were in the dishwasher, the leftovers stashed in the refrigerator. Travis wasn't needed back at the newsroom until the next afternoon. We were cuddled on the couch, half watching a rerun of NCIS. Sashkatu was stretched out along the spine of the couch, the other cats were dozing around the room. Within two seconds of the front door opening, they were gone, except for Sashki, who must have figured I'd protect him. Travis jumped up too, ready to take on any intruder with the remote as his weapon. He wasn't yet accustomed to my aunt's unannounced visits.

She marched in wearing her new orange Day-Glo sneakers, a pie carrier in her hands. The marmot bounded after her, followed by Merlin. It didn't take long for his presence to register with my scaredy-cats. They crept out of hiding, torn between the draw of the wizard and concern about the strange creature with him.

Tilly stopped at the edge of the living room. "Oh my, sorry to barge in. I didn't realize you had company."

"I'm not company," Travis said, walking around the couch to plant a kiss on her cheek. "And it's not barging in when you bring one of your pies." Tilly's cheeks pinked up and a smile spread across her face.

"If I were just a few decades younger…"

"What's the occasion?" I asked, joining them.

"Merlin has chosen a name for his familiar and wishes to commemorate the day."

"As good a reason as I've ever heard." Travis hunkered down to introduce himself to the marmot, who sat up on her hindquarters and sniffed his hand.

Sashki picked his way down the couch to the floor, stopping a few yards away from the interloper to assess the situation. The marmot sidled closer to him, but Sashki stood his ground. I was poised to scoop him up if things turned dicey. The marmot leaned slowly toward him, until their noses touched and they both jumped backward. "They will be fine," Merlin declared, "let us commence!"

We trooped off to the kitchen, the two new friends side by side. "I think romance is in the air," Travis whispered to me.

"But apparently not for us," I whispered back.

He squeezed my hand. "We'll make quick work of the pie and send them packing."

Tilly took a beautiful cherry pie out of the carrier, while I set out paper plates, utensils and a carton of vanilla ice cream that I kept on hand for unexpected pies. We all took seats around the table and waited for Merlin to announce his familiar's name.

He rose, a frown pinching the bridge of his nose. "There is a disappointing lack of fanfare," he said with a sigh.

Travis sprang out of his seat. "I know just how to fix that." He pulled open the cabinet where I kept my pots and hauled out two large ones. He found two big serving spoons in a drawer and gave Tilly and me each a pot and a spoon. "Give the man his fanfare," he said taking his seat.

What resulted was closer to an ear splitting cacophony than medieval fanfare, but since we had no trumpets it was the best we could do. Merlin got into the spirit and plucked his marmot off the floor. "I hereby name you Froliquet, my familiar till the end of time—or the end of us." We all applauded and Froliquet chattered her teeth as if she understood what a big deal she was. Tilly served up huge quadrants of pie topped off with snowball-sized scoops of ice cream and we gamely made our way through most of it.

Trudy called as Travis and I were cleaning up from the naming celebration. She said she'd be happy to talk to me about the ghost, but she sounded like she'd be happier going for a root canal or two. I wondered what Beverly was holding over her head.

According to Trudy, both of her parents worked, so she was home all day with her son, Jackson. I could come to see her the next morning at ten, during his nap. The time could not have been more convenient, since Travis would be able to accompany me.

We were at her door at ten on the dot. Trudy let us into the small foyer. Greetings were awkward. She and I weren't cheek kissing friends, but I leaned in for a friendly hug at the same time she reached out to shake my hand. We laughed uncomfortably. I was glad to have Travis there to introduce.

Trudy brought us into the living room, where Travis and I settled on the couch. She took a chair across from us. "I'm glad you were available during the day, because nights are difficult for me." When we didn't ask why, she went on to tell us anyway. "I'm taking courses at night to become a paralegal. Once I get a job, I'll hire a sitter or put Jackson in daycare."

I think she wanted me to know that she wasn't a failure, that she hadn't come home to freeload off her parents. She was in the process of remaking herself into a strong single mom. I smiled. "Sounds like you have it all together. Your little boy is lucky to have you for a mom." If I was overdoing the praise, she didn't seem to mind. I was sorry to complicate her life by dragging her into the investigation, but she'd seen the *ghost* and that meant we had to talk to her. "Trudy," I continued, "were you at the lake the night Scott drowned?"

"Wait, I thought you wanted to talk to me about seeing Scott's ghost recently, not about what happened ten years ago." Her eyes flitted from me to Travis and back to me.

"That's correct," he said in his deep newscaster voice that could assure you he personally had every crisis under control. "However we have reason to believe that the ghost sightings and Genna's death may all be connected to what happened back then."

"Tony Russo was run down and nearly killed the other night," I added to impress her with how serious things were.

Trudy was blinking fast. I could almost see the wheels spinning in her head as she put things together. "Tony was at the lake that night too. Am I in danger?" A roundabout admission, but at least we had the answer.

"We don't know," I said, "but the sooner we figure out who's behind these attacks, the sooner everyone can rest easier. Do you recall if there were any arguments or disagreements at the lake?"

"I just remember the guys goading each other to do stupid stuff the way guys always do—trying to be all macho."

"Like what?" Travis asked.

She thought about it for a while, longer than she should have if she actually recalled something. I was starting to wonder if we could trust her answer. Travis glanced at me with the same concern in his eyes. "They dared each other to eat some of the plants at the edge of the lake and in the water," she said finally.

Plants were my domain, I had a degree in botany. Most of the plants at the lake weren't toxic, but eat enough of the wrong ones and they could get you pretty sick. "Did anyone throw up after eating them?"

"I don't think so," Trudy said. "Mostly they just made faces, gagged and spat them out. But even if they had thrown up, it could have been from the booze."

"Did Scott go into the water by himself?" I asked.

"I don't know, it wasn't like I was being paid to watch him," she said, attitude building in her tone. "We were laughing and silly and probably too drunk to think straight. Nobody jumped up and said, *Wait, that could be dangerous.* Death was the furthest thing from our minds."

She had a point. Travis and I were looking at that night from a narrow angle, focused solely on Scott's drowning. But until he disappeared under the water, they were just kids on the brink of adulthood partying hardy.

"Thanks for putting things into perspective," I said. I'd learned that agreeing with a testy witness could take the fight right out of them. "Who was the first to notice Scott had been gone for too long?"

"I'm not sure," Trudy said, "but we all ran down to the water, calling for him. When he didn't respond, a few of the guys went in to try to find him. But it's a deep lake and it was dark. Someone called 911. It got scary fast. I remember thinking, 'This can't be happening. He's going to pop out of the water any second, laughing at us.'"

Tears filled her eyes. She blinked them back. "Divers found him the next day. Some of the kids went back there to watch, pay their respects. I didn't want to see Scott that way. I knew it would stay in my head forever." She'd crossed her arms, holding herself. "I guess that makes me a coward."

I wanted to reach out and put my hand on her arm to comfort her, but I was sitting too far away. "Everyone has a different threshold for things like that. There's nothing wrong with accepting your limits." Trudy nodded, looking down at her sandals.

"Nothing could have changed the outcome at that point," Travis added. We were quiet, waiting for her to collect herself. She scrubbed the tears from her cheeks and looked up.

"Do you think Genna was killed as payback for Scott's death? Did she do something to cause it? Did Tony?" There was desperation in her tone. She wanted to believe she had no reason to fear a similar fate.

"We don't know yet," I said. "But vengeance seems like the best explanation when you consider that the people being targeted were at the lake that night."

"We'd like to hear about your sighting of Scott's ghost," Travis said.

A tremor shook Trudy. "It was the freakiest thing that's ever happened to me. The first time, I'd just gotten Jackson to sleep. I went over to the window to pull down the shade so the sun wouldn't wake him too early. Scott was standing in the flower bed looking in."

"Did he run away or did he vanish?" It was an important distinction.

"I don't know. I screamed and grabbed my son out of his crib. I wouldn't go back in there. My parents helped me set up his stuff in my room. I realize it makes no sense. That ghost thing could look into the other windows too, but I needed my baby with me. My folks didn't say anything, but I could tell they thought I'd gone over the edge. You probably think I'm nuts too."

"We don't," Travis said, although he'd been a world-class skeptic not so long ago. "Strange things have been happening for as long as there have been humans to document them." And my ancestors were no doubt responsible for any number of them.

"Thank you for that." She took a long shaky breath before continuing. "The second time I saw Scott, I was coming back from class about ten at night. My folks park in the garage, and I usually leave my car at the curb to be out of their way. After that first sighting, I was so spooked, I ran from the car to the front door every night. I had it down to ten seconds flat. He came out of the bushes a few feet from the door. He was so close I was sure he was going to grab me. I screamed and ran past him into the house. I've never been so scared in my life."

I wished I could ease her fears and tell her that a real ghost couldn't grab her. Spirits aren't dense enough to do that. They vibrate at a much higher speed than we solids do. If the Scott-ghost had grabbed her, he wasn't a spirit at all, just a well made-up impersonator. But if I tried to explain it all to her, she'd wind up more frightened than she already was.

"Did these sightings happen around the time of the reunion?" I asked.

"Yes, and now that the weekend is over, I'm praying that will be the end of them."

I wanted to give her something to hold onto, something that would prove she wasn't crazy. "Trudy," I said, "you're not the only one who's seen Scott." Her eyes widened. Travis sent me a what-the-hell-are-you-doing frown. I understood his concern, in fact I shared it. I was gambling that Trudy would be grateful enough to keep the information to herself. "You're not the only one and you're not going crazy. That's all I can say without compromising the investigation. I need your promise not to tell anyone, not even your parents." If we broadcast the fact that the Scott-ghost had been seen by a number of people, in no time we'd be inundated with phony copycat sightings. In the age of social media and instant trends, people wanted to be part of the action.

"I promise, I swear. Thank you so much. You have no idea how much knowing that means to me." She was crying again, tears of relief. Travis and I stood up to leave. Trudy hugged us both. "I won't betray your trust," she said with a hiccup.

Chapter 12

"Kailyn, dear." Bronwen's voice was startling in the still of the early morning. I jumped in my chair, knocking over my cereal bowl. Cheerios, milk and banana splashed across the table and dribbled onto the floor. My grandmother popped into view, her energy cloud tinged with apologetic blue. "Sorry, I was aiming for a quiet entrance."

"That's okay, grandma." I grabbed a wad of paper towels from the dispenser on the counter and began cleaning up the mess. One of my early riser cats was already on the job, lapping up the milk. "How's my mom?" I asked from where I was squatting on the floor. The last time I'd seen her, she'd been whisked off for almost revealing why they hadn't been around as much.

"She's doing fine. It's not like she's in a Russian Gulag you know. In fact I'm checking on you at her request. But that's not to say I wouldn't have come to see you of my own volition."

"I don't doubt that." I tossed the sodden paper towels in the garbage and washed down the tacky table and floor. "Will she be done with her grounding soon?" I asked, having no idea what her present state should be called.

"If there's something you'd like to tell her, I can be your go-between," Bronwen said, being properly circumspect. I wanted to kick myself. If she'd answered me, she might have been whisked off like my mother.

"I do have a question either one of you could answer, but now that I think of it, I'm afraid it might make matters worse for her or get you in trouble."

"There's never a problem with asking a question. It's the answering where we may run into a problem. Go ahead and let me decide if I can answer it." That sounded like a reasonable solution, assuming Bronwen had a good handle on the rules. I spent a moment trying to word my question in the safest possible manner, before I laughed at my idiocy. Was I seriously thinking I could slip one by the powers on high?

"Spit it out dear," Bronwen said. "I don't have all day."

"Okay, here it is, I've been under the impression that spirits can only appear to the living in the form of energy clouds, the way you and my mother do. But recent events have made me wonder if there are other options."

"Hmm, that does tickle the edges of forbidden knowledge. I'll have to find out if I can answer that question. I'll tell Morgana you send your love."

I sat in the kitchen lost in thought, until a brigade of cats, under Sashkatu's leadership, demanded breakfast with a barrage of meows. Where would we be without the animals to keep us on a schedule? I fed them and promised myself an egg sandwich on a buttery croissant at the Breakfast Bar near my shop. There were enough calories and fat in it to carry me until dinner, or there should be. In the back of my sinful mind, a little voice was reminding me that Lolly's chocolate shop could provide any additional calories I might need.

At the top of the day's to-do list was a call to Charlie Desmond to set up a meeting. If an opportunity presented itself, I also intended to let him know his mother missed him and her granddaughter. It wasn't the usual stuff of an interview, but I'd known the family long enough to take some liberties.

I had a steady stream of customers all morning, locals, day-trippers, and an engaged couple from Ohio who'd come to check out the Waverly's wedding package, and spend the night previewing the bridal suite. I could almost hear my grandmother bemoaning how much things had changed since her time.

When the clock reached noon and Abracadabra was finally empty, I closed for the lunch hour and called Charlie. He remembered me right off the bat, which was probably because his mother had mentioned my recent visit. His greeting was tepid, which I expected. I wasn't the police, but I was still investigating a homicide that had potential links to his family. No one jumps at the chance to be questioned in connection to a murder. I had to make it sound like Charlie could reap some benefit by cooperating with me.

"You may have heard that an alum from Scott's graduating class was murdered at the reunion this past weekend," I said.

"Yeah, so what does it have to do with me?" He wasn't wasting any time pulling up the drawbridge. But I don't give up easily.

"It presents us with a unique opportunity to revisit your brother's death and possibly find out more about what transpired that night. A buffer of ten years can often loosen lips."

"It won't change a damn thing." His words were clipped and bitter.

"The ME's report labeled Scott's death an accidental drowning. What if it wasn't accidental? If someone was responsible for his death, shouldn't they be held accountable?" *Or are you busy settling that score on your own?*

"Ten years ago I was desperate to know," Charlie replied. "It was all I could think about. But now it would just dredge up painful emotions for me and my mother. I didn't have any choice about talking to detective Gillespie, and now that Duggan's back from vacation, I have to give him equal time, but I'm drawing the line there. If you continue to harass me, I'll file charges with the police!" He was stocking the moat with alligators as fast as he could.

"Charlie, you've known me all your life," I said, hoping to reset the tone of the conversation. "I would never want to hurt you or your mom. But she told me the other day that she's haunted by the feeling there's a missing piece to Scott's death."

"I can't say it any plainer than this, Kailyn, don't make the trip here, because I won't talk to you." He slammed down the receiver. He still had a landline, maybe for the sole purpose of hanging up on annoying solicitors and amateur detectives.

I sat there wondering if I should storm the Desmond family fortress or find a back way in to get what I needed. I went with plan B. Even if I made the trip to visit Charlie in Pennsylvania, and even if he agreed to talk to me, the odds weren't good that he'd tell me what I needed to know—where he was the Friday evening Genna was killed and on the Sunday morning when Tony was mowed down. There were other, more circuitous ways to get at that information, but first I had to call Charlie back. As expected, he let the call go to voice mail, which served my purpose just fine. "Your mother misses you and her granddaughter," I said after the beep. "You're all she has left, Charlie—man up."

Chapter 13

The most logical place to find Charlie Desmond's alibis was on detective Duggan's computer. While filling in for the vacationing Duggan, Gillespie had probably worked from his computer in the Watkins Glen Police Station. But there was another computer in the New Camel substation, from which the cop on duty could access files from the Glen. The latter had the added benefit of being manned by a single officer. If he happened to be out on an emergency call, the building was protected by a security system and a lock on the door. From what I'd observed, cops on duty in New Camel rarely bothered arming the system. And locks posed no problem for me.

I worked it out with Tilly. She would call the substation at a preplanned time, hysterical because Merlin was missing. It wouldn't be the first time. She would do whatever it took to keep the officer on duty from returning to the substation, until she received my all clear signal.

The hard part would be getting past Gillespie's password. Merlin had offered me a spell to circumvent it. He claimed to have used it successfully himself, but he refused to say whose computer he'd hacked into that way. The obvious contenders were mine and Tilly's and the answer was probably *both*.

"I don't know, this is pretty dark," I'd said after reading his spell.

"You want a snow white solution to a dark problem. Such a thing is not possible." After he left, I reworded the spell into one I could live with. If the watered down version didn't work, I'd have to try to create an entirely new spell.

I practiced teleporting back and forth between my house and Tilly's to be sure my skills were at the ready. All systems were *go*. Paul Curtis was the cop on duty. My family had a nice rapport with him. He'd do all he could to help my aunt. Plus he loved her baked goods, which made stalling him easier.

After feeding Sashkatu and the five other would-be familiars, I returned to my shop. At six sharp, Tilly would call the stationhouse. Although I couldn't see it from there, I would see Paul as he drove by on his way to Tilly's.

At three minutes after six he passed my shop. I closed my eyes, cleared my mind, hooked into the mitochondrial power of my cells and recited my teleportation spell three times:

> From here and now to there and then,
> Attract not change nor harm allow.
> Safe passage guarantee to souls
> As well as lesser, mindless things.

I opened my eyes in the main room of the substation, just steps away from the desk. The computer was always on. Crime and emergencies don't stick to a nine-to-five schedule. I plunked myself down in the padded desk chair and found Gillespie's file without a problem. Time to see if the watered down spell worked. I thought of the TV shows where brilliant psychologists could figure out a person's password based on the color of their eyes or the make and model of the car they drove. It was crazy that the same viewers who bought into that premise, refused to believe in magick. *Focus,* I scolded myself. Make or break time.

> With best intentions do I seek
> The information that you keep,
> So that justice we may reap.
> Not to harm and not for gain,
> Only to relieve the pain.

The computer screen didn't change. The white rectangle still demanded a password. I took a deep breath and exhaled slowly, centering myself. Before I could repeat the spell for the fourth time, my cell rang with Paul McCartney's "Silly Love Songs"—the ring tone I'd set for Tilly. It was way too soon for her to be calling. I grabbed it out of my purse.

"He found Merlin," she said grimly. "Or to be more precise, Merlin forgot why he was supposed to be hiding in the basement and came upstairs to ask me. Curtis and I were standing in the foyer at the time. Not only did he foil our plans, he made me look like an utter fool." I understood she needed to vent, but personal grievances would have to wait for a later date. I needed more time.

"Has Paul left?" I asked, poised to race out of the building.

"No, he's in the bathroom, probably trying to decide if I need to be admitted to a psychiatric hospital or a nursing home for patients with dementia."

"Aunt Tilly, you have to find a way to stall him. Bake him something."

"I've got that covered. I'm heating a coffee cake as we speak. Oh, I heard the toilet flush. I've got to go."

I repeated the spell with all the pathos in my being and this time it worked. Wow!—I ought to experiment to find out how big a part emotion played in the success of a spell. But that would also have to wait. I opened Gillespie's file on Genna's murder and scanned it quickly. On the next to last page I found what I was looking for—her interview with Charlie Desmond.

"Silly Love Songs" rang out again. Since I subscribe to the saying that no news is good news, I dreaded answering the phone.

"I must be losing my charm," Tilly lamented, "because he asked if he could take a piece of cake to go. You've never seen a person cut and wrap a piece of cake as slowly as I did."

"He's headed back here?"

"Sorry, I tried everything short of tying him to a chair." Knowing Tilly, I was sure she'd given that some thought before admitting defeat.

I said a quick *goodbye,* sent Gillespie's file to my home computer, and cleared the screen. I had to get out of there before Paul caught me. I tried to settle my mind. One minute became two. *Stop thinking about the time!* I heard a car drive into the station's parking lot, but the engine didn't shut off. Judging by the sound of the tires, the car made a U-turn and drove away. I finally quieted enough to begin the spell. I recited it once, twice—another car pulled in, tugging at my attention. The engine shut off. I finished the third recitation as the door of the little station house opened and Paul walked in. If I hadn't made a last second move into the storage area, he would have witnessed my vanishing act.

Back in my shop, I locked up, set the alarm and walked home. I didn't need Morgana or Bronwen to tell me I should never have cut it that close. Instead of being relieved I'd gotten away, I started to worry. In my hasty retreat, had I left evidence of my visit? At the very least, my fingerprints had to be all over the computer keyboard. I hoped the purloined file was worth what I might have to pay for it.

Gillespie's interview with Charlie turned out to be thorough and boring. He answered the detective's questions in as few words as possible, as if an attorney friend or relative had advised him not to say more than was absolutely necessary. His alibis seemed reasonable. At the time Genna was poisoned, he was at home with his wife and daughter. When Tony was run down by the SUV, he was paying his respects at the wake of a coworker. Gillespie noted the date and time that she confirmed the alibis with the appropriate parties. I would have liked to speak to them myself. Words on paper couldn't give me the tone of voice, the look in the eye, the little tells that came with lying. I didn't know the detective well enough to judge how insightful her findings were.

Of course even if Charlie's alibis were true, he could have hired someone else to mete out justice in his stead. But that option usually came with a hefty price tag, and a man with a young family wasn't likely to have lots of extra cash at his disposal.

I brought Travis up to date, when he called after signing off from the evening news. "A wife can refuse to testify against her husband," he said, "so I wouldn't waste time trying to press her about his alibis at this point. Have you gotten any more leads from that first email blast you sent out after Genna was killed?"

"Mostly repetitions of what we already know or wild speculations about who the killer might be, based on absolutely nothing. Wait—I almost forgot. There was one response I've been meaning to tell you about. It was from this guy Conrad—a loner who never seemed to fit in with the nerds, the jocks or any other group."

"What did his email say?"

"That Genna wasn't the girl I thought she was. Like he knew one of my closest friends better than I did. Maybe he had a secret crush on her back then and couldn't stand seeing her flirting and hanging out with other guys. But ten years after graduation?"

"Loners—they blend into the background until you don't see them. But they tend to be keen observers. I've had informants like that. You'd be surprised by what they can tell you. It might not be a bad idea to find out what Conrad's deal is." Travis was right. I'd been ready to dismiss the guy too easily.

Chapter 14

I replied to Conrad, thanking him for his email and asking where he called home these days. He got right back to me, his excitement vibrating through the computer screen. I'm not always sensitive to remote feelings, but I read his loud and clear. He said he lived on the outskirts of Burdett. It was a town with a population of less than four hundred. It came as no surprise that he'd chosen to live where people wouldn't chafe against him.

When I asked if I could talk to him in person with regard to his comment about Genna, he didn't immediately reply. I'd scared him off. I sat down in the living room and found reruns of Modern Family and the Big Bang Theory to help me relax. By nine o'clock the sun had finally set and my eyes were closing. I dragged myself through the nighttime ritual of pulling down shades, closing blinds and turning off lights. I left the kitchen for last so I could take a glass of water. I reached for the wide shade over the bay window in the dinette and jumped back with a shriek. The shade flew out of my hand and rolled all the way up with a loud thackity-thack. My heart tripped and thudded in accompaniment. Scott was framed in the window, looking back at me.

Why was I so sure it was Scott? With the bright kitchen lights on, it was hard to see details out in the dark. I backed up slowly, trying not to spook him, which was only funny later in the retelling. When I could reach the light switches, I swiped them off with the palm of my hand, not taking my eyes off his image. In the darkened kitchen, there was no longer any doubt in my mind that the man on the other side of the glass was the Scott-ghost. But there was nothing ghostly about him, except the fact that he was dead.

He held his right hand up in front of his face, palm outward in the universal sign meaning *stop!* Stop what—the investigation into Genna's death or looking back into his? And why would he want me to stop either one? Could I be missing the point entirely? Questions swirled in my head, but didn't make it to my mouth. It wouldn't have mattered. My mouth was so dry, I couldn't swallow and my tongue wouldn't work right.

We stared at each other for another minute or two before he vanished. He was there and then not there. I was inching toward the window to see if he had only ducked out of sight, when the front doorbell rang as loud as church bells in the silence. I shrieked again, my nerves on a hair trigger. Had he gone to the front door? Was he asking to come in? It was one thing for my mother and grandmother to visit, but in spite of how close Scott and I had been, this was freaking me out.

As I approached the front door, I managed to call out *"Scott?"* in a hoarse, wobbly voice. So much for sounding strong and unafraid.

"Are you okay?" came the muted answer. I couldn't get the door unlocked fast enough. I swung it open and flew into Travis's arms with so much momentum I knocked him over and we went down in a heap on the porch. I was laughing and crying. Travis untangled himself from me, then helped me up. *"Are* you okay?"

"I will be, now that you're here." I made tea and we sat at the kitchen table while I told him about Scott's visit.

"We've got to go out back and look for footprints," Travis said, already out of his seat. I hadn't thought of it, but he was right. If we waited until morning, raccoons, possums and smaller animals would run through the flower beds and disturb whatever evidence there might be. We left our tea on the table. Armed with a flashlight, we went out the kitchen door into the backyard and I pointed out where the Scott-ghost had been standing. Beneath the kitchen window were four small perennial bushes and between them, the dozen impatiens I'd planted back in June. None of them had been flattened or damaged in any way, but they were droopy.

It hadn't rained in days, leaving the soil dry, the wrong medium for holding onto prints. I didn't know if I was disappointed or glad. Footprints would have meant that someone very much alive was dressing up to look like Scott. A lack of them would have pointed to a ghost, a spirit, with no weight to leave evidence. But the hard ground told us nothing, except that my impatiens would die if I didn't remember to water them.

Travis was worried about my safety. But now that Scott wasn't staring at me in the dark, I was able to be more philosophical about it. "The others he's visited haven't been harmed," I pointed out. "Besides, Scott has no reason to blame me for his death. We were friends since forever and I wasn't even at the lake."

Travis ran his fingers through his hair, tousling the hair stylist's work. "I still don't like it."

"No need to worry. I can take care of myself."

"Wiping me out on the porch—was that you taking care of yourself?" he asked with a smile that crinkled the skin around his eyes.

"That was me being thrilled to see you." I tried to keep a straight face, but failed by a mile. "Come to think of it, you never told me why you drove out here tonight."

"I got these insane vibes that you were in danger and needed me," he said in the weighty voice he trotted out for the world news.

I laughed. "You know magick isn't contagious, right? You can't become prescient by hanging out with me or Tilly, so 'fess up."

"I missed you and I'm off tomorrow. I figured why not start tomorrow tonight?" He reached across the table and covered my hand with his. He understood how big the small things were to a woman. I wondered how many women had been his teachers and decided I didn't need to know.

First thing the next morning, I checked my email. Still no response from Conrad. I must have triggered something in his hermit soul when I asked to visit him. Hounding him with more emails was definitely not the way to go. I had to give him space; let the need to tell his tale build up in him. Just as well. It was going to be a crazy day with two tour buses due in, their schedules overlapping for an hour. New Camel could be overwhelmed by one busload. In the past, overlapping tours had just about brought us to our knees. When I explained this to Travis, he pulled a sulky face.

"If you had called, I would have told you I'd be busy," I said.

"I know the drill. All the merchants here depend on tourism, especially during the summer and the holiday season, to carry them through the winter." The way he rattled it off, I must have said it a few times too often. "So hire me on," he said. "I'm a quick learner and I'll work for free. In addition, I come with some perks that I will leave to your imagination. You'll never get a better offer." I had no doubt of it.

"You've got a deal. You do the grunt work. Leave the magick and all questions to me." By the time the second bus arrived, I was spoiled. My grandmother used to say that a luxury becomes a necessity in a month. I guess I'm easily spoiled, because we were only working together for five hours at that point.

Travis found his niche at the register. He chatted with customers, paid them compliments and charmed them with his mischievous little boy smile. If people recognized him from his stints filling in for famous anchors in the New York metro area, he played it *aw shucks* humble, but the light in his eyes beamed a bit brighter each time.

When there was a lull in foot traffic, he went off to the Breakfast Bar and brought us back coffee and brownies. We ate between customers like kids stuffing their faces with Halloween candy before their parents could ration it. He took a napkin and gently wiped the chocolate residue from around my mouth, then I returned the favor.

At that precise moment, Beverly walked in and caught me at it. The woman had radar for gossip worthy tidbits she could embellish and feed to the grapevine in her salon. "Sorry, I seem to have come at an awkward time," she said pointedly.

I had to unclench my jaw to respond. "There's nothing awkward about wiping chocolate off someone's face, Beverly. What can I do for you?" I saw Sashkatu open one eye when he heard her name. After satisfying himself that Travis was nearby to take care of any Beverly related crisis, he dozed off again.

"According to the word on the street, your shop is the place to be today. The tourists are all abuzz about your new hire." She turned her smile on for Travis's viewing pleasure. I think she may have batted her lashes at him too. He moved closer to me and slid his arm around my waist in an *I'm-here-if-you-need-me* gesture. I appreciated the show of solidarity, but Beverly was nothing more than a nuisance, like crabgrass or a swarm of gnats.

"Who does your hair?" She gave Travis's locks a thorough appraisal, shaking her head and muttering bits of criticism under her breath. "You should be coming to me."

"Not my call," he said, taking her rudeness in stride. "The network keeps a stylist on retainer."

Beverly plucked a business card from a pocket of her tight green capris and held it out to him. "If you ever want a free trial cut, you know—for comparison." He accepted the card and thanked her. I admired his willpower. I was irritated enough for both of us.

"*We'll* be sure to keep that in mind," I said in the way women understand to be a warning shot, but men take as everything's A-okay.

Beverly leaned toward me. "Can you afford to lose me as a source?" she asked in a stage whisper, before turning on her heel and sweeping out of the shop. I pitied her customers, who were about to get an earful of anti-Kailyn venom. I wasn't worried in the least about losing her as a source. She wouldn't let it go that far, because she was hooked on my antiaging products. This wasn't our first go-round.

"What just happened?" Travis asked after the door closed behind her. I shrugged. "We don't bring out the best in each other." He looked no less mystified, but before he could delve into it further, one of the women from the senior center bus tour, called out to him.

"Yoo-hoo, Mr. Anchorman, I'm ready for you to check me out." She had white hair, dimples and blue eyes that danced with audacity. The woman standing behind her in line giggled, her cheeks on fire as if she'd uttered those words herself.

Travis gave me a wink. "My public awaits."

By the time the second bus pulled out, we were both exhausted. My aunt hobbled in from her shop. Her curly red hair had lost its bounce. Her frothy lavender muumuu had deflated like a bad meringue. Travis vacated the customer chair for her, and she sank into it with a groan. "Were those two busloads more demanding than usual or am I just getting too old for this?"

"They were definitely up there on the charts," I said. "I was lucky to have Travis helping me. But are you sure you didn't just schedule too many readings and teas for one day?" I didn't like seeing Tilly so drained. It was an uncomfortable reminder that she was part of my mother's generation and I wouldn't always have her around. As if his subconscious had read my thoughts, Sashkatu awoke with a start and climbed down from his window ledge, without bothering to stretch. He padded over to Tilly and she helped him into her lap. Although he was an independent, often aloof cat, his emotions ran deep. And he'd always subscribed to the theory that one should never let a good lap go to waste.

Chapter 15

Tilly and I sat together on the couch in her family room, watching the evening news and waiting for the medical examiner's report on Genna. Although there was little doubt in my mind she was poisoned, I was hoping there might be other details that would prove useful to our investigation. The camera was focused on Travis, who'd staked out a corner of the Watkins Glen pressroom to recap the circumstances of her death. The room was filled to capacity, the hubbub around him forcing him to shout.

When the camera swung away to capture the arrival of the officials, Travis did a neat segue from providing backstory to naming the men as they filed out of the anteroom. Chief of police Gimble, detective Duggan, and ME Cuthburton took seats at the back of the raised platform. Mayor Tompkins walked directly to the podium, where he waited for silence before beginning.

"Hello everyone. I know there's been a lot of anticipation and speculation with regard to the death of Genna Harlowe. I applaud our fine medical examiner for refusing to be rushed in this case, despite the pressure brought to bear by certain factions. His dedication to excellence has provided us with a report in which we can all have full confidence. Dr. Cuthburton."

The two men switched places, bumping shoulders in an awkward do-si-do. Cuthburton, who was a good foot taller than the mayor, spent a moment raising the microphone.

"Thank you, Mayor Thompkins. I appreciate your patience. I won't keep everyone in suspense any longer. Genna Harlowe died from ingesting potassium cyanide. The poison works by interfering with the body's ability to take in oxygen. Aside from a faint almond smell, it's difficult to taste and therefore easy to disguise in other liquids. At first the victim feels dizzy.

That's quickly followed by convulsions, seizures, and the stereotypical foaming at the mouth most of you have seen on television and in the movies. The final stage is complete organ failure.

"In all likelihood, the poison was concealed in an alcoholic beverage and virtually undetectable. The time frame suggests that she ingested the poison at the reunion. My complete report will be available online. All questions should be directed to the police. Thank you."

A dozen arms shot up in the air, but Cuthburton left the podium without looking back. The mayor hurried back to the lectern to introduce detective Duggan, before the members of the press became bloodthirsty.

"I'm surprised Gillespie isn't there," Tilly remarked. "After all she was in charge when it happened."

I wasn't at all surprised. "Duggan's back and Duggan does not like sharing control or credit. I'm sure he dragged every bit of information out of her. And if he gets anything wrong, she'll serve as his scapegoat."

A reporter shouted out his question. "How hard is it to buy potassium cyanide?"

"Far too easy," Duggan replied. "You can order it on any number of websites and have it shipped to you." A barrage of voices drowned out his last words. "Let's do this in an orderly manner, folks. Raise your hand if you have a question." Hands shot up again. He called on a reporter near the stage.

"Have you talked to the bartenders and other personnel who were working at the Waverly Hotel the night she was poisoned?"

"Yes we have, but I can't go into our findings at this time." He acknowledged a woman several rows back.

"Have you identified anyone in her life with a grudge against her?"

"Again, answering that question could jeopardize the investigation. Rest assured that we will leave no stone unturned, until we have her killer in custody." He called on Travis in the back of the room.

"Do you consider the accident that nearly killed Tony Russo that same weekend to be related to the murder of Genna Harlowe or strictly coincidental?"

Duggan took a moment before responding. Watching him grapple with the question, I had the impression Gillespie may have glossed over the part about Tony when she brought Duggan up to speed. Maybe it was her way of teaching him a lesson in teamwork and civility. Whatever her reasons, I enjoyed watching him squirm.

"I'm not in a position to address that at this time," he said finally. "This press conference was called for the express purpose of releasing the ME's report. The fact that I've made myself available to answer some questions should not be taken as an opportunity to engage me in an arbitrary game of twenty questions." He turned on his heel and stalked off the stage. The mayor and chief of police looked at each other, shrugged and followed him off.

The camera came back to Travis for a wrap up. "I don't think anyone is surprised by the ME's findings. As for detective Duggan, although he asked for questions, he didn't seem eager, or perhaps able, to answer them. After he left the podium, we weren't any better informed than when he started." Ouch. Travis could spar with the best of them. His relationship with Duggan had never been great, but I couldn't help wondering if the detective's antipathy toward him was fueled by his association with me.

* * * *

"He fired the first round across my bow," Travis said when I asked him later about Duggan's response and his critical remark.

"I hope it doesn't have a negative effect on your career."

"If anything it increases my name recognition. My boss was grinning from ear to ear when I got back to the studio."

"Come have dessert," my aunt called from the kitchen. "I made dark chocolate brownies—the chewy kind."

"Did someone say brownies?" Merlin's voice came from the backyard where he'd been teaching Froliquet the ins and outs of proper household behavior. She'd proven to be quick and smart, but with a stubborn streak that confounded the wizard.

Travis laughed. "Hey! I want a brownie. No one does *chewy* like Tilly!" I promised to save one for him.

I joined my aunt in the kitchen. She'd set the table ahead of time and was pouring the tea when I sat down. The wizard appeared a moment later, followed closely by his new familiar, who was followed by Isenbale, Tilly's Maine Coon. According to my aunt, the cat had developed quite a crush on the newest member of the household. He didn't seem to care that the marmot was an entirely different species. Most of the time, Froliquet tolerated his affections, but there had been a few nasty skirmishes that resulted in Isenbale losing tufts of his luxurious long coat.

Between forkfuls of brownie and vanilla ice cream, I told Tilly about the email from Conrad and what I'd written in my reply. "I haven't heard back from him yet."

"I'm surprised he wrote to you at all. He was a strange boy even as a toddler. His mother and I were friends of a sort back then. Not close friends by any means. She didn't relate easily to people. She did seem to enjoy spending time with me, but then she went months avoiding my calls. From what I've heard, Conrad suffers from worse social anxiety than she did, poor boy."

I sipped my tea. Tilly had chosen her mild licorice blend to pair with the brownies. It was a digestive aid that worked wonders if one overindulged.

"Didn't his mother die young?" I asked.

"She was only forty two, which would have made him twenty. At least he was spared the foster care system. I can't imagine what that experience would have done to him."

I wiped brownie crumbs off my chin. "I don't want to pressure him, but I have to find out what he meant about Genna. To be honest, I wouldn't mind having a look around his house too. If he had issues with Genna, I have to consider him a suspect. I'm thinking of showing up unannounced."

Tilly shook her head. "Bad idea."

"Well I do have another plan, but it relies to a great extent on your help. Are you game?"

Her eyes lit up. "Ready, willing and able!"

"As am I," said Merlin, dribbling ice cream into his beard.

Chapter 16

The next morning, Tilly, Merlin, Froliquet, and I headed out to Burdett. My aunt called shotgun, leaving Merlin and his familiar the whole backseat. Since it was the marmot's first car trip, Tilly worried the animal might succumb to motion sickness and ruin her new apricot and aqua muumuu that went well with her sneakers. Tilly had always marched to the beat of her own fashion drummer.

We made it to Burdett in an hour. My last trip there was on a cold day in late fall, when Elise and I were investigating another murder case. Back then the town had been desolate, and dreary, a study in gray. Only a handful of stores had been open for business. Summer had resurrected the place. The shops were all spruced up, freshly painted, windows sparkling. Their doors were flung open to welcome the tourists who'd come to vacation in the Finger Lakes. Colorful banners and flags beckoned. People filled the streets. They waited in line for homemade ice cream and freshly squeezed lemonade. The tiny town was bustling.

For a couple of years following Scott's drowning, I hadn't been able to go anywhere near the lake or the town without grief swelling in my heart. Genna's death at the reunion was making it hard for me to be there again. But I was older, more experienced with loss, and determined not to let anything or anyone stand in the way of the investigation, least of all me.

Once we left the town behind, I pulled off on the shoulder of the road and asked Merlin to take Froliquet out for a bathroom break. He'd modified a dog harness to fit her for trips outside. But whenever he put the contraption on her, she spent the whole outing trying to pull it off. They clambered back in the car ten minutes later with nothing accomplished. Merlin muttered that he should have opted for a cat, and Froliquet chattered angrily back at him with what I imagined was marmot four-letter sentiment.

Although Travis wasn't with us, we would not have known where to find Conrad without his help. He'd called in a favor from a buddy who worked for the local electric company and within minutes he was reading me Conrad's address.

"That sounds like the address where his mom and he moved right after graduation," Tilly said when she heard it. "Money was always tight. I know she had a hard time holding onto the house in New Camel". She smiled wistfully. "I went to see them at the new place a few times. Whenever I visited, I brought his mom a lemon meringue pie—it was her favorite. And blondies for Conrad, hold the nuts."

I was lucky Tilly had been there and still had an agile memory, because even though I had the address, the house was not easy to find. She directed me down a dirt road with no street sign, where we bounced along through potholes and ruts for the better part of a mile.

I was beginning to wonder if I'd put too much faith in her memory, when she pointed to a thicket of evergreen bushes and old gnarled trees with roots bulging out of the ground. I turned off the dirt road into a driveway that was equal parts gravel and dirt.

We were facing the clapboard, windowless side of a small ranch house, which suited me fine. I didn't want Conrad to see us ahead of time. If I craned my neck, I had an oblique view of the front yard with its patches of grass stubborn enough to grow without any encouragement. A silver Chevy from the mid-nineties sat in the front yard, rust slowly consuming its body.

"I was right," Tilly said as if she hadn't been all that sure herself. "He never left his mother's house. It's a lot more overgrown than it was back then and the trees are taller, but this is the place I remember."

The initial part of the plan rested squarely on my aunt's muumuu clad shoulders. Merlin, Froliquet and I would remain in the car, while she tried to work her magick. First up was getting in the door. We were counting on the fact that Conrad had fond memories of Tilly's visits with his mother. She was carrying a plastic cake holder with two dozen of the blondies he once loved, to grease the process.

Her next move would be to gently probe Conrad's mind for information about Genna. She had warned me that a person as closed off to social interaction as Conrad probably had his subconscious locked down tight. If she was right, she had one last card to play—hypnosis. Since it was a skill she didn't often use, she practiced it on Merlin, who proved to be easily entranced.

If the hypnosis worked, Tilly would let the rest of us into the house. I would check around for any evidence he might have been involved in Genna's murder. Merlin and Froliquet had no purpose in our plan, but Merlin insisted on coming along, until he wore us down.

Armed with the blondies, Tilly marched up to the front door and knocked. No one came to the door or asked who was there. She waited a minute and knocked again. If he was in the house, he must have heard her. I heard her from my car with the AC blasting. She was starting to walk away when the door opened. She turned back and a few seconds later disappeared inside. My heart quickened, but not with the excitement of a plan in motion. It was more like anxiety. Maybe it wasn't such a good idea to have sent her in there alone. What if Conrad had developed homicidal tendencies during his years of solitude? I wanted to run to the door and pound on it until he let me in, but Tilly would be furious if I ruined the plan because I didn't trust her to take care of herself.

Each minute that ticked by was torture, and Merlin made matters worse. While I fretted silently, he pulled out all the stops in an Oscar worthy performance. "My dear sweet Matilda," he wailed. "What is to become of me without you?" Froliquet was doing her best to provide harmony with high-pitched whistles inches from my ear. But when I looked at her whisker twitching muzzle and big dark eyes, it was impossible to be annoyed with her. I stroked her head and she leaned into my palm, quieting.

"Tillie opened the door," Merlin sang out with enthusiasm as if he hadn't been the one wringing his hands moments earlier. "I never doubted her ability for a second."

"You are to follow me, touch nothing and keep quiet—both of you!" I reminded him.

"You suck all the joy out of things," he complained, carrying Froliquet out of the car and setting her on the ground.

We found Tilly and Conrad at the dining room table. His eyes were closed. Apparently the attempt to probe his mind hadn't worked. My aunt put her finger to her lips, a reminder not to make any noise that might snap Conrad out of his trance. I sat down beside her. Merlin ambled off to look around the house with his marmot in tow.

Conrad looked pretty much as I remembered him. He'd gained some weight since being on his own. Takeout and junk food no doubt. His skin was a pasty white as if he spent most of his time indoors, gaming and bingeing TV. The high school yearbook had almost named him *most likely to become a serial killer,* but Mr. Hemming, the teacher in charge of the yearbook, made the pranksters change it. They finally settled on *most likely to write horror novels.* To the best of my knowledge, he'd never shown any interest in writing.

"Conrad," Tilly began, "why did you say Genna was not the person Kailyn thought she was?"

His brow lowered. His jaw clenched. Either he had trouble remembering or he was fighting her suggestion to explain his words. "Relax," Tilly said in the calm monotone she used for hypnosis. "You are safe. Nothing can harm you." His expression softened.

"She wasn't nice. She did things girls shouldn't do."

"What kind of things?" Tilly asked.

"She went with any boy who wanted her," he said. "Any boy but me." A tear ran down his cheek. He dashed it away with his fist.

"The truth is Genna thought you were *too* good for her," Tilly said to soothe him. With Genna gone, there was no one to contradict her.

I whispered a question in Tilly's ear and she asked it for me. "How did you know those things about her?"

"I liked being around her, so I went where she went and I watched what she did."

Tilly and I exchanged looks of horror. Goosebumps flashed along my arms.

"Did she realize you were doing that?" I blurted out, covering my mouth after the fact, which did as much good as closing the barn door after the horse has galloped off. Maybe Conrad wouldn't hear the difference in our voices. No such luck. He sat up straight, his eyelids fluttering. Tilly swooped in for damage control. I held my breath as if that would make up for what I'd done.

"Your eyes are too heavy to open," she crooned to him. "Everything is fine. You feel very relaxed and safe." His shoulders slumped forward again. I let out my breath as quietly as I could.

"Conrad," Tilly resumed, "did Genna know you were following her?"

"I don't think so. I was good at it. I didn't want to scare her or anything."

Tilly consulted the list of questions we compiled ahead of time. She had it beside her on the table. It's easy to forget something important when the subject's answers take you far afield.

"Let's talk about the night of the senior prom, Conrad. Were you at the lake the night Scott Desmond drowned?"

"Genna went to the lake, so I went too. It was nice and dark there. I finally got up the nerve to ask her out."

"What did she say?"

He didn't respond immediately and when he did, his voice was higher and thinner as if he was being strangled from inside. "She laughed like it was a joke, and then she said, 'That's not going to happen. That's never going to happen.'" His voice cracked on the last words.

I didn't know how to feel. I was horrified and repulsed by the way he'd stalked her, but I ached over the way she'd treated him. I knew Genna could be self-involved and thoughtless. I'd never known her to be purposely cruel.

Tilly must have been dealing with the same mix of emotions as I was. She drew in a deep breath before continuing. "Conrad, I want you to put Genna out of your mind for now. Can you tell me what the kids at the lake were doing? What they were talking about?"

Conrad shook his head. "All I cared about was getting the chance to talk to Genna. Nothing else mattered. And after...after she...I left."

Tilly looked at me and raised her eyebrows. I nodded. We'd heard enough. Tilly had told me years ago that confessions from people under hypnosis weren't reliable and usually not allowed in court.

"You're tired, Conrad," Tilly said. "You deserve a nice long rest, while I keep watch over you." His head slumped forward onto his chest. Time for me to look around.

Conrad kept a tidy home, every drawer and closet in perfect order. No dust bunnies under the bed. No toothpaste in the sink. I found Merlin sitting on Conrad's bed, watching television with the volume down low. Froliquet was asleep by his side.

I searched the two bedrooms, the china cabinet in the dining room, even the bathroom vanity. A laptop was on a desk in the smaller of the two bedrooms. It leaped to life as soon as I moved the mouse. Conrad was logged into his email account, Facebook, Twitter and Instagram. A quick perusal of the sites showed me that he didn't interact much with other members. His friend count on Facebook was eight and included an aunt in New Jersey, and a cousin in Alabama. Nothing I saw raised any alarms.

I went down to the unfinished basement. There was a washer and dryer, a dehumidifier, a shredder, and a couple of large plastic storage containers. One was filled with old photos, the other with tax returns and other financial papers. If he'd written out a plan to poison Genna, I couldn't find it.

Coming up the stairs to the kitchen, I heard the sounds of a scuffle. I ran up the last few steps to find what could have been a scene from an old silent film. Tilly and Merlin were fighting over the box of blondies. They didn't say a word, but they looked like they were engaged in mortal combat. Before I could intervene, Merlin pulled the box out of Tilly's hands, knocking over a chair in the process. The crack of the chair on the tile floor was like a crack of thunder in the stillness. Conrad's head jerked up and he opened his eyes.

"This is all a dream," Tilly said to him. "You're still asleep. Close your eyes." His eyelids started to droop, then flew open again. He seesawed back and forth, one moment yielding to the powerful tug of the hypnosis and the next, fighting it off, until he finally broke through to full consciousness.

His eyes widened and his breath caught in his throat as he took in the three of us standing around him. We had to calm his fears, before he called 911. If Duggan found out what we'd been doing there, he would throw us all in jail.

"What is this? Why are all of you here? Who's that old man?"

I set the chair back on its feet and sat down beside Conrad. "You know me, don't you?"

"Yes...yes, Kailyn."

"I knew my aunt was coming to visit, so I popped in to say *hello*. This gentleman is a cousin of ours visiting from England." I leaned closer to Conrad and whispered, "He's a bit eccentric."

"I want you all to go," Conrad said, despite my attempt to engage him. He was about to rise when Froliquet jumped into his lap. The three of us went to grab her, but Conrad put his arm around the marmot. He smiled, cuddling her closer to his chest and murmuring endearments.

"I've never held a marmot," he said, eyes beaming. "What's her name?" Even his voice had changed. The hollowness had been replaced by a softer, sweeter tone. I'd never heard of a therapy marmot, but she seemed like a natural.

Merlin looked quite pleased with himself, as if her empathy was his achievement. "It's Froliquet."

"Froliquet!—it's perfect." Conrad didn't take his eyes off her. "Can I keep her?"

"Of course not," the wizard said indignantly. "She belongs to me."

"I'm willing to pay for her – whatever price you think is fair."

"It's simply out of the question." He looked crushed.

"I'm sure our cousin would be delighted to bring her to visit you," Tilly said, giving Merlin what I called *the look*. He opened his mouth, no doubt to refute her offer, when *the look* made him freeze. He knew what it meant—more chores, less freedom, and no dessert.

"It would be my pleasure to bring Froliquet to visit you, my good fellow. Shall we say once a month?" He glanced at Tilly with a hopeful little smile. Her brow lowered. His mouth drooped. "Silly me, what I meant to say was once a week?" He stole another glance at Tilly, who inclined her head in approval. Of course if Conrad proved to be the killer, a prison sentence would get the wizard off the hook.

Chapter 17

When I opened my eyes, I was still seated at the computer desk in my study. I didn't feel any different and everything around me looked the same. The spell hadn't worked. Perhaps I didn't have the ability to travel through time after all. I was disappointed, but also relieved. Had I let Travis's fears become my own? That wasn't acceptable.

I could tweak the spell I created and try again. No, not *could*—I *would* work on the spell and the next time I tried it, I'd succeed. I'd had to build my teleporting muscle, and traveling through time was no different. It would take work. I had to be patient and trust myself. Doubt was the enemy of magick.

Although I failed, my efforts had exhausted me. All I wanted was to crawl beneath my sheets and sleep. I signed out of my email and was about to shut down the computer when I noticed the date on the tool bar. My heart lurched in my chest, wiping the breath from my lungs. The date was yesterday. I looked down at my clothing and saw that I was wearing yesterday's sundress and not the capris I had on when I sat down at the desk two hours earlier. I'd done it! I actually traveled back a day. My thoughts were in a whirlwind. I couldn't separate the elation from the anxiety, the thrill from the fear.

I'd had some hefty qualms about tackling time travel from the get-go, but I felt obliged to attempt it while I was still in my twenties. According to Morgana and Bronwen, any untried magickal talents I possessed would go dormant once I hit thirty. Although I'd mastered teleportation, it was child's play compared to the dangers of time travel. If teleportation went awry, I could wind up anywhere on the planet, but I'd eventually find my way home. If time travel misfired, I could spend the rest of my life dodging dinosaurs, caught up in war, pestilence, famine, or in some desolate future beyond my imagining.

If *I* had misgivings about time travel, how could I expect Travis to ever be okay with it? I thought about not saying anything, but that was the coward's way out. Besides, if I just disappeared one day, he would be left to wonder what had become of me. Not that knowing the why and the wherefore would help him. There would be no way to rescue me, if I alone possessed the unique ability.

I had finally broached the subject at the table, after one of Tilly's dessert tastings–old-fashioned charlotte russe and a chocolate pecan tart she was considering for her teas. I hoped the comfort food would make him more amenable to the prospect. I was wrong.

"Are you out of your mind?" he said. His words were measured, but his eyes were dark beneath his lowered brow and his jaw was clenched so tightly I thought his teeth would crack from the pressure.

I tried to make it sound reasonable. "It's the natural progression after teleportation. And it's a very rare ability. How can I pass up the chance to find out if I possess it?"

Travis ran his hand through his hair. "It's the *rare* part that really worries me. There are no guidelines to help you, no books to warn you about dangers, teach you how to navigate through time, offer suggestions on how to get back home if things go south." He shook his head. "I can't believe we're even discussing this. I liked it better when I didn't believe in magick."

He pushed back from the table hard, causing his untouched coffee to slosh over the rim. He paced around the room, before stopping abruptly to take the empty seat beside Tilly, as if he were playing musical chairs to music he alone could hear. "Aunt Tilly, please tell her this is craziness."

For a woman of often dramatic emotions, my aunt had been very still as she listened to me and Travis. She looked into his eyes. "I'm afraid it's not crazy," she said. "If Kailyn feels the need to stretch to her full potential, how can we stand in her way?"

"By saying you won't support her in this and by asking her mother and grandmother to stand with us."

"They would be the first to encourage her." She patted his hand on the table. "It will be fine," she said with the tiniest wobble in her voice.

My heart caught in my throat thinking about that night. Yet here I sat having accomplished what no one else on Earth had, with the possible exception of one ancient ancestor, and all I wanted was to be back in my aunt's dining room, eating cake and discussing time travel in the abstract. But wishing wouldn't make it so.

For ninety miserable minutes, every time I reached a meditative state, a bubble of doubt popped into my mind. I had never struggled with it so badly before. But then I'd never been in such a precarious situation before either. The more tired I became, the harder it would be for me to successfully make the journey forward to my proper time. If I'd taken Sashki with me, he might have enhanced my magickal strength–after all that's what familiars did. But at his advanced age it could have proven too much for him and I didn't want to risk his life. I drew him close in my thoughts along with all my loved ones–Morgana and Bronwen, Tilly, Travis, Elise, and the other four legged members of our clan. As I focused on them, they seemed to close ranks around me, until I was finally able to banish the doubt and reach a state of calm.

The spell I'd created to go back in time was different from the one I needed to take me forward again. *There's a first time for everything,* I told myself. *Believe in the magick. Believe in yourself.* I recited the spell three times.

> Take me to the time I know,
> Nothing changed nor rearranged.
> White light gather all around
> For safekeeping as I go
> Through the darkness in-between
> This time and the time I know.

I was afraid to open my eyes. Time travel to and from the same exact location didn't have the *whoosh* of sound I'd come to expect from teleporting. What if I'd failed? *Oh for heaven's sake,"* my subconscious snapped at me. *You can't procrastinate forever. Open your eyes! Face whatever you have to face, Nancy Drew! When did you become such a ninny?*

My subconscious knew how to get to me. I immediately opened my eyes and looked at the computer monitor. I was home. Time travel had expanded my definition of *home.* No longer was it simply the place where I lived, now it was also the time in which I lived there.

I hadn't told Travis or Tilly the date of my maiden voyage, but they understood it would be sooner than later. The moment I realized I was back, my fatigue fell away like a heavy coat I'd shrugged off. I wanted to share the good news. I walked over to Tilly's house to tell her in person. She was rhapsodic.

"Not that I had any doubts," she said after singing my praises and looking me over to assure herself I was in one piece. "You must call Travis. The poor man is so besotted with you that this time travel issue has taken its toll on him."

"And you know that because?"

"I didn't read his mind, if that's what you're implying," Tilly said indignantly. "But the evening you first told us you were going to attempt time travel, love and terror were coming off him in waves so huge they almost knocked me over!" I apologized for jumping to conclusions. "That's better," she said, "now go home and call him. I have some celebratory baking to do!"

When I told Travis, he didn't respond for several beats. "Are you there?" I asked, thinking the connection had been dropped.

"Yes, yes I'm here. I'm glad you were successful." He sounded like he'd had the wind knocked out of him after going seven rounds with a heavyweight bruiser. I felt guilty for having put him through what was clearly an ordeal for him. Tilly was right to warn me. Everyone has a breaking point. If I didn't want to lose him, I had to keep my priorities in balance.

Chapter 18

The chimes over the door jingled with the arrival of the day's first customers. The couple who walked in reminded me of the twin theater masks of comedy and tragedy. The man appeared to be in his late sixties, but his wife looked a good ten years younger. He was dour; she had a ready smile. He answered my *hello* with a stiff nod and headed for the chair near the counter as if his radar had homed in on it the moment he walked in the door.

The woman introduced herself as Vera and her husband as Ted. "I've wanted to come to your store for years," she said, her eyes and her voice brimming with excitement. "Now that I'm here, I feel like a kid on Christmas morning—no, no, like a kid at Disney World for the first time—no wait, like a kid getting her first puppy."

Ted was wagging his head. "If you don't pull her plug, she'll keep it up till midnight."

"I'm very glad you made it here," I said to her, trying not to laugh. "What can I do for you?"

"I hardly know where to start. My friends rave about so many of your products. I nagged at poor Ted until he couldn't take it anymore—and here we are!"

"Five hours, thirty two minutes and eleven rest stops later—here we are," he said dryly.

Vera was rummaging through a vast purse like the one Tilly carried. In my aunt's case, one could usually find some freshly baked goods in its depths.

"My list," Vera said triumphantly pulling a piece of lined notepaper from her bag. "Her intention is to leave here penniless." Ted's delivery could have bought him a career on stage or on TV. But I sensed something amiss with him. I gave Vera a basket and sent her off down the first aisle on her treasure hunt. She would have more fun finding the items on her list than if I handed them to her. Besides, I wanted a chance to speak to her husband.

I hopped up on the counter near him. "You're very funny," I told him.

He looked me up and down as if he were measuring me for target practice. "I've been called a lot of things, but never that."

"You're also hurting. If you tell me what the problem is, I may be able to help."

"You've got a cure for old?"

"Not exactly—but I have some very effective herbal mixtures that can take the sting out of the condition."

He narrowed his eyes at me. "I'll have no truck with illegal drugs."

"Neither would I."

"Well I've tried all the rest, so unless it's magic you're peddling, I'm not interested."

"Funny you should say that sitting here in this ancient magick shop."

He dismissed my words with a wave of his hand. "It's all a gimmick to sell expensive products that work the same as the cheaper ones you can find in those big chain drugstores. You may fool Vera and her friends with all the trappings of magic, but you don't fool me, not for one minute. It's all smoke and mirrors."

"Great. Then it can't possibly hurt for you to give them a try."

He glared at me, momentarily outmaneuvered. "That depends. How much are these magical cures?" I could see by the gleam in his eyes that he thought he'd bested me.

"I'm going to give you free samples." *Try to argue with that, Ted.* I came off the counter, checked on Vera, who was enjoying her journey down the aisles, and grabbed two products for Ted the nonbeliever.

"This one is a cream," I said, opening a small jar and holding it out for him to inspect.

He sniffed it and shrugged. "Looks harmless and pointless." He gave me permission to rub a bit of it into the inflamed arthritic joints of his hands. "What's it supposed to…" His voice petered out and he looked up at me with a frown. "The pain…it's some better. You and I both know that's not possible. I've tried everything the medical profession can offer and none of it did a bit of good."

I smiled. "That's why this is called magick." I gave him the sample tea to try at home and an easy spell to help his body make the best use of the samples. When I used the word *spell,* I thought I'd lost him. He squirmed in his seat as if he were having a hard time suppressing a sarcastic remark. To his credit, he bit his tongue and wrote down the words I dictated:

Mind and body, I accept
Healing magick with respect.
Temper pain and protect so
Further damage won't collect.

Ted returned my pencil and pocketed the spell. He leaned closer. "Can I ask a favor?" I was pretty sure I knew what was on his mind.

"You want to keep this between you and me for now?"

He smiled. "If you don't mind. I don't think I should spring a change like this on Vera all at once. After forty-eight years together, the shock of me suddenly becoming open-minded may be more than her poor heart can take."

I gave him the grin he expected, but I had my doubts about just how open-minded Ted had become in the space of five minutes. Relief from chronic pain had the power to change a belief system, but Ted was a long time, hardwired skeptic. It wouldn't surprise me if he took my products to a chemist to find out what was *really* in them.

"All right," I said, "but only for the short term. Vera deserves to know that you're feeling better and why."

"To be honest, I need time to prepare myself before I tell her. The arthritis has kept me off the dance floor for years. I'll have to come up with a new excuse now."

They weren't gone two minutes when detective Duggan appeared in the doorway. He and Beverly vied for the title of my least favorite person in New Camel, and I knew they were every bit as sour on me. The detective never came into my shop if he could avoid it, which suited both of us. I wondered what urgent matter brought him in that day.

I stayed behind the counter and let him come to me. "Ms. Wilde," he said, after scoping out the shop to see if we were alone.

"Detective, how may I help you?" Had he been anyone else, I would have asked if he'd enjoyed his vacation, but he'd never shown any interest in sharing social niceties with me.

"As you're aware," he said, "I was away at the time of your friend's tragic death." I nodded. "My condolences, by the way."

"Thank you."

"I know you were interviewed by detective Gillespie, but I have a few of my own questions. Do you have the time now?" I was surprised he hadn't told a junior officer to call me down to the station house.

"As long as no customers walk in."

"If that happens, we'll set up a time that's convenient for you." An affable Duggan? Had he vacationed at a brainwashing facility? Or had dealing with Gillespie given him some much needed insight into dealing with someone else's obnoxious personality?

"That's fine," I murmured, expecting the old Duggan to reassert himself at any moment.

"Good, good. He pulled a notepad and pen out of his shirt pocket. "Playing catch up is not my favorite game," he said with a smile that was more creepy than pleasant. I smiled back, low wattage, feeling my way. "What can you tell me about Genna's parents and any siblings?"

I shrugged. "Growing up they weren't any different from my other friends' families." I couldn't use my family for comparison. No other family was like mine. Duggan was looking at me with his pen poised over his notebook. I tried to come up with more. "Father, mother, younger sister. I'm not sure what you're looking for."

"Where are they living these days?"

"Genna's folks moved to California when Genna stayed there after college. Her dad died a few years ago. I don't know if her sister is out there too." I didn't mind throwing him a bone, as long as it wasn't one with a lot of meat on it. I wanted to find the killer before he did.

"Do you have the mom's contact info?"

I shook my head. I could easily get it from Charlotte, but if he wanted to speak to Ada Harlowe, he could have one of his underlings do the legwork. When he didn't ask if Genna had been married or had kids, I figured those facts were in Gillespie's report. I'd raced through it when I was looking for Charlie's alibis.

"Any estrangement between Genna and her parents in recent years?" Duggan had exceeded his quota of a *few* questions, but I wasn't going to test our détente by quibbling.

"I wouldn't know."

"There seems to be a lot of conjecture around town about Genna's death being somehow related to Scott Desmond's drowning ten years ago. Do you know what that's all about?"

"People like to draw connections between events, tie things up in a pretty bow like a TV movie." A woman wheeled a baby stroller into the shop. I couldn't have timed her arrival better if I'd cast a spell to summon her. Duggan flipped his notebook closed. "Thanks for your help. I'll be in touch." He nodded at the woman as he passed her.

I spent close to an hour with the newcomer, whose family had recently moved to the Glen for her husband's job. She left with a large tote bag of my finest makeup and a gentle, but highly effective herbal remedy for her daughter's teething pain.

For a day without any tour buses, customers kept me hopping. A nice cross section of locals came in for refills, or because they had a new ailment, or a new wrinkle. With few exceptions, I enjoyed seeing people I've known all my life. They caught me up on the news in their families and they often waxed nostalgic about Morgana and Bronwen. I had to be careful not to speak about them in the present tense. Tilly and I never told anyone outside the family about their visits from beyond the veil. Travis knew because they'd popped in more than once when he was with me.

A number of day-trippers and overnighters added to the day's receipts. I liked hearing where they hailed from and if they'd heard of Abracadabra before coming to New Camel. At five o'clock, I was at my desk behind the counter, shutting down the computer. I'd already put the *Closed* sign in the window. All I wanted at that moment was to go home and put my feet up. After feeding Sashki and the rest of the cats, of course. When their stomachs were grumbling, they had no interest in the state of my feet. But I had one more thing to do before I left for the night.

Chapter 19

Calling the Waverly Hotel had been on my to-do list since the ME released his report on Genna's death. If she ingested potassium cyanide by way of a cocktail the evening of the reunion, I had to find the bartender who prepared the lethal beverage and served it to her.

According to the hotel's automated system, I could reach the catering manager, Hugo Humphrey, if I pressed three. Humphrey answered my call in a defensive tone. "Catering, how may I help you?" The Waverly's catering business must have suffered an abrupt downturn after the ME linked Genna's death with the drink she was served there. Most of the calls he was receiving were no doubt cancellations and demands for refunds. He probably dreaded getting out of bed in the morning.

Once I introduced myself and explained that I was investigating Genna's death, he adopted a clipped, officious tone. "We have worked closely with the detectives on the case to answer all their questions and accommodate all their requests. I'm not aware of any obligation on our part to provide the same assistance to private investigators."

Instead of sniping back at him, I went with a more laid-back, confident approach. "My partner and I have cleared every case we've taken on, before the police were able to. Given these results, I think it's fair to say that the Waverly board of trustees would want all their employees to show us the same *hospitality* they've accorded the police. This is small town America, Mr. Humphrey, and my family has been in this town from the very beginning. Our name is synonymous with a job well done." I could lay it on with the best of them.

There was a long pause on the other end while Humphrey weighed my words and considered his options. "I see no reason why we can't help you out," he said, spinning a one-eighty. He was trying to match my easy manner, but the nervous squeaks in his voice undermined the effect. "Exactly what is it I can do for you, Ms. Wilde?" That was more like it.

"I want to speak to the bartenders who worked the Friday night reunion dinner."

"Not a problem. Did you have a day and time in mind?"

"As soon as you can round them up. How many were tending bar at the reunion?"

"There were two that regrettable night. In my experience, two was sufficient for the number of guests expected. We were going to add a third for the larger dinner dance the next night, but..." His voice cracked and trailed off. He was probably craving a drink himself at that moment, one not laced with potassium cyanide. He cleared his throat as if it was a postnasal drip and not nerves plaguing his larynx. "I'll let you know as soon as I can set it up."

I put the phone down, thinking the conversation went better than I'd hoped. Humphrey could have stalled me for weeks until he spoke to higher ups in the hotel chain, but despite his initial statement, he proved easy to handle. A catering manager without any catering to manage had to be worried about losing his job.

Sleeping wasn't easy that night. A string of rough thunderstorms kept the cats awake, which kept me awake. All that electricity in the air frayed their nerves and they sought comfort by nestling on top of me. There was a nasty skirmish when one of them challenged Sashkatu for the coveted position of curling around my head like a scarf. I doubt any of them will ever make that mistake again. I wasn't likely to forget it either. The battlefield always bears the scars.

The next day dawned fresh and sunny as if the storms had been figments of our collective imaginations. At his advanced age, Sashki suffered from interrupted sleep more than the rest of us. He dragged himself to the door for the short walk to the shop. I took pity on him and carried him there against my shoulder like a colicky baby. His little tongue flicked across my nose as I set him on his tufted window ledge—a proper *thank you* in my book.

It was cool enough in the shop to turn off the AC. I propped open the door with the large ceramic dragon Bronwen had bought for that purpose. The air wafting in carried the scent of newly mown lawns and Lolly's chocolate. Two clouds popped up in front of me as I walked back inside. I shooed them away from the open door and into the supply room where they wouldn't be seen.

The edges of my mother's cloud were turning purple, a mixture of sadness and anger. "I thought you'd be thrilled to see me," she said. "Of course I am. I'm *overjoyed* to see you again." I had missed her, even if I hadn't missed the frequent arguments. I would have embraced her if I could, but as long as we resided on different sides of the veil, coming into contact was not an option, especially if I wasn't ready to join them. "You have got to be more careful where you materialize. We can't let anyone else see you." What a horror show that would be with cell phone cameras and social media. We'd be under siege by every news outlet, every kook and phony evangelist. "Remember, you two are proof that the soul survives physical death."

Morgana's cloud shook the attitude and returned to white. "Forgive me. I've been so immersed in spiritual learning, I forgot about the limits and pettiness of life on Earth." And yet she'd gotten her figurative nose out of joint, because I sent them to the supply room. Her learning on the other side was clearly a work in progress.

It occurred to me that Bronwen hadn't said one word. "Are you all right, grandma?"

"I'm enjoying being with two of my dearest again. Besides, I've discovered that words aren't always necessary. In fact they often get in the way and lead to misunderstanding." *Can I get an amen?*

"However I do have something to tell you. It is permissible for us to explain that spirits may choose to appear to the living as energy clouds or as they looked in life."

"Then I don't understand why you and my mother have chosen to appear as generic energy clouds."

"At the outset, you and Tilly were so devastated by our sudden passing that it didn't seem wise or kind to appear as ourselves. We wanted to visit with you, but keep a certain distance between us to help you move on." I held my breath, worried my grandmother might have revealed too much. But as the seconds passed without her being snatched away, I relaxed.

"We are only given the choice once," Morgana added. I didn't say anything. I wasn't sure I agreed with their choice, but at least I understood it now. As much as I would have loved to *see* them again as I'd known them in life, they had chosen what they thought was in Tilly's and my best interests at the time.

"How is my sister?" Morgana asked. "And Merlin?"

"They're in Tilly's shop. I'll get them."

"No need," Bronwen said, "we'll get there faster ourselves." Before I had a chance to warn them about Froliquet, they took off for the teashop like sloops catching a fresh wind. Cats had a long history as familiars for sorcerers and wizards. As such they were rarely put off by magickal occurrences. Marmots were another story.

I followed Morgana and Bronwen into Tilly's shop where apples, cinnamon, and sugar were bubbling away in the oven. My mouth started watering for my aunt's strudel. Merlin was on his stool keeping track of the timer, with Froliquet asleep at his feet.

When the clouds sailed in, the marmot must have felt a disturbance in the plane, because she awoke with a start. She jumped to her feet and backed away from them with an awkward gait. It occurred to me that I'd never seen her squirrel relatives move in reverse. If they wanted to change direction, they simply spun around. But Froliquet didn't seem inclined to turn her back on the indoor clouds for even a moment. Instead she sat up on her haunches and issued a high-pitched whistle alarm to those she considered members of her madness—namely us.

"Merlin," Tilly yelled from the tearoom, "Make her stop! She's your familiar. Teach her some manners! My poor ears!"

When Tilly came around the corner and saw her family gathered there, a smile split her face, plumping up her cheeks. Although the clouds couldn't smile, they twinkled, bouncing up and down with delight. With good feelings abounding, Froliquet caught the spirit, quieting to an occasional hiccup-like chirp.

Sashkatu appeared in the doorway. He regarded us all with an aristocratic disdain that conveyed his feelings as well as any words could—*you're all noisy and ill-bred peasants.* He turned and strutted back to Abracadabra, his tail straight as a flagpole. Once he was out of sight, we all cracked up. Froliquet chattered along, trying to mimic us.

Chapter 20

Hugo Humphrey called the next day. He had the two bartenders scheduled to meet with me at the hotel that afternoon. Maybe he'd taken my little speech to heart. If I could catch Genna's killer, her story would quickly be replaced in the news by the other myriad horrors around the world. The public's memory of it would quickly fade, courtesy of their shortened attention span. Hugo might stand a chance of saving his job after all.

How could I tell him I couldn't make it, after I'd demanded the meeting ASAP? But I'd forgotten that a group of seniors were coming to New Camel from the senior center forty minutes away in Corning. At least a dozen strong, they made the trip a couple of times a year. They were active, clear minded, and fun to be with. When they were younger, they must have been hell on wheels.

The words were barely out of my mouth, when Tilly offered her services. "Yes, I'm free. I'll do it, whatever it is."

"Don't you want to know what you're signing up for?"

"No, not necessary." I explained the situation anyway. "Wonderful! I'll leave Merlin home with his marmot. It will be like a vacation. I know that group from Corning—they're a hoot. When I get older, I want to be just like them." I didn't point out that she was already as old as some of them, ran a business, and took care of a house, not to mention a mercurial wizard. Arthritis and bunions may have slowed her down, but nothing had made a dent in her forward-ho spirit.

The catering manager's office was one floor below the main lobby, where one could also find the Waverly's spa and gym. Although I was early, I was the last one to arrive. Three sets of eyes turned to the door when I walked in. Humphrey was seated behind his desk, looking much like I imagined him during our phone conversation—forty something with a jawline already melting into his neck. He was wearing a lightweight blue suit, white dress shirt with a collar that cut into his beefy neck, and a blue and red striped tie.

Two young men, still south of thirty, lounged in chairs across from Humphrey's desk. They looked like print models.

Humphrey pushed his chair back and stood up to offer me his damp hand. The bartenders smiled, and nodded, as relaxed as Humphrey was tense. When you're good at tending bar, there's always another gig to play. Catering manager positions were in far shorter supply in Schuyler County. If the killer wasn't caught soon enough, Hugo might have to uproot his wife and two girls, who were smiling at me from the photograph on his desk.

"Please, Ms. Wilde," he said, indicating the empty chair.

Before sitting, I set it at an angle to face all three of them and introduced myself. Humphrey turned beet red when he realized he'd failed to perform that basic courtesy. He seemed to shrink in stature as I watched him. He mumbled an apology and as soon as my butt hit my chair, he sank into his.

The bartender who was farther away gave me a salute and a wink. "I'm Joey."

"Blake," said the one closer to me.

I pulled a mini legal pad and pen from the purse that had replaced my slim cross-body number. Another decade and I'd probably be toting around a satchel the size of Tilly's. "Thank you both for making yourselves available on such short notice."

Joey gave me a grin that could have been in an ad for teeth whitening. "Not a problem." Blake made do with another head bob.

I had decided to question them together. The detectives may have separated them, but that approach had clearly not netted them the killer. By speaking to the men together, I hoped to make them less wary, more willing to part with information.

"Do I look familiar to either of you?" I asked to start things off. It wasn't likely they recognized me. Although I'd been at the bar briefly, it was Genna who had ordered my club soda.

"Sorry," Blake said.

Joey asked me to stand up, and then he gave me a slow and studied appraisal, one that might have earned him a slap under other circumstances. "I must have been working the other end of the bar," he said finally, "because I'm positive if I had seen you, I'd remember you. And I would have asked for your phone number."

Humphrey cleared his throat and sent Joey a look of displeasure.

"Yeah, yeah, I know it's against the rules," Joey said, his eyes still on me, "but I would have made an exception. What good's a rule without exceptions?"

I resumed my seat and took out my phone. "What about this woman?" I handed Blake the phone with the picture I'd taken of Charlotte and Genna that night. He concentrated on it for a count of five, before saying *no* and passing it on to Joey.

"The one on the right—she's the one who was poisoned. I saw her on the news, but I didn't see her at the reunion."

"Here's the thing," Blake said, "when you're working an event, there's this sea of faces and you're busy making one drink after the other. In a bar or a restaurant things are usually slower. You have a chance to talk to people, joke around. That way you remember them."

"How hard is it for someone to get behind the bar during a party?" I asked.

Joey laughed. "Here? Not hard at all. Most places it's not an issue. But I worked at one bar with some pretty scary customers, guys who wouldn't think twice about smashing up the place if someone looked at them funny. The only way you could get behind that bar was through a little supply room that locked from the inside, so someone had to let you in."

Humphrey was aghast. "That's awful! I've never heard of such a thing." He'd apparently recovered enough from his embarrassment to throw in his two cents. He looked at me. "Why do you need to know that?" The man had no imagination.

"If the killer had access to the bar, then he could have made Genna's drink himself."

Blake took exception to my theory. "It doesn't matter how busy we were, we would have noticed if some stranger was suddenly working the bar with us."

Joey fixed his friend with a sly smile. "Not so fast."

Blake rounded on him. "What's that supposed to mean?"

"There *was* a guy who came behind the bar that night. He said he was there to spell us if we needed the restroom. I figured Humphrey arranged—

"I did no such thing," the manager interrupted. "There was no need for restroom breaks when the cocktail hour was just an hour." He didn't have a great way with words.

Joey gave a quick roll of his eyes for my benefit. When he was a kid, he must have spent a lot of time in the principal's office. "I didn't take the guy up on the offer anyway. And I didn't think about it again, until Ms. Wilde brought it up."

Blake laughed. "Hey Joey, I know someone who's got a bridge for sale."

There was no humor in Joey's expression. "Really? And what would *you* have done if that guy came over to you?"

"I would have told him he had to get out, he didn't belong back there. And if Humphrey sent him, he could tell me that himself."

Anger flashed in Joey's eyes. "Yeah right, your hindsight is twenty-twenty, but you wouldn't have done anything different from me. You talk big, but you back down from real confrontations."

I don't know if Humphrey or Blake understood what was happening, but I sure did. Joey didn't like being the one who may have let a killer get past him without even questioning his unlikely story.

Blake grabbed a Waverly brochure off Humphrey's desk, rolled it up and bopped Joey on the head with it.

"Cut it out," Joey snarled, pulling the brochure out of Blake's hand and tossing it behind him.

Humphrey opened his mouth, but nothing came out. He tugged at the knot in his tie. Beads of sweat blossomed on his upper lip. He'd be out two good bartenders if fists started flying, not to mention the potential for breakage. He glared at me as if it were my fault for demanding the meeting.

"Boys, boys," he cajoled, "there's no reason for animosity here. We're all on the same side. Fighting among ourselves won't help Ms. Wilde find the killer."

"Joey," I said, hauling the conversation back on track, "did you see that man again during the night?"

He combed his hair back in place with his fingers. "Matter of fact, I did. He was wandering around the room with a glass in his hand. I thought maybe he was working security too."

A mocking smile lit Blake's face. "Yeah I'm sure his resumé reads *security guard slash relief bartender.*"

"It's called blending in with the crowd."

Listening to them, reminded me of the way Elise's kids bickered. I suspected these two had been friends for years. "Did you see this guy doing anything suspicious?" I asked.

Joey shrugged. "I was busy and it wasn't like I was told to keep track of him. It was before that woman was killed. And it's not like he was wearing a blinking sign that said *KILLER.*"

Blake laughed. "Now *that* would have made for an interesting resumé." Humphrey tried to contain himself, but a chuckle got away from him. He covered his mouth and swallowed hard, trying to regain control.

I ignored him, determined to continue. "Joey, can you describe the man?"

He scratched his head. "Five-ten, gray hair, between fifty and sixty—that's all I got." It wasn't much. He could have been describing any middle-aged man. If your ambition was to be a hired killer, it was a description that would serve you well.

I thanked everyone for their time and handed out my card with the usual request to call if they thought of anything else related to that night.

I'd left my car at home and walked the mile or so to the Waverly. With the temperature in the mid-seventies it was a perfect day to be outside, and I needed the exercise. On the way there I'd hustled, because I didn't want to be late. Going home, I took my time. Tilly would have called if she needed me sooner.

I replayed the meeting in my head, trying to tease more information from what Joey and Blake had said. The man who went behind the bar may well have been the one who poisoned Genna. He might have taken a cocktail glass and poured the poison into it, waiting for the perfect moment to add it to her drink.

Halfway home I forced myself to put the case on a back burner and focus on the simple pleasures of walking when there were no appointments to keep. A lawn mower growled in the distance, birds sang their unique melodies, tea roses sweetened the air, and sunlight sparkled off a freshly washed red convertible that made me think of open roads and wind in my hair. I didn't hear the soft footfalls behind me, until it was too late.

Chapter 21

He slapped his hand over my mouth and shoved a gun into my back. "If you want to live, keep quiet!" His words were low and gravelly, the way men in movies sound when they're trying to disguise their voices to scare you. He was taking a huge chance by attacking me out in the open in daylight. As if he'd read my thoughts, he hurried me off the main street and into an alley between a hardware store and a dry cleaner's. He pushed me to go faster, making me stumble over my own feet. When I fell forward, he jerked my head up and back with the hand that was over my mouth. I thought my neck would snap.

This was no impulsive attack, no thief looking for quick cash and credit cards to fund a drug habit or he would have snatched my purse and run. No, he'd studied the area. He knew he had to grab me before I reached the tourist part of New Camel, where people were always in and out of the shops, especially in the summer.

What does he want from me? The question beat at my mind, but I couldn't let myself go there. Fear was this guy's wingman. I couldn't let it paralyze me. I tried to center my mind to invoke a spell, but I couldn't hold onto the words and their rhythm.

When we reached the end of the alley, he pulled me roughly to the right, behind the cleaner's. There were no windows or security cameras. Toxic vapors from the solvents they used vented there, mixing with the fetid smells of rotting food in the garbage cans. When I gagged, my attacker hissed at me to cut it out. In my head I yelled, *it's an involuntary reflex, moron.*

I was having trouble breathing through my nose alone. I was light-headed; darkness crept around the edges of my mind, closing in. Panic rose in my throat tasting of bile. *Forget about the gun,* I told myself, *fight while you still can.*

His palm over my mouth had shifted enough for me to snag the meaty part between my teeth. I bit down hard, the metallic taste of his blood making me gag again. He yowled in surprise, but didn't pull his hand away. If he had, for even a second or two, I would have screamed at the top of my lungs and spun around, going for his vulnerable spots like the experts tell you to. But he jammed the gun deeper into my back, up against a rib until I thought the bone would crack. He leaned close to my ear, "You try that again and I'll knock your teeth out. If you're a good girl, you'll get out of this without any permanent scars. Now pay attention—I'm only going to say this once—stop playing detective or someone else is going to die, someone you love and it will be your fault!" He snickered as if he were enjoying this game. It tripped a switch in me.

Anger surged through me, stronger than panic. My mind cleared long enough for me to focus and gather my life force. Long enough for the right words to tumble into place. I just had time to recite the spell once:

From here and now to there and then.
Attract no harm nor change allow.
Safe passage guarantee to souls,
As well as lesser mindless things

I landed in a heap in my storeroom, gasping for air. My right knee and elbow had taken the brunt of my graceless entry, but they would heal. I'd chosen the storeroom, because no one was likely to be in there when I appeared out of thin air. It was bad enough that there was now a man with a black heart who knew I was no ordinary woman.

I pulled myself up from the floor on rubber Gumby legs. I didn't dare leave the storeroom, until my legs had steadied and I regained some of my composure. Otherwise Tilly would want to know what happened, and if I told her, she might insist I stop the investigation. I wasn't going to do that. Not even for my aunt's peace of mind. I decided to give her an expurgated version of the attack.

I found her sitting in the chair near the counter with Sashkatu in her lap. They both had their eyes closed. She was petting, he was purring. Seeing them in such a serene and loving pose, I came unglued. After my knees had stopped wobbling, I'd thought I was fine, but the attack must have left a deeper emotional wound. Tears streamed down my cheeks. I was headed back to the storeroom to wait out the deluge, when Tilly opened her eyes.

She stood up immediately, forgetting she had a cat in her lap. Sashki landed on his feet, none the worse for his rude awakening, but he stalked off in the direction of his window ledge, too miffed to bother greeting me.

"My dear girl," Tilly said, "what's happened?" With the flair of a master magician, she pulled a tissue from a hidden pocket in her muumuu and held it out to me. Knowing my aunt, she probably had a muffin or a scone hidden somewhere in its folds as well. She liked to be prepared for any emergency.

I blotted my eyes with the tissue and blew my nose. "I'm fine," I assured her, "I just had a scuffle with a guy who tried to steal my purse."

Tilly raised a critical eyebrow. She wasn't buying it. Why did I think she would? She'd known me all my life, and except for my entrance into the world, I'd never been much of a crier. "How about the whole, unabridged version?" she said.

I didn't have the energy to fight her intuition. I broke down and told her everything. I wouldn't have lasted long in the spy business. When I was done, she gathered me into her arms, the muumuu enveloping both of us.

"The good news," I said, taking a step back, "is that I was able to teleport away before anything worse happened."

"The bad news," my aunt countered, "is that you're not going to stop the investigation, are you?"

I looked her in the eye. "Since when does a Wilde crumble before a threat?"

"Maybe a Wilde shouldn't act alone. This thug wouldn't have attacked you if you were with someone else."

"Travis can't always be with me, Aunt Tilly. He has to earn a living too."

"Who's talking about Travis? *I* could have been with you." I didn't see that one coming.

"And who would have been here to keep my shop open?" It was a lame attempt to win an unwinnable argument.

"You would have closed for half a day." I had nowhere to go from there. Tilly's phone rang, like a bell ending the round in a boxing match. The judges would have given her that one. She fumbled around in her muumuu, looking for the pocket with the phone. The conversation itself took a matter of seconds. "That was Merlin," she said with a sigh. "My vacation is over." She put her hand on my forearm, "We'll continue this discussion later. In the meantime, try to stay out of trouble." I promised I would, but it wasn't as if I'd been looking for trouble, when it had come from behind to accost me.

Chapter 22

Travis had been on assignment in D.C., covering a state visit by China's president. Although we talked every night, I decided not to tell him about my little misadventure until he returned. He didn't need to be distracted by my *all's-well-that-ends-well* tale, which is how I decided to characterize it. I was fine. I handled the matter and I seriously doubted my attacker would ever come near me again.

"When are you coming home?" I asked. I was missing him like crazy. A little over a year ago, I hadn't even known he existed.

"Hormones," is all Elise had to say when I'd made this observation to her.

"I know, but they're just a fancy cocktail of chemicals!"

She'd laughed. "With the power to control you like you were some mindless drone. Romantic isn't it?"

"You've been on my mind all week," Travis said, plucking those hormones like the strings of a harp. "I'm flying home tonight. I could come straight to you, but it will be late."

"I'll cast a little spell to unlock the door for you, in case I fall asleep. Just stand on the doormat and say your name. But keep an eye out for my attack cats."

"Maybe I'll stop at a pet store and pick up some catnip."

"I wouldn't do that, unless you want to deal with a bunch of hyped up kitties."

Determined to wait up for Travis, I put on the late show that came on after the eleven o'clock news. One minute I was lying on the sofa listening to the comedian's monologue and the next, I was waking to the feel of Travis's lips on my cheek.

"I guess I didn't make it," I murmured, pushing myself upright. Travis sat down and put his arm around me to keep me propped up against him.

"Hard day?" he asked.

"Sort of. But you must be exhausted."

"Not really. The flight was short and my car knows the way here. It practically drives itself. If I ever get a new girlfriend, I'll probably have to buy a new car."

"A new girlfriend?" I repeated, coming fully awake.

Travis grinned. "That worked better than caffeine—apparently I now have my own magick words."

"I wouldn't use them too often if I were you. Magick can backfire when used indiscriminately. Are you hungry? Can I make you something?"

"I grabbed dinner before the flight, so unless you have some fabulous Tilly dessert with which to tempt me, all I need is you." And, in spite of his denial, a decent night's sleep.

I was up at seven to feed the feline masses who had clocks for stomachs and not a stitch of compassion for their indentured help. Travis slept until after nine. When he couldn't find me in the house, he walked across the street to the back door of my shop and knocked.

"You should install a doorbell," he said when I let him in.

"Tilly and I are the only ones who come in the back way and we both have keys."

"I think I should have a key. For the house too."

"Done." I liked hearing him talk long term. He followed me up to the front of the shop where we took our usual seats, I on the counter, he in the chair. If I intended to tell him about the attack, I should get to it before customers arrived.

"A strange thing happened yesterday," I began. Travis sat up straighter, instantly on alert. I've been told I often minimize bad things. In fact Travis was one of the people who'd told me that, so it was no surprise when he interpreted *strange* to mean *nearly fatal or death-defying.* I started at the beginning, summarizing my meeting with the bartenders and Humphrey, hitting all the salient points.

"When do you get to the *strange* part?" he asked. A lot of people might have given my tale short shrift, until I got there, but not Travis. If I quizzed him on everything I'd just told him, he would know it cold. Remembering was his stock-in-trade.

"Strange part coming up now." I recounted the attack from beginning to end. There was no point in leaving anything out. He had a journalist's mind and a journalist's ear. Not much got by him. He listened without interrupting me, his expression growing darker and more troubled as I drew toward the end. When I reached the part where I teleported out of the attacker's grasp, the tension didn't drain from his face like I thought it would.

He didn't give me a high five or a thumbs-up. There was no victory cheer in his voice. "You were lucky. It could have gone very differently."

"But it didn't, because I have certain abilities to call on."

"What if he knocked you unconscious or used chloroform, and then kidnapped you? Or killed you outright by slashing your carotid artery?" His sobering words took me down a peg or ten. Served me right for being arrogant.

"You're right. I am lucky to be alive."

"Look Kailyn, I'm not trying to undermine your confidence and courage. But I don't want you to be so sure of yourself that you're not sensibly scared when things like that happen."

"Then you have nothing to worry about. When I couldn't remember the spell I needed, I was scared enough for both of us and my aunt Tilly." Judging by his deepening frown, I might have overdone the honesty. He looked like he had more to say, but was restraining himself.

Since I had no interest in coaxing it out of him, I nudged the conversation in a less personal direction. "I'm sure the guy was hired to scare me off the case. We just need to figure out who paid him."

"The same person who's been playing avenging angel by killing Genna and trying to kill Tony. They may have more people on their hit list and they don't want to be stopped before their work is done. It could be any one of our suspects. He ticked off the names on his fingers, "Lillian Desmond, Charlie Desmond, Conrad Williams or Ashley Rennet."

"Don't forget Scott," I added, "or at least his ghost." Travis compressed his lips like a kid refusing to eat his broccoli. He'd learned to accept the existence of magick and ghosts and individuals like me, who straddled the real and supernatural realms. He might have convinced himself that the magick was an elaborate trick, the ghosts merely holograms, but there was no explaining me away or the impossible things he'd seen me do. But an avenging ghost was clearly more than he could stand.

"You don't think Scott's ghost came back for revenge, do you?" The look on his face begged me not to tell him that.

"No, to the best of my knowledge, ghosts cannot kill the living—except maybe by causing a heart attack. A ghost might enjoy scaring the people who did him wrong, but that's about it."

"Speaking of which," Travis said, "have you found a common thread between the people who have seen him?"

"Nothing definitive. Everyone he's visited was at the lake the night he drowned, except for me. So that can't be the link."

"Wait a minute. Scott may be visiting the others to scare them, but what if he didn't come to scare you? What if he came to *see* you? Pay you a visit?"

I started to laugh, but cut myself short as the memory of his visit replayed in my mind. "I was so freaked out that night and so thrilled it was you at the door, I forgot to tell you this—Scott looked straight at me and held up his hand. Not like he was waving. More like he was telling me to stop."

Travis's brows inched together. "'Stop' as in stop the investigation?"

"I can't imagine what else it could have meant."

"But if this is his ghost, why wouldn't he want you to figure out who was responsible for his death?"

I shook my head. "One more question to add to all the others that still need answers."

"If you're right about his gesture, he dropped by to give you a message and that does set you apart from the others who saw him. Being at the lake *is* the common thread."

"Not so fast," I said. "I got an email this morning from another person who saw Scott. I have to talk to her, before I make that commit—" The door flew open, and Beverly stumbled in and collapsed on the floor, gasping for air.

I jumped down from the counter and Travis launched himself out of the chair. We reached Beverly as she was trying to stand up. "Are you okay?" he asked once we'd helped her to her feet.

"Now I am, thanks to you." She gave him a smile that nearly triggered my gag reflex. But her breathing was still ragged and she was trembling.

"Was someone chasing you?" I asked, thinking of the man who accosted me.

"Not someone, something! Your crazy cousin was walking this…this… giant squirrel creature. The thing was trying to get at me and pulled the leash right out of his hand. I had to run for my life. That's why I dodged into the first shop I came to. Whatever you do, don't let him in here. He could be rabid!"

"The marmot or Merlin?" I asked evenly. Travis tried not to laugh, but he finally lost it.

Beverly lifted her chin with indignation. "Laugh all you want, but I bet my life it's not legal to keep a beast like that as a pet in this state, and I intend to find out!" The situation went from funny to grim in five seconds flat. Merlin would never agree to give up Froliquet. An image of them sitting together in a jail cell popped into my head.

"I'm sorry, Beverly," I said with as much sincerity as I could muster. Travis followed my lead. "My apologies as well. I have no idea why it struck me as funny, but that was totally inappropriate."

I saw the calculated look flash in her eyes and realized she was about to ask about compensation for her ordeal. I peered out the window past Sashkatu, who was absorbed in cleaning his paws. "Oh no, here they come! Merlin's gaining on the marmot," I called it out like a play by play of a sporting event. "He's about to catch her...oh no, she zigged when he zagged. She's running him around in circles. He stumbled. Is he going down? No, he's still on his feet—what a save. Now he's herding her this way!"

Travis grabbed Beverly's arm, hooking into my improv and running with it. "Quick—come with me. I'll get you out the back way." For a moment she seemed torn between standing her ground and wanting to flee. I helped her make the right decision by throwing open the front door. Beverly didn't even look over her shoulder as Travis rushed her out the back door.

For the rest of the morning, whenever we happened to glance at each other, we burst into laughter at what would come to be known, among family and friends, as Beverly and the Attack of the Giant Squirrel.

Chapter 23

We should have known that Beverly would follow through with her threat to report Merlin and Froliquet to the police. But we had a lot more pressing matters on our minds, not the least of which was earning a living. We were in the thick of the summer season, with bus tours filling our calendars and tourists filling our shops. We had little time to restock merchandise, and none to waste worrying about when Beverly's theatrics might come home to roost.

Tilly was baking for so many hours a day that her feet were perpetually swollen and couldn't be stuffed into even her most comfortable stretched out slippers. Merlin and I tried every herbal poultice we could think of. He massaged her feet until his fingers were numb. I wrote a spell that worked for five minutes, but then her feet ballooned up again. It was Merlin who finally came up with a solution.

"Mayhap we need more power behind the spell to make it last longer." We were in Tilly's shop where she was seated with her feet up on another chair. I ran back to Abracadabra to fetch Sashkatu. He wasn't happy to be plucked off his sundrenched windowsill mid nap, but I rarely made such demands of him. Besides this was for Tilly, whom he loved dearly. When he realized she was ailing, he dropped the put-upon attitude. With everyone on board, Merlin, Froliquet, Sashki and I formed a circle of sorts around my aunt. Those of us who spoke English repeated the spell seven times for good measure.

Heal the feet of she who ails.
Be gone the pain and swelling.
Let her finish all her work

Just like a girl of twenty.

Like time-lapse photography, Tilly's feet returned to their normal size right before our eyes. Five minutes passed and they remained unchanged. Ten minutes passed, then twenty, and thirty. No one dared call the fortified spell a success yet.

"Hold it," I said. "Tilly needs to be standing. Otherwise how can we tell if the spell is really working?"

"Oh dear," Tilly mumbled, "we should all be ashamed of ourselves."

She set her bare feet on the floor and stood up. The vigil of her feet began again. When the results were in, Tilly could stand for two hours at a time before the swelling returned. Although that was far from perfect, she could manage to do her baking between periods of rest. The hope was that with practice she might only need the rest of us to provide a booster shot of the spell once a day.

With Tilly literally back on her feet, I returned to my storeroom. I was rushing to fill bottles with poison ivy remedy when the bells over the front door jingled. I screwed the cap on the last bottle and went to greet my customer. I found Paul Curtis poking his head down the aisles, looking for me. "Hi Paul," I said, giving him a start. "Sorry, I didn't mean to sneak up on you."

He broke into an easy smile. Since he'd started dating Abigail Riggs, things had finally become less awkward between us. If Travis hadn't come into my life at the same time Paul got up his nerve to ask me out, I might have been the one dating him. He was a nice guy, but I'd known him most of my life. He never had a chance once Travis showed up on my doorstep.

"Hi. I stopped by to give you a heads up."

"About what?"

"Beverly Ruppert filed a complaint against your cousin Merlin. She didn't know his last name. It seems he has a new pet that chased her down the street?" His voice rose in a question as if he knew Beverly might have exaggerated the incident. "Does Merlin have a new pet?"

The answer was an easy *yes*, but it would lead inexorably to a reading of the town code with regard to harboring animals. I'd read the code a few times over the years, whenever I thought about getting a more exotic pet than a cat, dog or canary. I was fairly certain that marmots were not on the list of animals permitted to dwell in New Camel residences. Even if the police tried to look the other way, marmots chasing people down the street was a hard *no*. "He has a wonderful new pet," I said wishing that could be the end of the conversation.

Since Paul wasn't telepathic, he kept it going. "What did he get?"

I considered saying it was a mutt of questionable ancestry, who suffered from a curvature of the spine that affected its gait and could have benefitted from the help of a skilled orthodontist. But Paul would see right through my ruse the moment he laid eyes on the marmot. I swallowed a sigh. If Merlin was forced to send Froliquet back to wherever she'd been, he would come unglued. I was on the verge of admitting the truth, when a better idea popped into my head. "Why don't you come by this evening to meet our new addition? You should see her with your own two eyes." We settled on 7:30. He would be off duty, and I'd have plenty of time to get Tilly and Merlin onboard with my plan.

When I explained the situation, I made sure Froliquet was busy fending off the lovesick Isenbale. Merlin flew into a tizzy at the mere thought of losing his familiar. My aunt managed to calm him down by threatening not to serve dessert for the next two days if he didn't behave. He feigned an attitude of calm by compressing his lips and remaining seated, but his frantic energy needed an outlet. His foot pumped up and down on the floor to the beat of his anxiety and his fingers drummed an accompaniment on the tabletop.

Tilly fixed him with her eyes. "This plan will only work if you're in possession of your faculties. Do you understand?" Merlin's head bopped up and down.

"Merlin," I said, "how long can you maintain a glamouring before it starts breaking down?"

"An hour, maybe three."

"There can't be any *maybes* for this to work. We'll keep it under an hour. You cannot mention this to Froliquet. If she knows what's coming, she could sabotage it." Merlin mimed locking his lips and throwing away the key.

We all agreed that glamouring the marmot so that she appeared to be an acceptable species under the town code would be less risky than actually transmuting her into that form. We also agreed she should look like a dog. We rarely agreed so easily and that alone made me worry about impending disaster. If anything did go wrong, Merlin could be exposed for the wizard he was, and I would lose my status as an honest and upstanding citizen. And that was only the tip of the iceberg that could sink us all.

The doorbell rang at seven thirty on the dot. Merlin, Froliquet and I remained in the living room while Tilly went to open the door. I wanted Paul to see us as a normal family gathered together after dinner to chat. If it hadn't been the middle of summer, I would have asked Tilly to light the gas fireplace to add another element of cozy warmth to the scene.

Froliquet had no idea she appeared different to the world. To me she looked like a small dog with an overbite and coarse brown fur. Merlin's spell had changed her tiny ears into long, floppy ones and elongated her nose and mouth into a doglike snout. She was the homeliest pooch I'd ever seen, but we weren't planning to enter her in any dog shows.

Tilly ushered Paul into the room and offered him a seat. "Thanks, but I can't stay. Isn't somebody going to introduce me to the new member of the family?" He hunkered down close to where Froliquet was snoozing.

Tilly took care of the honors. "Paul this is Froliquet. Froliquet meet Paul." The marmot didn't bother to open her eyes, for which I was grateful.

"Nice to meet you, Froliquet," he said, stroking her back. "Merlin, where did you get her?" Paul was really pushing the due diligence.

I jumped in before the wizard had a chance to say the wrong thing. "He got her at the animal shelter. She was there for two years, but was always passed over for the prettier dogs. Merlin insisted on saving her."

"You did a good thing, Merlin," he said, getting to his feet. "Oh, I should tell you that according to Beverly, this little lady chased after her with a bloodthirsty look in her eyes and saliva dripping from her jaws."

"Does that seem likely?" I asked.

He laughed. "No, but it has Beverly written all over it. In any case, I have to inform you that all dogs must be up to date on their shots and leashed when out in public."

Merlin had started to doze off. Tilly shook his shoulder. "Did you hear that?"

"How's a fellow supposed to sleep with you bellowing in his ear?"

"A *fellow* isn't supposed to sleep when entertaining guests," she whispered loudly enough for the neighbors to hear. I looked at Paul and mouthed the word *sorry*. He winked at me.

"It's all good. I'm going to head out and let you folks get on with your evening." He leaned down to give Froliquet a last pat. With the worst possible timing, dragon spikes suddenly sprouted along her spine and in a second were gone again. Paul jumped back, rubbing his eyes.

"Are you okay?" I asked as if I had no idea what happened.

"You didn't see that a second ago?"

"See what?"

"There were…I mean, it looked like—" he stopped, perhaps realizing there was nothing he could say that would sound rational. "I guess I'm overtired."

"You put in long hours," I commiserated, taking his arm and turning him away from Froliquet, whose snout was in the process of stretching to the length of an anteater's, before snapping back to its original size. I steered him toward the door. Merlin's spell was going haywire and we couldn't have Paul there to witness it. There was just so much he would chalk up to fatigue. It bothered me how good I'd become at deflecting questions and flat-out lying to hide the true extent of our magick. But as my grandmother Bronwen always warned me, "Don't assume the witch trials can't happen again."

I closed the door behind Paul and hurried back into the living room where poor Froliquet was growing and losing animal parts too quickly to count. Tilly gave Merlin a well aimed kick in the shins to wake him again.

"Good Lord, woman," he sputtered, "what has possessed you?"

"If you're not alert enough to monitor your spells, they seem to lose cohesion," I said now that he was awake. I kept my tone even, trying to bring calm and reason to the situation. "You need to be more careful in the future."

"Nonsense, that's never happened before."

"But it's happening now," Tilly said. "Wake up and smell the coffee."

He sniffed the air. "Coffee? I could use some coffee. Might there be any more of that lovely banana bread to enjoy with it?"

Chapter 24

At the end of the day, Sashkatu and I headed home. The five other cats gathered around me the moment I walked in. No one complained about starving, so I plunked myself down on the hardwood in their midst and spent a good twenty minutes cuddling them. I enjoyed the interlude as much as they did—okay, probably more. It was nice to be needed for more than my opposable thumbs at mealtimes.

The only one who didn't enjoy the love fest was Sashkatu, who'd spent the entire day with me. He sat down outside the circle of his peers to remind me with frequent, irritated *meows* that he was at death's door and only an immediate infusion of food could save him. It was a contest of wills and he eventually won. But he didn't play fair. When he didn't make any headway with me, he let the others know, in ways cats alone understand, that they'd better get with the program—his program. I often wondered what he held over their heads to get his way.

The only chore I set for myself that evening was to call the last alum who had responded to my email. I remembered her as soon as I saw her name on the reply. Carina Ardsley. We were close friends for a time in middle school, but drifted apart in high school. Looking back from my adult perspective, the only reason I could attribute to our parting of the ways was the fact that she became a cheerleader. The girls in that group were a tight clique and Carina had always liked fitting in as much as I shied away from it.

When she answered the phone, the years fell away and I was swept back into my adolescence. "You sound exactly the same," I said with a laugh, forgetting about any sort of greeting. And it was quickly obvious that identifying myself wasn't necessary anyway.

"Oh Kailyn—so do you!" We spent the next fifteen minutes reminiscing. "I was so bummed I couldn't make it to the reunion," she said, "at least until I heard about Genna. I get the chills every time I think about it. And now you're investigating her death. Do you have any suspects?"

"I'm sorry, I can't talk names at this point. I really appreciate your responding to my email. You wrote that you've seen Scott's ghost."

"Yes. Scared me half to death. He was outside my bedroom window one night. I haven't told a soul, other than my husband and my sister, and now you. I don't want people to think I'm losing it, you know. But I've always felt like I could trust you. Besides, you wouldn't be asking if I'd seen anything *unusual*, unless something weird was going on."

"Well you're right. He seems to have visited a number of the alums."

"Do you have any idea why he's chosen to *haunt* some of us?" She whispered the word as if someone might overhear her and cart her off to a padded cell. "I never did anything to him to deserve payback."

"We have a working theory, nothing solid yet. It seems that the people who have seen him were at the lake the night he died. Can you tell me what you remember from that night?"

"Not that much really. It was very warm and somebody suggested continuing the party down at the lake. All the cheerleaders were going, so I hopped in one of the girls' cars and off we went. There was a lot of drinking and laughing at the lake, but I recall thinking it was maybe getting out of hand—the drinking part. I was actually looking for a ride home when I heard the screams. The cops came and ambulances—all the flashing lights. It felt surreal, like a dream you should be able to wake up from."

"Thank you," I said. I remembered how warm it was. And it made sense that Carina had chosen to go to the lake if the other cheerleaders were going. Not having been there, that was as much as I could corroborate.

"Is it possible Scott somehow blames me for his drowning?" she asked. "I swear I wasn't anywhere near him at the lake. And I never went into the water." She was pleading her case to me as if I were a judge and could set him straight in some afterlife court.

"I'll let you know if I figure out why he's visiting people from the lake. At this point, all I can say is that everyone who has seen his ghost was at the lake that night." Except for me, but I'd already told her too much. I still had a soft spot in my heart for Carina and our once upon a time friendship.

The phone rang again before I could put it down. "Hi, how're you doing?" Travis said and barreled on without waiting for me to reply. "When are you available to make the trip up to see Ashley? I feel like we've been coasting on that."

I'd had similar thoughts of late. "Name two days you're free."

"We can drive up this Thursday and meet with Ashley either later that day or Friday. If she opts for Friday, we'll spend another night and leave for home the next morning."

"Okay, I'll call to see if she's willing to talk to us on either of those dates." I'd wait until she was onboard, before asking my aunt to take care of my beasties. "If we can make it work, I want to stop on the way back to talk to Tony." Aside from a few quick calls to make sure he was on the mend, we'd never had a chance to talk to him at length after the hit and run.

"We'll make it work. I'm convinced Genna's killer is the one who went after Tony. We have to find out what set the two of them apart from the others at the lake."

I filled Travis in on my conversation with Carina. "So your theory about the ghostly visitations is still holding. There's something else I want to run by you."

"Shoot."

"We never discussed the question of Genna's murder and Tony's close call being tied to the hauntings. But I've certainly been thinking of them as two ends of the same search for revenge and justice."

"I have too. Otherwise the odds of them playing out at the same time would be way too high."

"Then we're on the same page. Let me call Ashley before it gets too late. I'll get right back to you." I found her number in my list of contacts, but I didn't immediately dial it. When I asked to visit her, I had to word it the right way. She had to be aware that Duggan considered her a suspect. Subtlety was not his strong suit. She had nothing to gain by speaking to me, unless she thought I was on her side.

I spent ten minutes working and reworking my pitch. Primed and ready, I punched in the numbers. Waiting for her to pick up, I felt like an actor waiting in the wings for her cue. When the voice mail came on, it threw me. "Ashley, hi, it's Kailyn." I wanted to sound casual, but I sounded stiff, like I had a knife at my throat. "I'll be up in Maine for a couple of days and I'm hoping we can get together." Way too perky. The message sounded like Dr. Jekyll and Mrs. Hyde. I didn't mention Travis, because we'd already decided I would see her alone. She was bound to be more open and trusting without my journalist boyfriend in tow.

She returned my call an hour later as I was drifting off to sleep. She seemed upbeat about my visit. "My time is kind of limited though. I spend most of the day baking and working in the shop. I leave around two and there's someone who takes over until closing. Would three o'clock Friday work for you?" I told her it would. What she didn't know was that any time she proposed would have worked for me. She was the sole reason we were driving to Yarmouth, Maine.

Chapter 25

We were zipping along I-95. The car smelled like breakfast. We'd stopped at a fast-food drive-thru for eggs, ham and cheese on biscuits with large coffees. Travis ate his while he drove, alternating between the sandwich and the coffee without taking his eyes off the road.

"It's a kind of braille you learn on road trips, when you're chasing down a story." he said, when I tried to convince him to eat before getting back on the highway. "Broadcasting from the site of breaking news before the other outlets is the name of the game. Stopping to eat can knock you out of the running. Speed has always been important, but in this hi-tech age it can make or break you." When I didn't say anything for a few minutes, he asked why I was so quiet.

"I was thinking about how everyone's always rushing to get somewhere. If I could teach teleportation, I'd be the next instant billionaire."

He stole a worried glance at me. "You can't teach that, can you?"

I laughed. "No, teleportation isn't possible without the right DNA."

"Hey wait a minute, what about the time you tried to take me with you? Were you experimenting?"

"I don't know if I'd call it experimenting," I said. "I was trying to save your life."

"For future reference, I don't know if I want to live without all my parts in the right places."

"I was almost certain you'd be fine. I've tried it with inanimate objects and plants, even a frog I caught in the garden. Everything came through unscathed."

"If I were an amphibian or a ficus that might be more comforting."

"What happened to my courageous reporter who throws caution to the wind to catch a killer and sweep a girl off her feet?" I was enjoying his discomfit more than I should have. "I'm teasing you," I relented. "It's actually in the scrolls Merlin's been translating. 'As long as the sorcerer holds fast to another, both are protected during the process of teleportation.'"

Travis wasn't ready to put the question to rest. "Just how good are Merlin's translation skills? He's not always what I'd call *a hundred percent.*"

"They've been spot on so far. Don't forget, it's not really translation for him. He lived before the scrolls were even written."

"Good point." Travis reached for my hand and held it tightly. "Let's try to stay away from the subject of magick for the rest of this trip. I want to concentrate on being courageous and romantic." I would have been a fool to argue with that.

We made it to Yarmouth in the mid afternoon and after checking into our hotel, we took a walk through the Village Center. According to the online guide, the center had cafes and shops, including Baked to Perfection, Ashley's pride and joy. But we almost missed it altogether. It was a narrow little shop, wedged between a variety store and a soup and salad cafe.

"Ashley should be gone by now," I said to Travis. "I want to nose around inside."

He laughed. "And maybe sample a thing or two?"

"Well you can't grow up with an aunt like Tilly and not be addicted to sugar. But I also wanted to chat with Ashley's one employee."

Bells over the door announced our arrival. An elderly woman with snow-white hair wound into a bun on top of her head was behind the counter. A plastic nametag pinned to her blouse read *Connie.* She was nibbling on a cookie when we walked in. She stiffened and shoved the remainder of the cookie into her mouth as if we'd caught her doing something illegal. For all we knew, she'd been told to stop eating the wares. She put her hand over her mouth and tried to chew subtly. Travis and I browsed the glass counters and pretended not to notice.

Some of the trays were empty, except for crumbs, others nearly so. The shelves on the back wall held a few breads and rolls. In a small refrigerated counter were pastries with whipped cream and custard. Breakfast had been hours ago. I didn't realize how hungry I was until I saw the éclairs. I asked for one with dark chocolate icing. Travis succumbed as well, taken down by a large cream puff.

"Shall I put your goodies in a bag or a box?" Connie inquired now that she was able to speak.

"A bag will do," I said, knowing we'd attack them the moment we left there. If not for the fact that I wanted to engage Connie in conversation, I would have told her not to even bother with the bag.

She handed me the change from my purchase. "You folks down from Portland? We've been getting more and more customers from there every day. Twelve miles is nothing when you've got a craving."

"We're from out of state," Travis said.

Connie bobbed her head, but continued on without missing a beat. "Our business is growing by the day—word of mouth to be sure. Ashley...she's the owner—she has quite a following. I keep asking her why she doesn't invest in a bigger space. With the money coming in, this is the time to expand, maybe even open a tiny branch in Portland. She just shrugs and says she likes things fine the way they are. But she deserves more than *fine*, poor girl."

We could simply let Connie keep talking. Sooner or later she was bound to tell us everything we might ever want to know. But in the interest of saving time, I jumped in.

"Poor girl?"

"I guess you wouldn't know." She leaned over the counter, her voice dropping to low and confidential. "Ashley's high school sweetheart drowned the night of their prom." She wagged her head. "So tragic."

I copied her spy-like whisper. "What happened?"

"No one knows for sure, but Ashley doesn't believe it was an accident," Connie said ominously. "And if it wasn't an accident, it must have been murder." All that was missing was melodramatic music in the background.

"Does she have a theory about who's guilty?"

"She's never said, but if you ask *me*, I think she's finally figured it out."

"What's she planning to do about it?" Travis was trying to mimic us, but his delivery was jarring. It broke the mood. Connie straightened, morphing seamlessly back into the kindly purveyor of baked goods. She'd missed her calling. She could have had a career on the stage or screen.

"You folks enjoy your stay here in Yarmouth," she said, handing me the bag of pastries with a smile.

Chapter 26

We found a bench and sat down to devour our sugary lunch.

"Don't ever leave your day job," I said, wiping the last of the éclair off my mouth with the napkins Connie had put in the bag. Travis looked confused, but his mouth was too full of cream puff to question me.

"Leave the acting to naturals like Connie."

"Yeah," he said when he could speak. "I was pretty bad—I heard it myself." Travis was more self-aware than most men I'd known. It was one of the things I loved about him. He never saw himself through rose-colored glasses. "Connie is quite a character. She'd be perfect for a local acting troupe. And based on the cream puff I just inhaled, Ashley's one hell of a baker."

"Not to mention a good candidate for the role of revenge killer," I added. "I think it's safe to say she has no idea about the gossip well-meaning Connie is spreading." We wandered through the rest of the Village Center, before heading back to the hotel. Travis sank into the armchair facing the TV and grabbed the remote off the nearby table. He clicked through the channels until he found a baseball game.

After I unpacked my toiletries, I went over and perched on the arm of his chair. "So watching baseball is your idea of a vacation?"

"It certainly is. I bet I can even make you a fan."

"Not likely."

"We'll see," he said. "Step one, find a comfortable seat." He snaked his arm around my waist and pulled me into his lap. "Comfy?" I nodded.

"I'm beginning to see what you mean. What's step two?"

"Don't get pushy. Step two, relax until your team gets on base." He moved my hair aside and kissed the nape of my neck. He was right, I was becoming invested in the game. A few minutes later, the batter hit a ground ball past the shortstop and outran the throw to first base.

"Step three?" I asked.

"We celebrate."

"How does one celebrate a base hit?" In response Travis turned off the TV.

* * * *

I didn't feel bad about leaving Travis behind the next day, when I left to see Ashley. He had his whole afternoon planned. He'd hit the gym, swim laps in the pool and watch another baseball game, although he said it wouldn't be as much fun without me.

I arrived at Ashley's house at the designated time. The house was a small Cape Cod that hadn't been dormered like its neighbors. The front yard was tidy. The bushes had been trimmed, although not recently, and the lawn was mowed. On closer inspection, there were as many weeds as there were blades of grass, but since they were all green, it worked. This was the house of someone who had more work to do than hours in which to do it. I gave her a mental thumbs-up for effort. I was about to ring the bell, when she opened the door.

"Ashley, hi," I said. "Good to see you!"

"You too, Kailyn," she said, but without any real warmth. "Come on in."

We touched cheeks, but I didn't try to draw her into a hug. Our relationship had never been that close. The only interest we'd had in common was Scott. Maybe she regretted agreeing to see me. She might have found out I was investigating Genna's death, but was afraid if she canceled it would raise my suspicions about her. Speculating wasn't going to net me any answers, so I dialed up my smile and walked inside.

The foyer was barely big enough to hold the two of us. Directly in front of us was a steep narrow staircase that bisected the house, with the living room to the right and the dining room to the left. Ashley led the way through the dining room, where a folding table was piled high with papers, and into a small, but updated kitchen with white shaker cabinets and a gray and black granite countertop. She'd set the breakfast bar for two with cups, spoons, napkins and a plate with chocolate chip cookies that smelled like they'd just come out of the oven.

It was a cozy setup with the two of us sitting side by side. The only other option would have meant cleaning off the folding table, but even I could see that would have been a huge undertaking.

She poured the coffee and urged me to try the cookies. It didn't take a lot of coaxing. They were better than Tilly's, both chewy and crisp. If I ever mentioned that to my aunt, she would fly into a tizzy and start baking around the clock until I said hers were better.

The conversation was slow in starting. Ashley spent a lot of time adding sweetener and milk to her cup until she was satisfied with the taste. I asked the usual inane questions. How was she doing? Where in Florida had her parents settled? Why had she chosen Yarmouth for her bakery?"

She sipped her coffee. "Finances. I couldn't afford to live in Portland *and* rent a place for the bakery there. A friend suggested Yarmouth, because it's a quick fifteen minute drive south on I-295."

I reached for another cookie. "My friend and I stopped in your bakery yesterday and it's no surprise why you're succeeding." My compliment was sincere, even though I was using it so she would let down her guard.

She smiled, a blush rising in her cheeks. "My parents warned me I'd wind up in debt, but I was determined to make a go of it, even if I had to peddle my wares on a street corner."

"Scott would have been proud of you."

Her smile dimmed and she looked down into her coffee. "Thank you. I like to think so too." When she looked up again, there was a sheen of tears.in her eyes.

"You know," I said, "it's always bothered me that his death was deemed an accidental drowning."

"Me too," she murmured. "It wasn't like Scott to go swimming alone at night. He used to talk *me* out of reckless behavior. But the ME found alcohol in his blood—a lot of it."

"That wasn't like him either," I said.

Ashley tucked her hair behind her ears. "The questions still haunt me."

"But you've managed to move on with your life." I lay my hand on her forearm. "That's huge—impressive."

A smile flickered across her face, but didn't take hold. "I've moved on in my career, yes, but not in my life."

"Have you put yourself out there to meet people?"

"Friends fixed me up a couple of times with blind dates," she said with a short joyless laugh. "The guys were nice enough, but I couldn't wait for the dates to be over." She swiveled in her seat to face me. "I actually felt disloyal."

"I knew Scott for almost all of his eighteen years and I can tell you that he would want you to live your life to the fullest."

"Believe me, I'd like to. I get really lonely sometimes. But I think I need to see him get justice first."

"What if the ME was right, and Scott's death was simply the result of tragic decisions?" Although she was a suspect, I couldn't help wanting to ease her mind. "He wasn't a drinker, but he drank too much that night—like he was trying to prove something to himself. And he knew better than to go into the water in the dark, but the alcohol messed with his thinking."

"But why did he drink so much? Maybe if I'd been there…"

"Don't do that, Ashley. No way was it your fault."

She finished her coffee and made a face. "Coffee should either be piping hot or ice cold, not room temperature." She rinsed her cup at the sink and refilled it. "Can I refresh yours?" She held up the carafe that was still half full. I declined. "Have you made any progress in finding Genna's killer?" she asked, returning to her seat.

I shook my head. "We're working with the theory that her murder is related to Scott's death." I watched for her reaction.

"You mean like a revenge killing? That would mean the killer knew Genna was to blame." Connie had said her boss had finally figured out who was responsible for Scott's death. Did Ashley think if she spoke openly about it, I would conclude she had to be innocent? For now it served my purposes to let her believe she'd succeeded.

"What we can't figure out is why Genna would have wanted to harm Scott in the first place," I said, "or why her killer believed that she had. It's a puzzle with a lot of missing pieces." I thought I saw relief cross Ashley's face, softening her features. Her back that had been ramrod straight, relaxed into the curve of the barstool. I wished Travis could have been there to corroborate my insight or tell me I was projecting what I was thinking. "Not to worry," I added with an optimistic uptick in my voice, "I'm pretty good at solving puzzles. It's just a matter of time before I figure out this one. Maybe then you'll be able to move on." *Or into a prison cell.*

Ashley produced a wry smile. "I guess we'll have to wait and see."

Our visit was winding down. Any minute she would excuse herself to run errands or do any of a dozen things that needed doing. "I'm curious what you would consider justice served for Scott?"

"The guilty party tried and properly punished. No early release for good behavior."

"I assume you mean a prison term. There's no death penalty in New York."

"I know, but maybe there should be."

* * * *

Tilly called when I was on my way back to the hotel. "I spent the whole day debating whether or not to call you. I didn't want to interrupt your time with Travis or your investigation, but I can't seem to get it out of my mind."

"Get what out of your mind?"

"The dream I had last night. You know what, forget I called. It's probably nothing. I'll let you go."

"No, Aunt Tilly, wait." I found a place to pull over to the curb so I could concentrate on what she was saying. "I really want to know what's troubling you."

"Well if you insist. I had another one of those dreams—like the ones that have predicted death." There was a nervous hitch in her voice like a single hiccough. I wasn't psychic, but I knew what was coming. "This time it was about somebody away on vacation." A sob punctuated her words.

"I think worry and fear planted that dream. Do you remember telling me that whenever I had a nightmare as a kid?"

"Yes, but this is different. I can't explain it. Just promise me that you'll be careful on the road and wherever you go. I have no idea where or when this danger will strike. I love you." She hung up before I could try to reassure her, although I suspected that would have been an exercise in futility.

Chapter 27

I called Tony Russo on our way home from Yarmouth to see if we could stop by for a chat. I try to avoid the word *interview* whenever possible. It immediately puts a person on edge and a person on edge is preoccupied with saving their butt, not helping you solve a murder case.

Courtney answered the phone and sounded happy to hear from us. We'd established a friendship of sorts with them through phone calls to check on Tony's progress. When I asked if we could visit them that afternoon, there was no hesitation or reluctance in her answer. That easy trust made me feel like a traitor. There were times I wondered if I was cut out for this type of work, despite the fact that I was good at it.

"You picked the right day to be passing by," Courtney said, ushering us into their home, an L-shaped ranch nestled among beds of brilliant flowers. "Tony is back at work part-time now, but he's always home on weekends." She took us into the family room, where Tony was ensconced in a brown leather armchair, his injured leg propped up on a hassock. His face split into a grin when he saw us.

"Please don't get up," I said before he had a chance to make the effort.

"Thanks. Good to see you guys! Make yourselves comfortable," he said after I'd leaned down to kiss his cheek and he and Travis had clasped hands. We sat on the end of the curved couch that was closest to him. Courtney brought us tall glasses of iced tea, before joining us on the couch. We asked Tony how his recovery was going and commiserated with Courtney about the difficulty of trying to keep him from doing too much too soon.

He shrugged. "What can I do? I'm not a sitter. I can't binge a whole season of TV shows like some people. I get antsy. I'm used to being active."

"And you will be again," Courtney said as if she was reading a script she knew by heart. "As long as you stick to the doctor's schedule. Push it and you may be stuck in that chair for another month or two."

"See what I have to put up—wait a second," he interrupted himself, his voice dropping to a more serious register. "You probably haven't heard the latest."

"What's that?" Travis and I said in unison.

"The other night someone disabled the brakes in my car. I pulled out of the driveway to go to work—scary as hell when you put your foot on the brake and it flatlines. I totaled the mailbox across the street and took out a couple of their bushes."

"He might have gone into their house if not for the boulders in their rock garden," Courtney added. "The police were swarming all over the place, searching for evidence. They towed the car away too." Her voice was tightening as she spoke. "First Tony was run down and nearly killed and now this. What's next?" Her voice cracked. "Excuse me," she mumbled, hurrying out of the room.

Tony sighed and shook his head. "It's been tough on her. We were just starting to put the first incident behind us…"

"Can you think of any reason why someone might blame you and Genna for Scott's death?" I asked bluntly. The time for mincing words was past and then some. "There haven't been attempts on anyone else's life." We'd talked to a lot of people in this case, but Tony was the ultimate source, the horse's mouth so to speak. If I hit a sore spot with my question, he'd be smart to admit it. "Help me find the killer, Tony, before he succeeds in taking you down."

"Believe me, I've wracked my brain over it. Being laid up, I had plenty of time to think—too much time. That's why I needed to get back to work."

Travis was studying him. "And?"

"Nothing really, but if I had to take a wild guess, maybe it was the booze. A bunch of us were egging each other on to drink more. Stupid stuff, you know."

"Whose idea was it to go swimming?" Travis asked.

"I'm not sure about that. A lot of the details are hazy. Scott wasn't the only one who drank way too much that night. I remember hearing someone say, 'why did we come to the lake if no one's going in?' In my memory, the voice sounds like it could have been Genna's. But it was so long ago…"

Travis jumped in with another question. "Did you actually see Scott or anyone else go in?"

Tony's eyebrows pinched together. "You're beginning to sound an awful lot like a reporter. This is just between friends, completely off the record, right?"

"Sorry—absolutely off the record."

"All right. I didn't realize anyone had gone into the lake, until I heard splashing. It couldn't have been more than another minute or two, before the screaming started."

Courtney returned looking more composed, despite the red rimming her eyes. "I have a favor to ask," she said, taking her seat beside me. "I've been listening to you guys talk and I know how important this is, but can we please change the subject? The kids will be home from a birthday party soon. The brake incident was traumatic for them and it's still fresh in their minds. If Tony and I don't have it together, they're going to pick up on that and be even more frightened."

It wasn't an easy shift, but Tony dredged up every silly memory he had from high school. He'd loved being the class clown, even though he'd gotten into plenty of trouble because of his antics. I laughed harder than I had in a long time. Good therapy for us as well as them.

Travis and I said our goodbyes and made our way down the driveway, edging past Tony's rental car, to the curb where we were parked. A group of boys in their early teens were playing a rough game of dodgeball in the cul-de-sac. The ball missed its intended target and flew straight at Tony's car, smashing into the side. I was thinking *poor guy can't catch a break*, when the world erupted in searing light and ear-shattering noise.

Chapter 28

When I opened my eyes, I was in a hospital with no recollection of why I was there. The last thing I remembered was saying goodbye to the Russos. There was a big blank spot where the memories should have been. I had half a dozen small bandages on my arms and legs. My back hurt where it pressed against the bed and my head throbbed like a bad toothache.

Where was Travis? Whatever happened to me, must have affected him as well. Anxiety welled in my chest. I pushed myself up against the pillows so I could reach the curtain around my bed. The effort made my head spin, but I managed to move it enough to see that there was another bed in the room. It was stripped down to the mattress. A set of folded linens was piled in the center of it. Whoever had been in that bed, no longer needed it. With that thought came other questions that pumped up my anxiety until I thought it would burst through the walls of my chest. I needed answers and if I didn't get them in the next few seconds, I was going to climb out of the bed and track them down myself!

I found the button to call the nurse's station. I pressed it and counted to twenty. When no one appeared, I swung my legs off the side of the bed. The room tilted and spun. I gripped the edge of the mattress and waited for it to stop. I had to find Travis. I planted my feet on the cold floor and tried to stand on my own. Darkness closed in on me. I gritted my teeth and locked my jaw, determined not to succumb to it, but the darkness was swallowing me.

When I opened my eyes again, I was back in the bed. The nurse was taking my pulse. She smiled at me. "Welcome back. You got a little too adventurous."

"I can't just lie here. I have to find Travis. I have to figure out what happened to us."

"Your friend is here. He just went downstairs for coffee. Take some deep, slow breaths and try to relax. From what I understand, you were both very lucky."

A moment later, Travis walked in with a container of coffee. When he saw that I was awake, his whole face brightened as if a spotlight had been trained on him. I scoured him for injuries. There was a small bandage along his jaw and another on the hand holding the coffee.

The nurse finished checking my vitals. "Don't let her get out of bed again," she said to Travis as if it was his fault I wound up on the floor.

"Yes ma'am," he said with a salute.

I was nearly jumping out of my skin with the need to hug him to me and feel his arms wrapped around me. But he was taking the nurse's warning to heart. I had to make do with a gentle kiss on the cheek as if I might break from a more passionate one. He moved the only chair closer to the side of the bed and took a swig of his coffee.

"Please, tell me what happened," I said. "I can't remember a thing."

He closed his hand over mine. "Someone planted a bomb on Tony's rental. We were caught in the shock waves. I was farther from the blast, so it had less of an impact on me. You suffered a concussion and some second degree burns."

"What about Tony and Courtney?"

"They're fine. We've been texting. The fire jumped from the car to the garage by the time the fire department arrived. They lost some stuff they were storing in there, nothing important. There was no damage to the rest of the house. But they feel awful we were hurt trying to help them and they're really scared."

"They'd be crazy if they weren't. Whoever is out to kill Tony isn't going to give up."

"I told them to demand police protection. Give me a second. They made me promise to let them know how you're doing." While he updated them, I leaned back against the pillows and took a deep breath. The anxiety was slowly filtering away, but I still had no recollection of the explosion or the trip to the hospital. Merlin might have a spell to recall memories. I didn't know if I could trust any spell I created while my brain was busy healing. It wasn't the kind of question the nurse or doctor could answer.

Travis tucked his phone back in his pocket. "They send their best."

It dawned on me that the bomb must have been what Tilly had foreseen. "Does my aunt know what happened?"

"Yes, I figured you'd want me to call her. It took a lot of convincing to keep her from driving up here to take care of you herself. Being pigheaded seems to run in your family." I didn't have a clever comeback. "Listen," he said, a frown puckering the skin between his brows. "I spoke to the doctor before you woke up. He wants to keep you overnight for observation—to make sure all your organs are functioning properly. Shock waves pass through your whole body. They can do a lot of damage."

I was shaking my head while he was still talking. "No way. I'm fine. I'm not staying here tonight. I'll heal more quickly under Tilly's care." To emphasize the point, I threw back the covers and started to get up. Travis set his coffee on the bedside table, scooped me up and tucked me back in.

"Not so fast. People who are *fine* don't pass out from standing up. You've been through a traumatic event. You can't rush things."

"We've both gone through this before and I don't recall you listening to the doctor's advice back then or Tilly's for that matter."

Travis ran his fingers through his hair. "All right, all right. There's no use arguing with you once your mind's made up. Let's get some food into you. That may help with the dizziness."

I had to sign a form saying that I was leaving against medical advice. The nurse made it clear she thought we were both crazy.

Scrambled eggs and an English muffin later, he was helping me into his car.

We were quiet for the bulk of the trip home. Shock waves and fatigue are not conducive to lively conversation. Left to wander, my mind poked around the case. The multiple attempts on Tony's life led me to believe he was withholding information from us. He had to bear more responsibility for Scott's death if someone was hunting him like this. For that matter, we hadn't yet figured out what Genna's role had been. But she was beyond our help. If only there were some way to communicate with Scott. He had all the answers. I couldn't ask Morgana and Bronwen to look him up. Morgana had already undergone remedial training for a wayward remark to me. I didn't want to be responsible for getting her into more trouble.

I fell asleep for the last hour of the trip. Travis woke me when he pulled into my driveway. I was disoriented for a few moments, the remnants of a dream floating around in my head. I tried to piece it back together, but then the front door of my house flew open and Tilly did a neat little shuffle-run to the car. Merlin was behind her with Froliquet at his side. Although he'd left the door wide open, the cats remained at the threshold as if it was an invisible barrier. I caught Sashkatu peeking out of the living room window, but the moment he realized he'd been spotted, he disappeared. He had a reputation to protect.

Travis helped me into the house with his arm around my waist for support. Tilly claimed my free arm. Merlin tried to help too, but only managed to tangle his feet with Tilly's. Before we all went down in a heap, Travis picked me up and carried me straight to the couch. He looked exhausted.

"You have to stop treating me like I'm going to break," I told him, "or we'll need to start carrying you next."

He laughed. "You really know how to threaten a guy."

Tilly made me a mug of her whole body healing tea that she mixed with another tea of sage, turmeric, ginseng, lemon balm, and rennet to mend the brain. She forced Travis to drink a cup as well. Merlin recited a spell he'd come upon in the family scrolls and surprised even himself by remembering all the lines. Froliquet seemed to be having a beneficial effect on him.

Tilly fed all the animals, and Travis called to have pizza delivered for the rest of us. When we were finally alone again, he carried me up to bed and fell asleep beside me with his shoes still on.

Chapter 29

Travis and I slept for ten hours straight. My cats were pacing around looking for their breakfast, but Sashkatu must have made it clear that I was not to be disturbed. Although he often acted like their union representative, when I needed help, he was quick to change camps. Travis left for the Glen after two cups of strong coffee and my assurance that I was able to take care of myself. Even if I'd needed help, I would have called on my aunt or Elise before keeping him away from work. He was anchoring the evening news and had some catching up to do. Broadcast news could be a fickle mistress, always being wooed by younger, more attractive, better spoken men and women with rocketing demographics.

I didn't have to worry about losing my gig to some new sorcerer scrambling up the ladder to overtake me, except for a daughter of my own. And I would be rooting for her. As secure as my career was, whenever I was away from Abracadabra for more than a day, I felt the tug to reconnect with the ancestral magick at its heart.

Tilly had insisted on keeping the shop open for business while I was gone, saying she could do with a respite from baking. She was such a natural saleswoman that many of my products needed restocking. Dried herbs and plants had to be combined in the right amounts to create dozens of teas for different purposes. Beauty products required botanicals to be cooked down and mixed in precise quantities. And all my wares required the extra help that came from the addition of magick. But I had no right to complain—I'd come home to full coffers. Even so when the phone rang, I was glad for the distraction.

"Guess what?" was the response to my *hello.*

"Charlotte." I knew her voice by its breathless quality, as if she were calling while running a marathon.

"I didn't say *guess who?* I said *guess what?!*"

I laughed. "How about we try a normal conversation?"

"You're really no fun anymore." She sounded exasperated.

"I think you've forgotten. You always called me the party pooper, the buzz kill. I was never the fun one. You're getting me confused with Genna." Saying her name still made my chest tighten like a fist around my heart.

"Oh, you're right." Charlotte's voice flattened like a soufflé during a thunderstorm.

"All right, you leave me no choice but to give you the answer – not that you deserve it. I'm coming to pay you a visit."

In the ten years since graduation, Charlotte had never flown in from the west coast to see me. And now she was coming back so soon after the reunion? Something was up. "Any special reason?" I asked.

"Two of them. I'm going to be decorating a client's six thousand square foot *pied-à-terre* in Manhattan, so I'll be back and forth a bit."

"And the other reason?"

"We have to talk. Actually *I* have to talk. You just have to listen. Now I'm late for a meeting. I'll send you my itinerary."

I stood there staring at the phone as if the empty screen could answer all the questions Charlotte had prompted with her announcement. They would plague me until she arrived. It was futile to try to dismiss them from my thoughts. I never had the discipline to restrict my thoughts for more than a few minutes at a time. Morgana had claimed she had absolute control over her thoughts, to which Bronwen always replied *rubbish*. The truth was probably somewhere in between.

I was stirring the liquids that were bubbling away on the small stovetop, when the bells over the door chimed, and two male voices drifted back to me. I couldn't make out the words, but their tone was high-spirited. I turned off the burners. Ruining all the lotions and potions, unguents and creams this late in the process was not to be contemplated. A whole day's work would be lost and I'd have to replace the raw ingredients, not all of which were easy to come by.

"Hello?" one of the men called out. "Anyone here?"

I didn't shout a reply. My grandmother had drummed it into my head that even a sorceress should act professionally when dealing with the public. "Can I help you?" I asked as I approached them. They were in their late teens or early twenties, college boys on a summer road trip perhaps. They looked at each other, suddenly at a loss for words. The tall one with blond streaks in his hair found his voice.

"Yeah—hi. We heard you sell magick spells. If it's true, we'd like to buy one."

"It's true." I glanced out the window to see if there were others in their group who had dared them to come in. The street was empty.

"But do they really work?" asked the shorter, curly haired one.

"They can if you believe in the magick and have good intentions. What kind of spell are you looking for?"

"A…you know…a…love spell." Blond Streaks was blushing and shifting his weight from one foot to the other. He was telling the truth. Curly was having trouble keeping a straight face, but he wasn't mocking his friend. He was dealing with his own awkward discomfort. Expressions and body language often told me more than words.

"You want a spell to make girls fall in love with you?" I summed up.

"Yeah," he said, clearly relieved that I understood.

"I'm sorry. I can't help you. A spell like that is meant to subvert someone's will. It's black magick. But I'll tell you how to go about it without a spell."

Blond Streaks's shoulders slumped. "I know what you're going to say—the same thing my mom says. Be a gentleman, be thoughtful, be helpful, be her friend. I tried that, but it didn't work. I wound up being her friend. Now I have to listen while she goes on and on about how much she loves Matthew."

"Now there's a dude who must have found some serious black magick," Curly said, "'cause he's way out of Jessi's league. She belongs with Jared. You just have to look at them to know I'm right. It's a travesty, a regular travesty." I held myself back from telling him that there were better measures of a relationship than how a couple looked together.

Blond Streaks seemed so dejected, I ignored my better judgment and offered him hope. "I can give you a spell for patience. If Matthew and Jessi break up, you'll be there to pick up the pieces. It wouldn't be the first time love grew from friendship."

He perked up a bit. "Yeah sure, what do I have to lose?" I led him to the chair near the counter and gave him a pad of paper and a pencil. "What's this for?"

"You have to write down the spell. It helps to make it yours. I recited the words slowly enough for him to jot them down.

> Time is of no consequence
> For love that will not stray.

Patience grant me so I see
That what cannot be won today
May yet come to be.

"You will need to rewrite the spell each time you use it."

"When do I use it?"

"Whenever you get impatient," Curly supplied. "You've needed this spell since way before you fell for Jessi."

"You—shut up."

"Your friend is right," I said. "When you feel you're losing patience, rewrite the spell and recite it three times." He asked how much he owed, but I told him it was on the house. They were on their way to the door, when Froliquet came racing from the hall that connected my shop to Tilly's. I didn't know a marmot could move that fast. She was headed toward the door too.

"Grab her," Merlin bellowed as he came into view, running with a staccato gait like an ancient cartoon figure. But by that time, she'd passed me.

"Don't open the door!" I yelled to the young men, but Curly had already pushed the door open. Caught halfway out, the two of them kept going, closing the door behind themselves as quickly as possible. In the last second, Froliquet made her escape between the closing door and the jamb. Muttering a string of what must have been Old English profanities, Merlin barreled toward the door, another marmot on his heels. *Two marmots? What had the wizard done now?*

Tilly shuffled in at the end of the procession, mumbling. "I told him not to do it. I begged him not to do it. Did he listen? Of course not."

"Watch Froliquet," Merlin said, galumphing after the escapee. I hoped he could tell the difference between the two marmots, because I couldn't tell them apart. I scooped the remaining marmot into my arms and she cuddled against me, a good sign that she was indeed his familiar. Tilly plopped down in the chair by the counter.

"What the heck is going on?" I asked her.

"Our old great granddaddy was certain Froliquet was lonely, so he cast a spell to bring her a friend. I guess we should be grateful only one answered the call. On the other hand, if that marmot bumps into the *wrong* person the police may have no choice but to confiscate both of them. My head is spinning at the thought."

Twenty minutes later, there was still no sign of Merlin or the other marmot. I put Froliquet in my aunt's lap, intending to go search for them.

The wizard met me at the door, wheezing and carrying a cat. He headed straight for the chair, which Tilly vacated in the nick of time.

"All's well that ends well," he said, collapsing into it. "I don't wish to hear any more on the subject."

"Where's the other marmot?" I pressed him. "And please tell me you didn't see Beverly or Paul."

Tilly set Froliquet on the floor. "And what are we supposed to do with the cat?"

"You women don't know when to stop yammering. We didn't bump into anyone and the other marmot is right here."

"That's a cat, you old fool."

Merlin looked down at the creature in his lap. "Oh right, I transmuted the marmot into a cat while I was chasing her, in case we did come upon the wrong people." I prayed no one saw that transformation or we'd be in a lot bigger trouble than harboring marmots.

"When will the spell wear off?" Tilly asked. "You know Isenbale doesn't like other cats."

"I can withdraw it this very moment. It's a new one I perfected recently—quick, reliable, and easy to remember."

> Marmot, return to your true self,
> Let go of all things cat.
> No ill effects remain with you…remain with…remain…"

"Is there a problem?" I asked.

"No—why must you always think the worst?" he snapped. "It's merely taking me a moment to remember the last line." Tilly and I bit our tongues and waited. At the half hour mark, she retired to Tea and Empathy to bake away her distress. Ten minutes later, the marmot quietly reasserted itself. Where there was a cat, there was now a marmot. "Yes!" Merlin cried as if he finally recalled the spell in its entirety. "I forgot I built an expiration time into the spell. One can never be too careful when working with transmutations." I didn't bother asking why he hadn't glamoured her instead. He'd probably forgotten glamouring was less risky. The marmot jumped off his lap and the three of them headed back to Tilly's shop to await the fruits of her labors.

I was relieved to have the incident behind us, but for some reason it lingered in my mind. Hours later when I climbed into bed, it was still playing in a loop in my brain. As tired as I was, it took me a long time to fall asleep.

Chapter 30

According to Charlotte's schedule, she'd be spending two days in Manhattan working with her clients on the design for their new condo, after which she would take a car up to New Camel. She'd stay with me for one night, before heading back to JFK for her flight home. When I told Tilly about her impending visit, she wanted a list of her favorite desserts.

"For all I know, she's on a no dairy, no sugar, no gluten, air and water diet," I said. She'd looked pared down and super-toned at the reunion.

"No, no, never mind," Tilly said, "I'll make a few different things."

Travis asked if he should be available for Charlotte's pronouncement in case it had to do with the investigation. "Just because she refused to discuss it over the phone, doesn't mean it's dark and mysterious. She tends to be overly dramatic. I wouldn't be surprised if she's coming to talk me into a different shade of lipstick. But whatever it is, she'll speak more freely if it's just the two of us." He said he understood, sounding more relieved than disappointed.

"Any place you want to have dinner?" I asked Charlotte when she was in the limo on her way up here. "Or I could cook something."

"Not to knock your talents in the kitchen, but I've been dreaming about having a burger and shake at the Caboose. It's still there, isn't it?" There was a note of alarm in her voice as if she just realized it might have gone out of business during the years she lived on the West Coast.

"It is and we can."

At five thirty Charlotte popped out of the limo with one medium sized suitcase on wheels. "What an endless trip," she groaned, hugging me. "I could have flown back to California in the same amount of time. Thank goodness for cell phones. Halfway here I made arrangements to fly from Ithaca to JFK tomorrow."

She came inside to freshen up. If I had less willpower, I would have tackled her and forced her to tell me what on earth she couldn't have said over the phone. But Bronwen, Morgana and Tilly hadn't raised a ruffian.

"I have to give you credit," Charlotte said as she brushed on more blush, "most people I know would have badgered me to death by now to reveal my mysterious news."

"Imagine that. Ready for dinner?"

We had a short wait for a booth in the restaurant that had started life as an actual train caboose. Between the diners, people waiting for tables and those picking up takeout, the noise was like a physical curtain. Whatever Charlotte wanted to tell me wouldn't leave our immediate space. It might not even make it intact from her lips to my ears.

We ordered our burgers. She went for a chocolate shake. I craved vanilla. The shakes arrived first. She was struggling to sip hers through the straw. "I forgot how thick these are! They barely qualify as a beverage."

I'd reached the limits of my patience. "Charlotte, can we discuss the reason you made the trip up here to speak to me in person?"

She laughed. "I'm sorry, I didn't notice the smoke coming out of your ears."

"Where there's smoke," I said, wondering if I could weave a gray spell that would force her to give up the goods.

She lost the smile and pushed the shake out of sipping range like she meant business. "Okay. The reason I wanted to tell you in person is that I need to *see* your reactions. It's very hard for me to break a confidence— especially this one. I have to know that what I say is taken the right way." A food runner dropped off our cheeseburgers and waffle fries. Charlotte waited until he was gone before continuing. "I think I know the reason Genna was murdered. I almost went to the police with it, but I felt like I was betraying her. Then I remembered I could tell you, and that's sort of like keeping it in the family, if you know what I mean."

"You do understand I might have to take it to the police anyway, right?"

"Yes, it's not six degrees of separation, but it will have to do," she said with a joyless laugh. "This isn't only about Genna's death, it's about Scott's death too. Maybe what I've been carrying around for the past ten years will help with your investigation." My mind was screaming questions, but I didn't make a sound. I had the feeling one wrong word could change her decision to tell me.

She took a deep, shaky breath and said, "Genna was in love with Scott. She was obsessed with him."

I could no longer contain the questions. "Since when? Were they ever a thing?" If they had been, Scott and the school grapevine had bypassed me.

Charlotte shook her head. She had a mouthful of burger. "Sorry—I was starving," she said after swallowing. "This is every bit as good as I remembered. That never happens." She slid the shake back and worked on it for another minute before blotting her mouth with a napkin. "Her feelings for him grew over the years. She thought fate was on her side, throwing them together at every turn. They wound up in a lot of the same classes and afterschool clubs. They were invited to a lot of the same parties."

How had I not known the extent of her feelings for him? Sure, I'd heard her say how cute he was on a few occasions, how smart and considerate. Maybe she refrained from taking me deeper into her confidence, because she knew Scott and I had grown up as close friends. "So her feelings grew slowly," I said, nibbling on a waffle fry. I was trying to make sense of what Charlotte was telling me. "It wasn't a sudden case of hormone fueled lust." Genna had had a reputation for being *fun*, but she'd had a more conservative side too. "So what happened?"

"During our senior year, she was stressing because she felt like time was running out for her and Scott to get together. She went back and forth about whether she should tell him how she felt, before it was too late and they went their separate ways."

"But he was already with Ashley. Everyone knew they were going to get engaged. Did Genna really believe if she confessed her love, he'd finally see the light? That borders on delusional."

Charlotte dredged up the last of her shake. "I know. I suggested she go to a therapist, talk it out with someone who could be objective. But she tossed her head that way she used to and said, 'I don't need a therapist. I just need to make Scott understand that Ashley isn't the right one for him.'"

"Did she actually confront him?"

Charlotte picked up the last third of her burger, brought it to her mouth, then put it back on her plate. "When she found out Ashley wasn't going to the lake that night, she decided it was fate intervening to give her one last opportunity. She was really excited about the prospect of telling Scott how she felt. When I couldn't talk her out of it, I just prayed she'd lose her nerve."

"Not likely with all the alcohol around that night." The drinking had started at the dinner. Kids had stashed water bottles filled with vodka in their cars. No color, no smell for the chaperones to detect.

Our waiter stopped by to ask if we wanted another shake or dessert. We groaned our *no thank yous.* He put the check on the table. "Whenever you're ready. Have a good night, ladies." He couldn't leave fast enough for me.

I leaned across the table. "Well what happened?"

"Scott didn't react the way she dreamed he would, the way she convinced herself he would. He told her off and not too kindly."

"That doesn't sound like Scott, but maybe it was the alcohol talking."

"Or maybe Genna was obnoxious and wouldn't take *no* for an answer. Anyway, when he went into the lake to clear his head, Genna went too. She still thought if she kissed him, he'd finally understand that they were meant to be together. It was pitch black. She grabbed him and kissed him, but he pushed her away. Their legs got tangled and they both went under. She bobbed right up, but he didn't. He'd hit the back of his head on an outcropping of rock, lost consciousness and drowned."

It had happened a decade ago, but listening to the details made it seem like it was yesterday; the wound in my soul as fresh and deep as ever. Plenty of people had blamed Genna for Scott's death, based on gossip I'd made a point of ignoring. Now I blamed her too. I lost two good friends that night.

Charlotte's shoulders slumped. "I thought I'd feel relieved to tell you and get this burden off my chest, but I don't."

"That's because telling me doesn't change any of it," I said. "It would be nice if things were that simple. How was Genna afterward?"

"She was on a downward spiral, grieving his loss and torn with guilt. I didn't think she'd ever recover. But somehow she convinced herself that what happened was meant to be and would have happened whether she'd been there or not. She couldn't wait to leave for college where she could reinvent herself."

"One last question and then we'll put that night to rest. We should try to enjoy some girl time and better memories before you leave."

"The sooner the better."

"Did Genna ever mention Tony Russo when she talked about the lake?"

Charlotte frowned. "Only to say he was one of the people who was there. Why?" I told her about Tony's close calls. "It sure sounds like the same person who killed Genna is after him too. I wonder if there are any other names on their list."

Chapter 31

Travis and I were in my kitchen making dinner—blueberry pancakes and scrambled eggs with sharp cheddar. He took charge of the pancakes, claiming he was a master flipper. By default I presided over the eggs. I'd had a busy day with back to back bus tours and the last thing I wanted to do was leave the house again. When Travis showed up on my doorstep to surprise me and whisk me out to dinner, I begged for leniency and takeout.

"I have a better idea," he said, his head in my fridge checking out the slim pickings, "breakfast for dinner and I'll do the dishes."

I nearly swooned. "You have no idea how great that sounds!" By some miracle of timing, the pancakes were plated at the same moment as the eggs. The English muffins popped up in the toaster and were buttered as the tea finished brewing.

"Was there ever a couple more perfectly in sync?" he asked as we carried our food to the kitchen table.

I laughed. "Matchmaking services take note—the key to a lasting relationship is timing—like everything else in life."

Travis reached across the table and took my hand in his. He was using the other one to tuck a forkful of pancakes into his mouth. "If I wasn't so hungry, I'd sweep you off your feet and carry you upstairs this very moment. Rhett Butler would look shabby by comparison."

"And if I wasn't famished, I'd dare you to prove it this very minute."

* * * *

Travis was on his way back to the Glen early the next morning, after a cup of coffee and one of Tilly's carrot muffins, so chock-full of carrots, raisins and walnuts it had been known to keep one sated until dinner.

Lately when Travis left, the house felt too big and empty, the way it had after I lost my mother and grandmother. The cats helped with their sweet silly antics, poking their heads out of holes in the cat trees or stuffing themselves into the tiniest spaces. But Sashkatu seemed to understand exactly how lonely I was feeling. That morning instead of heading for one of his favorite napping spots, he stayed by my side, curling up in one of the bathroom sinks while I showered, put on makeup and combed my hair. He followed me into the bedroom and made a nest of my quilt as I decided what to wear.

I chose the red sundress, then had to rummage through my closet for five minutes to find my red and white sandals. One day I really had to get organized. I glanced over at Sashki and was sure he rolled his eyes at me. When I was finally ready, we walked side by side to Abracadabra. He climbed the stairs to his tufted window seat and was asleep before I opened the door for business.

Weekday mornings without tours were generally quiet in my shop. I used the time to pay bills, order supplies, and dust the merchandise—a never ending chore. I could hear Tilly and Merlin arguing next door in Tea and Empathy, their voices punctuated here and there by Froliquet's whistles of disapproval—what passed for normal in my life.

Lolly stopped by to say *hello* and pick up a jar of her favorite facial cream. "I gave myself permission to open an hour later today," she said settling herself in the customer chair. "I've been in the backroom making candy since six. I figure I deserve a little rest. Most folks don't think about buying chocolate this early in the day anyway." She asked after my family, and told me how her growing brood was doing. "My grandkids sure keep me on my toes," she said.

"If you ask me, they keep you young." Lolly looked the same as she had when I was growing up. The same plump pink cheeks and twinkling eyes.

She laughed. "I simply don't have time to grow old. Speaking of not acting old, the other day I saw Merlin running after a marmot."

"Froliquet escaped again."

"This one looked smaller than Froliquet." Lolly was one of the few people who'd met the wizard's familiar, although she thought it was just a pet. "Does he have two now?"

"No, no that was Froliquet you saw." I hated lying to her, but since Merlin had sent the second one back from wherever it had come, I had no choice. "I think only marmot mothers can tell the creatures apart."

"I really must have my eyes checked anyway," she said. "One moment it looked like a marmot and the next it looked like a cat." Just what I'd been afraid of. I could only hope that anyone else who'd been privy to Merlin's little trick, also blamed it on their vision.

"Thank goodness it wasn't a cat," I said. "Isenbale won't put up with other cats, and I already have so many in my house I expect the town to declare it a shelter any day now."

"When I have all the grands visiting my tiny place at the same time, I feel like the little old lady who lived in a shoe!" Lolly laughed so hard, she cackled.

We talked a while longer, before she heaved herself out of the chair. "You must come by and taste my new chocolate coconut fudge!" she said on her way out. "It should be ready later today." I promised I would.

Lolly wasn't gone two minutes, when the bells over the door chimed again. I thought she might have forgotten something, but I looked up to find Courtney framed in the doorway. She had a tentative smile, the kind you might have if you were visiting a new dentist for the first time. Although you needed their help, you weren't especially happy to be there.

Courtney seemed to be stuck at the threshold, so I went over and took her arm in mine. "Hi, come on in. How is everything?" Since the car bomb, I had worried about her family.

"We're okay for now," she said. "Tony thinks I'm here visiting my mom. I don't like to lie to him, but I needed to talk to you alone."

"Please sit," I said, indicating the chair Lolly had recently vacated. I hiked myself back onto the counter. I'd been spending so much time up there lately, I wouldn't have been surprised to find an imprint of my butt in the wood.

"I'm not the kind of wife who goes behind her husband's back, but my family's safety is at stake." Tears filled Courtney's eyes. "My kids' lives." Her last word was choked off. She took a few shaky breaths. "I've been talking to some of the alums who've seen Scott's ghost, but until now we've been spared that nightmare. Not anymore. We've seen him at night and during the day. It's scary as hell, but we've been putting on a brave face for the kids. Thank goodness he looks like a regular person, not like their idea of a ghost. But regular people don't wander around your property at all hours and put their faces right up against the windows. The kids are so little, they shouldn't have to deal with stuff like this."

Whoever was after Tony was getting frustrated and attacking his family on a psychological level, while they plotted their next physical assault on him.

"Can I get you water or anything?" I asked. She shook her head. "Give me a second, I don't want anyone interrupting us." I jumped down, found the I'll be back clock behind the counter and put it in the window indicating I'd open at noon. Probably a lot more time than we needed, but I could always open sooner. I plucked the tissue box off my desk and handed it to her, before resuming my perch.

She thanked me and took a tissue to dab at the corners of her eyes. "That's not even the main reason I came here. Tony hasn't been completely honest with the police or with you and Travis," she said, a hitch in her voice. "When he told you about the night at the lake, he made it sound like all the guys were egging each other on to keep drinking. But he admitted the truth to me years ago. It was *his* idea, a game to see who could handle their liquor well enough to pass one of those dangerous fraternity initiations. He convinced the other guys they had to build up their tolerance to alcohol or they wouldn't stand a chance of getting into any decent fraternity. He blames himself for Scott's death and he's lived with the guilt of it all these years. He told me Scott didn't want to keep playing, but he goaded him into it." She broke down, sobbing.

Listening to her, I felt sick to my stomach. I had to remind myself that Tony and the rest of them were just kids at the time—seventeen- and eighteen-year-old kids who thought they were all grown up and invincible. Any one of them could have died that night. Besides, Tony wasn't solely responsible for Scott's death. Genna had played a role in it too.

Someone with justice and vengeance on their mind had put the pieces of the puzzle together—or made an educated guess. They'd already taken Genna's life and were clearly determined to take Tony's. Although I couldn't bring Scott or Genna back from the dead, I could try to save Tony and keep his innocent family from paying a price they didn't owe.

"I had to tell you the truth," she said, "even if it means the end of my marriage. I believe you and Travis have the best chance of finding the killer and saving Tony's life, before he takes the rest of us down with him." She had good cause to worry. The car bomb could easily have killed them all.

I slid off the counter and knelt down next to her. "We will do everything in our power to find the killer. Is there any safe place you and your kids can stay until then?"

"I've already made arrangements for the three of us to fly down to Atlanta and stay with my sister. I told Tony he's not welcome to join us there. As long as he's the target, he cannot be near the kids."

"How did he take it?"

"He said he understood, but I could tell it hit him hard." She blew her nose. "I know this isn't his fault and has nothing to do with the man he is today, but the situation has put us in an awful position. I have to take the kids away even though I can't help worrying about him being alone."

I took her hand in mine. "We're on it and I'll be in touch." We both stood up and Courtney grabbed me in a hug that was equal parts desperation and gratitude.

After she left, I called Travis and brought him up to date. "That explains a lot," he said, "but it doesn't get us any closer to the identity of the killer." He was right of course. All we'd gained was the likely reason Tony was on his hit list.

"No matter how many times I go over it, I can't see Lillian, Charlie or Ashley killing anyone. That leaves Conrad. He stalked Genna, but that doesn't automatically make him capable of murder. Besides he has no beef with Tony. What are we missing here?"

"If you were burning with vengeance, but couldn't bring yourself to kill someone, what would you do?" Travis asked.

"Hire someone who could. I had the same thought, but it takes money, and I don't think any of them is sitting on that much cash."

"We don't know what we don't know," Travis said. "Maybe one of them inherited money, or socked away a secret emergency fund or is bartering for the killer's services."

"I guess there are bargain basement killers out there too, which could explain why Tony is still alive. You get what you pay for. Oh, I almost forgot, Courtney also mentioned that the Scott-ghost has been showing up. Even her kids have seen him. Between that and the car bomb..."

"She's doing the right thing by taking them down to her sister." He paused, then cleared his throat. "I can't believe I'm going to ask you this, but on the off chance that Scott is actually a ghost and not an impersonator, do you think Tilly could hold a séance and talk him into going back where he belongs?"

"Sorry, Tilly doesn't conduct séances. She once told me that calling ghosts is one of the worst things anyone can do. Even if every person in the circle has the purest of motives, when you open a channel to the other side, all sorts of malignant spirits can sneak in."

"What about when your mother and grandmother visit you?"

"I don't reach out to them. They always come to me. They would never take the chance of endangering me, so I have to assume they've learned how to prevent others from hopping on their coattails."

"More than I wanted to know. From now on, I think I'll keep my questions to myself."

Chapter 32

My heart was racing, my forehead beaded with sweat. I was trying to catch Froliquet before the police did. Something wet flicked across my nose. I opened my eyes and found myself staring into the green depths of Sashki's eyes. He licked my nose again and I fell back against the pillow, relief making me giggle at my own silliness. I'd been dreaming of the other day when I thought the marmot had escaped. Sashki shook his head at me and went back to curl up on his pillow.

I didn't have that luxury. There was a bus tour due in at ten. Some of the shopkeepers had put up websites, so they wouldn't be as dependent on foot traffic. I'd toyed with the idea myself, but the arcane charm and magick of Abracadabra were a huge part of its success. People loved the shop, they loved talking to me, they loved telling friends about their experiences. Travis had cautioned me that a website might increase business to a point where I spent all my time filling orders, instead of running my shop. When I polled Tilly and Elise they agreed. For now the ancient magick shop would remain brick and mortar, or whatever it was actually made of.

Although I spent the day selling beauty and health aids and the occasional magick spell, my subconscious was still playing with the dream from which Sashki had awakened me. I was talking to a customer, explaining the difference between two night creams, when it nagged at me to pay attention.

"Are you all right, miss?" the woman inquired. I realized I'd stopped talking in the middle of a sentence and was staring off into space.

"I'm so sorry," I said, having a hard time focusing on her again. "I just remembered something I have to take care of later." After I helped her decide which cream to try, I answered questions from three other people.

By then a line had formed at the register, and I rushed over to tally up their purchases.

"You really should think about hiring someone to help you," the cream buyer whispered when I was ringing her up.

"I appreciate the suggestion," I said, "and I'll give it some serious thought." When Bronwen and Morgana were alive, there was never any reason to think about hiring help. And although I was often overwhelmed during the bus tours, I wasn't busy enough the rest of the time to warrant paying an employee. In any case, even if I were that busy and even if had money to spare, I couldn't have someone work in Abracadabra where they would see and hear far too much about my family's talents. I'd probably have to put a muzzle on Merlin for starters—there was no way to tell what might come out of his mouth or what new crisis he would create with his misbegotten spells.

Someday when I had a daughter and she was old enough, we would work side by side in the shop the way I had with my mother and grandmother. It was a lot more than wishful thinking. Without a daughter to carry the Wilde magickal DNA into the next generation, it would be forever lost.

When the bus pulled out of New Camel, I made sure Sashkatu had ample water and I ran next door to tell my aunt I was driving over to the Glen during my lunch hour. Now that she and I were the only living members of our family, we were careful to keep each other apprised of our comings and goings. Merlin would be quick to point out that he should also be counted among our living family. But he belonged to the past and might one day go back to his rightful place in history.

I parked in the lot at town hall and went straight to the office of the town clerk. The public files were computerized, so I sat down at one of three computer terminals and entered the name Scott Desmond. The record of his death was easy to access, but the system didn't seem to have any record of his birth. Maybe it was my error, or whoever had input the data had missed that document. I wasn't about to give up, not after driving all the way there. Considering the problems with computers, their reliance on electricity, and how vulnerable they were to hackers, the original paper records were probably stored away somewhere. I needed help, but lunch hour was the worst time to find it.

I walked around the building, but it was like a ghost town. Elizabeth Hathaway, the town clerk, was my last hope. Her office door was closed, but when I knocked, she said to come in. The office wasn't spacious, but it was large enough to accommodate a standard desk, a couple of filing cabinets, two visitor chairs, a table holding a coffee maker, and shelving filled with books and personal knickknacks. Elizabeth was an attractive woman in her forties. When I walked in, she was eating what looked like a turkey sandwich. My stomach grumbled to remind me it was empty. I hoped she didn't think I was coveting her food.

"Sorry, I didn't mean to interrupt your lunch," I said with no intention of leaving.

She put down the half sandwich she was holding and brushed the crumbs off her hands onto the tinfoil that held the other half. "Not a problem." She paused to take a quick sip from the straw in a can of diet Pepsi. "I could have ignored your knocking if I didn't want to be disturbed. Please have a seat and tell me what I can do for you."

"Thanks, but I just have a quick question. Why would a person's birth certificate be missing from the computer records?"

"They may have been born in a different municipality or it may have simply fallen through the cracks when the data was being input. Where human beings are involved, there's always room for error. The only thing I can suggest is looking for the original certificate in the old filing cabinets stored in the basement."

"That would be great."

"Unfortunately it's not that simple. We're shorthanded today, and I'm working on a project I have to complete before I leave. Would it be possible for you to come back at another time?"

"There's no need to bother anyone else. I'll be fine going down there myself."

She smiled. "I'm sure you would, but the public isn't allowed in the basement. It's a matter of safety and liability. The stairs are old and uneven, as is the floor. There's a host of problems with old buildings like this. Plus the filing cabinets haven't been anchored to the wall. The custodian has had too many other things to attend to. She picked up the half eaten part of her sandwich. "It would be a good idea to call in advance next time to make sure we can accommodate you. Now if you'll excuse me…"

"Yes, of course," I said, "another time." Another time, I thought—preferably after hours.

* * * *

I waited until I'd fed the cats. I had no appetite for my own dinner. More to the point, I'd never teleported on a full stomach and this wasn't the time to experiment. I'd visited the building afterhours once before and I'd had trouble navigating in the darkness. I needed a flashlight. I kept a small one in the kitchen and tucked it into the pocket of my jeans.

I closed my eyes, drew deep calming breaths, and pictured the public computer area inside town hall.

> From here and now to there and then
> Attract not change, nor harm allow.
> Safe passage guarantee to souls
> As well as lesser, mindless things.

I knew I'd reached my destination before I opened my eyes. Town hall had a particular odor I associated with old wooden buildings. It was the mustiness of time, layers of time piled one upon the other that the most thorough cleaning could not eliminate.

When I did look around, I was exactly where I intended to go. In the spirit of better safe than sorry, I recited another spell I designed to shut down any motion detectors or cameras on the premises.

> Disarm alarms, detectors off,
> Disable now the circuitry.
> Cameras down, transmissions end,
> Scrub memory and never send.

Time to find the stairs. Given that the basement was off limits to the public, access to it was most likely behind a door. I'd never noticed before how many doors there were in town hall, apart from the main offices. I counted four supply closets, and a couple of small bathrooms, before locating a door that was locked. This had to be the one. A simple spell from my childhood opened it.

The stairs were immediately in front of me. If someone opened the door with less caution, they could easily tumble straight down them. I pulled the door closed behind me, so I could turn on the basement lights without anyone outside noticing. The clerk was right. The steps were uneven, some more shallow than others, and the risers weren't a uniform height. I held onto the banister, but even that wasn't all that well secured to the wall. No wonder they didn't want the public to go downstairs. It was a series of accidents and lawsuits waiting to happen.

The basement itself was a slapdash affair with an old linoleum floor and peeling green paint on the walls. The filing cabinets shared the space with stacks of extra chairs, some folding tables, and a metal shelving unit crammed with items no longer needed, but too good to throw out—it was like a retirement home for things past their prime, but not yet dead.

I went through the *Ds* for *Desmond,* making sure none of the certificates were stuck together. Again I came up empty. I went through the *C* and *E* files in case the certificate had been mistakenly placed there. Scott must have been born somewhere else. The one person who could provide that answer was his mother.

Chapter 33

Lillian Desmond was surprised to find me at her door the next afternoon. I didn't call ahead to ask if I could visit. She asked me to forgive the current state of her house. "It's always a battle between the dust and my arthritis," she said, flexing the swollen joints of her fingers. "The dust has been winning lately."

"No worries. You haven't seen dust until you have six cats."

Lillian laughed. "You always know the right thing to say, my dear. Can I make you tea? I'm afraid I don't have anything sweet to go with it."

"No thank you. I can't stay long. I was nearby and just wanted to see how you were doing." It wasn't a lie even if it wasn't the primary reason for my visit. I had promised myself I'd check on her from time to time. If my aunt Tilly lived alone, I would hope someone would look in on her too.

We settled at the kitchen table, where women always seem the most comfortable. "You're a lovely girl to think of me, but I take good care of myself, if you overlook the extra pounds and pesky blood pressure," she added with a wink. In spite of her words, she didn't look well to me. Her hair lay dull and lank against her head, in need of shampooing and her eyes were sunken into dark hollows. On my last visit, she looked a whole lot better. Of course she'd known Elise and I were coming then and had had the time to whip herself into shape.

Lillian must have felt my appraisal, because she put her hand up to her head. "I *have* to get to the beauty parlor. With one thing and another I forgot about my last appointment. I've put off calling to reschedule, because I know I'll get a lecture from Beverly about not cancelling in advance. I ask you, how am I supposed to cancel ahead of time, if I've forgotten about the appointment?" She sighed. "If there was another salon nearby that was half as good, I'd switch in a heartbeat."

"I hear that from a lot of people, including my aunt," I said, wondering how I was going to turn the conversation in the right direction without arousing her suspicions. Regardless of the fact that I'd known her all my life, she was still one of our suspects in Genna's death and Tony's near misses. Grief changed people and not always for the better.

"A long time ago," Lillian said, "when you were a little kid, there was another place in that little strip mall just outside of town. It was owned by a lovely young couple, but Beverly and her friends bad-mouthed them out of existence."

By talking about the past, she had inadvertently given me an opening. "You know, the other day I was thinking back and I couldn't remember how old I was when you moved to New Camel."

Her eyebrows knit together. "That's a good question. You and Scott had to be...let's see...about three years old."

"Where did you live before that?"

"Marlboro, New Jersey." Her mouth curved up in a smile. "That's where I grew up. My husband and I were high school sweethearts. You remember Vincent, don't you?"

"Of course. I used to wish he was *my* father. So that's where Scott was born."

"It was a nice place to raise children," she said, without confirming my statement.

"Why did you move to New Camel if you were happy there?"

Her smile faded and she sat up straighter in her chair as if someone had called her to attention. "Vincent got a better job offer. Circumstances change, you never know where life will take you. I'm sure you didn't expect to be running Abracadabra on your own so soon."

"You're right about that." I was trying to come up with a way to keep the conversation going when Lillian drew herself to her feet, holding onto the table for support.

"If you'll excuse me, Kailyn, I'm not feeling very well. I think I should lie down for a bit."

I stood too. "Not at all. Is there anything I can do for you before I leave?"

"Thanks, but with a little rest I should be fine. Please give your aunt my best regards."

* * * *

I sat across from Tilly at one of the little tables in her shop, sipping a mug of her restorative tea. Merlin was in his usual spot, monitoring the oven from his seat just outside the kitchen. Tilly could have hired him out as a human timer. Nothing burned on his watch.

"Well you did say she wasn't looking herself," Tilly remarked after I told her about my peculiar visit with Lillian. "Maybe she's fighting a bug. I'll bake her favorite lemon bars and bring them over with a bottle of Bronwen's botanical antiviral medicine." Some people swear by chicken soup for what ails you. Tilly claims that what comes out of her oven works better, especially when coupled with Bronwen's healing spell.

We chatted until we heard the bells in my shop announce someone's arrival and I was off and running. There was barely a lull in the foot traffic all afternoon. Good for my bottom line, but it was evening before I could call Travis and tell him about my visit with Lillian. "So now we know that Scott was most likely born in New Jersey, but Lillian rushed me off before I could ask her if he was adopted. So...given all your many contacts in high and low places, is there anyone who can find out for us?"

"Let me see what I can do."

The phone rang a half hour later, too soon for Travis to be getting back to me. The Caller ID told me Courtney was on the line. "Hi, I'm sorry to be calling at dinner time," she said.

"No problem," I assured her, with a yogurt container in hand. "Around here dinner is hardly a formal affair."

"I'm in Atlanta with the kids, like I told you." Her tone was grim. "I just got off the phone with Tony. He says he's tired of waiting for other people to fix things. He's got his guns out and he's waiting for the Scott-ghost to make another appearance. When I asked him what good it would do to shoot a ghost, he said he had to do something so it would be safe for us to come home. I think it's all starting to affect his mind.

"Maybe I shouldn't have left him alone with his demons. But how can I even think of bringing the kids home if he's running around the house with loaded weapons?" Her voice broke. "Kailyn, I'm sorry to lay this in your lap, but I don't know where else to turn. If I call the cops, they might haul him off to a psych unit. Could you possibly drive up and talk to him?"

"I'm out the door," I said grabbing my purse and keys.

Chapter 34

I called Tony on my way up there, so he wouldn't mistake me for a ghost or other enemy when I walked from my car to the front door and rang the bell. He told me not to come. "I guess Courtney called you," he said. "You're wasting your time. I'm tired of being a target for ghosts or killers."

"You know you can't re-kill a ghost or scare away a ghost by shooting at it. On the other hand, if it turns out to be a person masquerading as Scott and you injure or kill him, you could wind up in prison for the rest of your life. Your kids would grow up without you. Please tell me how that fixes anything?"

"I have to stop being a victim and turn the tables on this whole thing."

"The ghost isn't even your biggest problem," I said. "Someone is out to kill you, remember?"

"What if they're one and the same, huh?" His tone was petulant.

"For what it's worth, I don't think they are."

"Yeah? What makes your theory any better than mine?"

"The night Genna was killed, the Scott-ghost was sighted too far away for him to be in both places at the same time. And with the exception of possibly causing heart attacks, ghosts can't actually kill people."

"In *your* theory."

It was becoming increasingly clear that Tony was past being reasoned with. I had to get the guns away from him. I told him to expect me and hung up. I dialed Travis, but stopped before it connected. He was anchoring the evening news. Besides, the more people who descended on Tony's house, the higher the odds someone would get hurt. I had centuries of magickal ability on my side. I could handle whatever Tony threw at me.

What I hadn't counted on was the rush hour traffic or the two fender benders that closed down lanes of the highway. I considered pulling off and leaving the car in a parking lot, while I teleported to somewhere near Tony's house. I scuttled the idea a moment later. What if I popped out of the ether in front of people? That was sure to make the headlines. I couldn't chance it.

By the time I arrived at his house, it was a small miracle I hadn't gnashed my teeth down to stubs. I parked at the curb and walked up the driveway, giving Tony's new car a wide berth. Killers often stood by their favorite methods.

Before I could ring the bell, I heard a scream, followed by shouting inside. The door was locked. I glanced around me. A woman was walking a little dog on the far side of the cul-du-sac while talking on her phone. Someone could cut the leash and steal the dog without her noticing. Satisfied that no one was watching, I opened the lock with what I'd come to think of as my lockpick spell. I left the door ajar, worried the sound of the lock engaging might give me away. I stood in the foyer long enough to pinpoint the location of the two voices. They were in the family room down the hall, where Travis and I had recently visited with Tony and Courtney.

"Man, you've got to do something or I'll bleed to death," a voice pleaded. "If that happens, you'll be facing murder charges. Did you think about that?"

"Or I could finish the job right now and get rid of the evidence," Tony snapped.

I didn't wait to hear more. I ran down the hallway, stopping short at the entrance to the family room. In spite of what I'd heard, I was stunned by the tableau in front of me. Tony was sitting in his chair, his gun pointed at a man who was crumpled on the ground, bleeding from a wound in his thigh. It wasn't an arterial hit, or the blood would have been pumping out of him with every beat of his heart, but he could still bleed out if the wound wasn't stitched up. It would just take a little longer.

Tony saw me before I could collect my thoughts enough to speak. "I told you not to come here. Don't take another step." His tone was cold and menacing. "I've got things under control. You'll only make matters worse by butting in."

The man on the floor dragged himself around to see who had arrived. His face was pale and bathed in sweat, each movement causing him to grimace in pain.

"Scott?" was all I could manage. If I were a fainter, I would have collapsed right then and there. Even though I was working on the possibility Scott was adopted and had a twin he didn't know about, seeing proof of it was unsteadying.

Tony snickered. "Let me introduce you. This is Brett Kosik. Take a real good look, Kailyn. It's been ten years since you last saw Scott, so the subtle differences between them may not be as obvious. It took me a minute too."

The longer I stared at the man on the floor, the better I could accept that he wasn't Scott. His face was fuller than Scott's and he was missing the crescent scar Scott had over his left eye from a playground accident. *Why had Lillian made a point of not letting anyone, including Scott, know he was adopted?*

"Kailyn?" Brett said, "Please help me—I need to get to a hospital." His words kicked me out of my stupor. "Tony, give me your belt!" He started to refuse. "Now!" I shouted, shutting him down. He stood up, dropping the gun onto the chair behind him, and grudgingly tugged the belt out of its loops. As soon as he handed it to me, he retrieved the gun. I knelt beside Brett and cinched the belt above the wound.

"Thank you," he whispered.

"You need to take a look at his phone," Tony grunted. "It's a real eye opener." He pulled the phone out of his shirt pocket and tossed it to me.

I scrolled through Brett's texts and calls. There were some to Ashley and Charlie, but the most by far were between him and Lillian.

"Was Lillian aware Scott had a twin brother?" I asked Brett.

"No and I didn't know about Scott either, until he died and I saw his picture in the paper. That's when I found Lillian and introduced myself to her." The phone chimed with a new text. I clicked on it. "It's from Lillian. It says, 'He's here.' Do you know what that means?"

Brett looked stricken. "She needs help." His skin was turning ashen and he was struggling to keep his eyes open.

"I have to know what's going on," I said.

"Too long to explain." He was breathless.

I pulled my phone out of my purse. "I'll get the police over there ASAP." Brett grabbed my arm. "No, no police. I was supposed to be there." Tears choked off his voice.

"Well maybe you shouldn't have been here trying to scare the hell out of me and my family!" Tony exploded.

Without saying a word, I hit 911. When the dispatcher answered, I gave her Tony's address. Tony leaped out of his chair. "What the hell do you think you're doing?"

I ignored him. "We need an ambulance for a gunshot victim ASAP. Possible hostage situation." He ripped the phone from my hand, but it was done. "I'm saving you from doing any more damage to yourself and your family." I held out my hand. "Give me the phone."

"Maybe I should have put a bullet in you too," he said, but without any heart. The impotent rage that had pushed him to shoot Scott's twin was fading away.

"Hang in there, Brett. The ambulance is on its way. I'm going to help Lillian." I had no idea what I'd be walking into or what kind of help she might need, but I would try to honor his request not to involve the police.

Chapter 35

I was almost back to New Camel when Travis called. He'd noticed my missed call after he went off the air. I told him what happened at the Russo home, keeping my voice even and reasonable—just another day in the life of a private investigator. If I'd let him hear the way I really felt, he might have carried me off to the tower next door to Rapunzel's.

"You just called 911 and walked out?" he sputtered, when I got to the end of my tale. "Tony could have put a bullet in you, shot you dead for doing that. He's not thinking rationally, and now I have my doubts about you. Who catches a man in a state of temporary insanity and decides to see how far he can be pushed?"

"I just knew he wouldn't hurt me," I said with no supporting evidence.

"I'd feel better if those words came from Tilly, but you're not psychic. You've told me that yourself."

"Can we finish this discussion later?" I asked. "I need to focus on Lillian now. She's in danger from this man, whoever he is. Brett was supposed to be there with her when he arrived, but he's busy bleeding to death in Tony's house. How can I leave her to deal with…whatever this is on her own?"

"You should have called 911 for her too. In fact you need to do it right now," Travis said in a tone that brooked no argument.

"I can't. Brett begged me not to involve the police for Lillian's sake." I realized how threadbare that argument sounded. Here I was, racing full tilt toward an unknown danger, on the say-so of a man who'd been masquerading as his dead twin to terrify people. "Okay I realize how crazy that sounds. Forget the request came from Brett. This is about Lillian. It doesn't matter that she's a suspect. In my eyes, she's innocent until proven guilty. She's been a friend of my family for decades, but even if I barely knew her, I would help her for Scott's sake."

Travis didn't have an immediate comeback. "I get it. I'll be there as soon as I can."

"No, I can handle this myself," I said with more bravado than I felt. "You didn't know Scott. This isn't your problem."

"We're partners—for better or worse, you're stuck with me."

* * * *

I called Lillian's number when I was a few blocks away. It rang and rang before going to voice mail. I hung up and slowed to a crawl, stopping two houses away from hers. Her car was in the driveway. An old black pickup was parked at the curb. Layers of weather and dirt had dulled its finish. The driver's side mirror was taped in place. It had a Delaware license plate that I committed to memory. I made my way around the garage side of the house where there were no windows. When I reached the back of the house, near the kitchen window, I paused to listen for voices. There appeared to be two, although I couldn't make out their words. Lillian and her guest were probably in the living room. Given Brett's distress over this meeting, I had to assume the man was not there to take Lillian out on a date. And he probably had a weapon.

I took it as a good sign that there was no shouting or screaming as there had been at Tony's house. On the drive there, I considered my options. I didn't have many. I could go around to the front door and ring the bell as an innocent neighbor who wanted to borrow a cup of sugar. Or I could use the lockpick spell to gain entry, but if they were in the living room the man might hear the lock disengage and greet me with a bullet. Or I could teleport into the living room and hope that the element of surprise gave me a brief advantage, maybe enough time to disarm the visitor. Of course arriving by teleportation meant two people would see me appear out of thin air. Stories like that are bound to spread like wildfire. Instead I went with a variation on the theme. I focused my mind on my landing site and repeated the spell three times:

> From here and now, to there and then,
> Attract not change, nor harm allow.
> Safe passage guarantee to souls
> As well as lesser mindless things.

When I opened my eyes, I was standing in the middle of Scott's old room. It seemed an appropriate way to enter the house where he'd grown up. It looked the same as it had when he was alive. Lillian hadn't changed a thing. A wave of nostalgia brought tears to my eyes. I wiped them away. A lot of good I was doing Lillian, crying up in her son's room, while she was in trouble in the living room.

I made my way to the staircase, wincing each time the hardwood creaked under my weight. I waited there for a minute, listening to what the two of them were saying.

"You are not getting another penny from me until you get it done." Lillian sounded like she was in control of the situation, but her voice was higher pitched than normal. She was putting on a good act, but she was afraid of him.

As soon as I heard him speak, I recognized the voice. It was deep and coarse, not a young man's voice, but that of a man in middle age, used up and with few prospects—a dangerous man who'd never grown a conscience. It brought to mind predators waiting for their prey in dark alleys, or in the backseats of cars, or out in the open on a bright sunny day where you'd least expect them.

"I need the rest if you want me to finish. It ain't my fault it's taking so long."

"Then whose fault is it?" Lillian demanded. "You agreed to do the job for the amount we discussed. You were quick enough to take the down payment. You don't get the rest until you complete the work."

"Or what? You gonna sue me? You gonna call the Better Business Bureau and tell on me?" He made a sound that was somewhere between a guttural laugh and a smoker's cough. "It's real simple, Lillian, I need to eat. I don't eat, I can't work. Hand over the rest of the money."

"Hold on, Norman. How do I know you won't take the money and run? I'll have no recourse."

"I guess you'll just have to trust me. It's not like we're talking about a new roof for your house. There's risk on both sides of this deal."

"Well I don't keep that kind of money here. I need some time."

"What kind of time we talking?"

"A week, maybe two, and while I'm getting it together, you can tie up that loose end on your side." Lillian was still bargaining, stalling, maybe in the hope that Brett would ride in like the eleventh hour cavalry. She didn't know that couldn't happen. I was her only cavalry and I was struggling to accept this new version of her, even though I'd known it was a possibility.

"You trying to beat me at my own game?" Norman snapped. "Here's a free tip. *Nobody* gets to pull the wool over my eyes, let alone an old biddy. You've used up my patience."

I heard Lillian's sharp intake of air. I had to assume he'd pulled a weapon. "That's not necessary," she said, her voice quavering. I sneaked a quick peek around the wall at the top of the stairs where I was hiding. Norman had his back to me, a pistol aimed squarely at Lillian. If she hadn't been so transfixed by the gun, she might have seen me. I was thankful she didn't. Norman would have seen her eyes shift and if he had any experience in his chosen profession, he would have followed her gaze up to me.

I crept to the top step and slowly descended. When I was close to the bottom, I focused my energy on the gun. I had to get it away from him, but using magick to pull it straight to me would be like saying, *Hey, look what I can do!* I settled for a telekinetic spell that jerked it out of his grasp and sent it spinning away to a neutral corner beneath the living room window.

"What the hell," Norman grunted, wasting precious seconds trying to process what had happened, while I leapt off the stairs and dove for the gun. I was on my feet, gun in hand before he could react. "You!" he said when he got a good look at me. "You got a death wish or something?" He was talking like he was still the one with the weapon.

Lillian had watched the action play out with her mouth hanging open. I took up a position between the two of them. Norman's eyes narrowed at me. "How did you do that…that trick with the gun?"

"I was about to ask you the same thing," I said. We stood there for a minute regarding each other suspiciously. "I know," I said. "Your hand was sweaty, Norm, and you were holding the gun so tightly, it flipped right out of your grasp like a fish." Norm didn't look convinced, but at least he wasn't blaming me anymore.

"You know," he said, coming toward me with a slow grin, "I don't think you have the guts to shoot me. So why don't you just hand over the gun right now, before you get hurt?" The doorbell stopped him in his tracks.

Travis! I'd told him not to come, but I was relieved he hadn't listened to me. "Lillian," I said, "would you please answer the door. I want to keep an eye on Norm here."

Lillian did as I asked, but she didn't open the door all the way. I wondered why, until I heard "Hi Lillian, dear." My aunt Tilly. My heart stopped for a beat before revving into overdrive. For a renowned psychic, Tilly had some lousy timing. Since she couldn't see Norm and me from her vantage point, she kept right on talking.

"I know you've been under the weather, so I baked your favorite lemon bars and brought along some herbal medicine. Together they're guaranteed to perk you right up." If she knew I was there and in danger, she would never walk away. I caught Lillian's eye and shook my head. Either Lillian understood or she didn't want to put Tilly in harm's way any more than I did.

"This isn't the best time," she said, her voice shaky. "Perhaps tomorrow?" She started to close the door, but I should have realized that Tilly on a mission was hard to dissuade.

"Nonsense," she said. "I have precisely what you need. I won't stay long." She squeezed past her friend into the living room, freezing when she saw me with the gun on Norm. "Oh my," she said, stumbling forward and nearly losing her balance as Merlin pushed his way in behind her. I wasn't surprised. Wherever the baked goods went, the wizard followed. Froliquet scuttled in between his legs, sat up on her haunches and surveyed the scene with little marmot mutterings.

Norman took advantage of my split attention. He rushed me, grabbing my gun arm and wrestling the weapon out of my grasp. "Unhand that woman!" Merlin demanded as if he had the power of King Arthur to back him up. "Else I shall turn you into a grasshopper." From the corner of my eye, I saw Tilly slam her elbow into his ribs.

"This place is a loony bin," Norman said with a disgusted curl of his upper lip. "But I'm not leaving without my money. So if you staged all this nonsense to get out of paying me, Lillian, forget it." *Did he seriously think any of this had been planned?* Froliquet must have finally sensed trouble. She let loose with a series of ear-shattering whistles.

"Make it stop that," Norman snapped, menacing all of us with a sweep of the gun.

"It's instinct," Merlin informed him in a haughty tone. "She won't stop if she feels her family is threatened."

"You wanna bet?" Norman cocked the pistol. I had to get it away from him, before he hurt or killed someone out of sheer pique. I saw Lillian slip out the door. I didn't want to think she was abandoning us to the hit man. Maybe she assumed he'd have no interest in us once she was gone. Seconds later, Travis marched her back inside, his face grim as he took in the room and its occupants.

"If you're carrying, toss it down and kick it away," Norman said. He seemed to have accepted the fact that this house was akin to a clown car, but with people pouring in, instead of clowns pouring out.

Travis put his hands up. "No weapons."

"If I find any on you, you'll be sorry you lied."

"No weapons, no lies," Travis assured him, backing away to stand near me.

I saw the realization bloom on Norman's face that his one-on-one bullying of a defenseless woman had turned into more than he bargained for and possibly more than he could handle. "Everyone on the other side of the room! On the floor! Now!"

We all complied, but since the room wasn't very large, the swath of floor between him and us was barely four feet wide—not much of a safety zone for him. If Travis stretched out his legs, they could reach the hit man's feet.

Norman must have come to the same conclusion. We were too close for comfort. He needed more control. In a tone devoid of emotion, he threatened to eliminate anyone who moved. But he had to make an exception, when he realized he should take away our cell phones or someone might call 911. After we slid them across the hardwood to him, he reiterated his warning.

"Excuse me, Norm," I called out, "I *really* need to use the powder room. It's sort of an emergency—stress, you know." I did my best impression of someone who couldn't hold on much longer. He looked annoyed, but on the fence. "It's right down the hall from the kitchen, and it has no windows," I added to sweeten the deal.

"Okay. Just don't get any ideas about attacking me or trying to escape. If you pull anything, someone you love dies. And you'll have a front row seat for the execution."

I thanked him and ran down to the bathroom like someone with an emergency and locked the door. I didn't have much time. I cleared my mind the best I could, gathered the power in my cells and started reciting the spell, aiming for the moment in the living room just before Tilly arrived:

> In time's stream do I cast
> From the present to the past.
> Anchored here deep and strong,
> While a tether holds me fast
> For as long as I'm gone.
> In time's stream do I cast.

When I opened my eyes I saw with relief that I'd made it. I was holding the gun and it was pointed at Norman. The doorbell rang. I asked Lillian to answer it. My family trooped in. This time I didn't spare them a glance. The hit man was watching me, waiting for a moment to spring for the gun. He ran at me, but before he could grab my arm, I pulled the trigger.

Chapter 36

The bullet grazed him a few inches above the knee. I'd aimed low on purpose. I didn't want to hit a vital organ. I wanted to stop him from hurting anyone else, but I didn't want to kill him and pay for it with the rest of my life. He collapsed on the floor, screaming and cursing, and trickling a few drops of blood onto Lillian's area rug. Travis ran to my side and took the gun out of my hand. Until that moment, I didn't realize I was trembling.

Everyone else was frozen in place. They seemed stunned by what they witnessed. Or was that confusion I saw on their faces? What if changing the past wasn't seamless? What if people retained some memory of the way things had gone down the first time around? It was a little late to worry about it now, but I'd have to give the possibility some serious thought once my life calmed down. And preferably before I felt the need to pop back into the past again.

Travis kept the gun trained on Norm, in case he realized he wasn't incapacitated. Having gathered her wits, Tilly joined us. "Do you think he needs a tourniquet on that leg?" she asked.

I'd gone most of my life without using the word *tourniquet* and here I was discussing it for the second time that day. "It's a superficial wound. It's barely bleeding anymore." Norman's screams had faded to a whimper. For someone who dealt out death with equanimity, he was deeply invested in saving his own miserable life. Maybe it hadn't yet occurred to him that he was likely to be spending the remainder of that life in prison.

Although I had promised Brett I'd try not to call the police, we were well past that option. As much as I liked Lillian, I'd heard enough to know she hired Norman to dispose of Genna and Tony for the parts they played in her son's death. She bulldozed right over the presumption of their innocence and a trial by their peers. She must have known there wasn't enough evidence to convict either of them, so she decided the only possible justice for Scott had to come at her own expense, both literally and figuratively.

Once Norman and the gun were no longer in charge, Tilly, Merlin and Froliquet made themselves comfortable on the couch, and Lillian sank into one of the wingback chairs, her expression a combination of relief and resignation.

Before I could ask Lillian one of the many questions on my mind, the front door flew open again. Our heads all snapped in that direction like synchronized robots. *Who else felt so much at home they could barge right in without bothering to knock or ring the bell?*

Charlie Desmond, Scott's older brother, appeared in the doorway. I hadn't seen him since Scott's funeral. Ten years had aged him. His hairline had receded; lines creased his forehead and bracketed his mouth. He stopped where he was, staring back at us and just as perplexed to see us there. "Mom?" he said.

In the wingback chair she was partially hidden from his view. She rose at the sound of his voice and emitted a strangled sob as he rushed over and gathered her in his arms.

"Are you okay, mom? I'm so sorry I couldn't get here sooner. What happened to Brett? He was supposed to be here with you." Had Lillian issued an all-points bulletin when Norman arrived? How many other people knew about her contract with the hit man? My head was spinning with questions.

"I'm all right," she said. "Kailyn came to my rescue." She turned to me. "But I don't understand how you knew I needed help." After I explained what happened at Tony's house, Lillian slumped down on the edge of her chair. "Poor Brett. What a horrible mess I've made of things. It all seemed so simple at first."

Charlie hunkered down beside her and took her hands in his. "Mom, don't say another word until we get an attorney. Do you understand?"

She nodded. The bravado that had seen her through the encounter with Norman had left her diminished. Her ramrod straight shoulders were curved inward, her determined chin drooped to her chest. She was curling in on herself like a hedgehog.

Charlie turned to me. "Thank you. You may have saved my mother's life. If there's ever anything I can do..."

I held up my hand to stop him. "Don't Charlie, by the time we leave here, you won't be feeling so grateful." I nodded to Travis, who already had his phone in hand.

"No, no." Lillian cried, springing out of the chair with renewed vigor. "Charlie has to make the call. He has to be the one who turns me in—I beg you."

I nodded to Travis, who put his phone away. Lillian released a wobbly breath. If Charlie called on a cell other than his own, it would raise eyebrows. Charlie took out his phone, looking like it was the last thing on earth he wanted to do. Before he dialed, I asked him to hold off for a minute. Lillian and Charlie exchanged bewildered glances. Travis frowned at me. "I want to speak to Lillian first," I said.

I took her by the hand and led her into the kitchen. I wasn't worried that she'd try to get away. This was her endgame and all that mattered now was protecting her loved ones. "How did you discover that Genna and Tony were involved in what happened to Scott?" I asked.

"I listened to what people said at the funeral and when they called and came to visit me. Little by little I put the pieces together. Maybe the police didn't have enough of what they call *hard* evidence to get indictments on those two, but over the past ten years I'd become convinced they had a hand in taking Scott's life."

"I promise to keep anything you tell me confidential, but I need to know more."

"Were you aware Genna didn't come to Scott's funeral?" I nodded. Genna didn't like funerals, so I'd chalked her absence up to the fact that she and Scott hadn't really been friends. "She never reached out to me in any way," Lillian continued, "not even with a sympathy card. On the other hand, Tony was at the wake and the funeral. He came to visit me a number of times before leaving for college. His concern for me was touching, but it was over-the-top for someone who played such a bit part in Scott's life. Guilt works differently on different people."

"Is that all?" I pressed her, wanting to understand what had made her confident enough that she could take justice into her own hands.

"I listened to what people said, all the gossip. Where there's smoke there is always fire, Kailyn. Even rumors are wrapped around kernels of truth."

"Why didn't you come to me? You know I would have listened to you even if the police wouldn't."

Lillian gave me a tolerant smile, the kind you might accord someone who believed the world was flat. "But how would you have changed the fact that the necessary evidence didn't exist?" she asked.

I had no answer. I considered pointing out that even if Genna and Tony were involved somehow in what happened to Scott, it was still an accident. They didn't kill him, and there was no reason to believe they ever meant him any harm. But it was clear that regardless of what I said, Lillian wasn't going to see things differently. She needed someone to blame, someone to punish.

"It's time," Travis called out to me. He was right. I could talk to Lillian for another three hours and nothing would change. We walked back into the living room, and he nodded to Charlie who grimly punched in 911.

Chapter 37

Merlin suggested holding what we had come to call our investigation *wrap-up dinner* at the lake. I usually tried to be flexible, but this time I used my veto power without a second thought. It might have seemed like the most logical place to celebrate the conclusion of the case, because it had started there ten years earlier with Scott's death. But that fact alone rendered it unthinkable for me.

When Tilly explained this to the wizard, he said he understood, but he walked off grumbling that people of the twenty-first century needed to grow tougher hides. In the end, I chose to hold the dinner in my house or backyard, depending on the weather. Mid-September in New Camel could feel like late summer or a harsh brush with fall. Scott and I had spent so many innocent, joyful hours playing here as children, it didn't matter if we held the wrap-up inside or out. And I decided the dinner should include a memorial. Travis seconded the plan. Tilly swung into action, delegating and baking.

The day dawned, gray and brooding, the temperature just shy of sixty. When it wasn't actively raining, the raw dampness permeated everything, creeping deep into the bones. Travis got a good fire going in the living room and pulled me out of the kitchen to show me the product of his labor. "Did I ever tell you that you're good to have around?" I asked.

He grinned. "Once or twice, but it never gets old." He drew me into his arms, my back against his chest so that we were both watching the flames. Standing there with him warmed my body and my spirit. I would have been content to remain there for hours, but there were things to do before my guests arrived.

"Can you keep the fire going so we can enjoy it after everyone leaves?"

He brushed my hair away to kiss the nape of my neck. "I promise, even if I have to chop down the old oak in your yard for the wood."

I shook my head and laughed. "Some boy scout you were. Don't you know you can't burn wood when it's green?"

He shrugged. "I figure you can come up with a dandy little spell that will age the wood in no time. One of the perks of dating Merlin's greatest granddaughter."

I turned so that I was facing him. "You could be accused of being too glib," I said, planting a leisurely kiss on his mouth. He tried to tighten his arms around me, but I ducked under them and scooted back to the kitchen.

I set the dining room table for seven. Although Elise hadn't been as involved in this investigation, I considered her part of our team as well as my extended family. Besides she was still seeing Jerry the dentist and he was good company for Travis, especially if Elise, Tilly and I got to chatting about girl stuff. I couldn't count on Merlin to talk work, the stock market or sports, at least not the kind of sports that would interest Travis. Elise's son Noah was coming, but her older son Jake had plans with his girlfriend. Time changes everything, but that was as it should be.

Tilly and Merlin were the first to arrive. The wizard carried the large crock-pot of beef stew, with carrots, potatoes, and green peas bobbing in the gravy. My aunt carried the chocolate cake and peach and blueberry pie. Elise brought her veggie lasagna, as well as vanilla ice cream to pair with the desserts. Travis was in charge of the hors d'oeuvres that included his signature guacamole, stuffed mushrooms and pigs in blankets as requested by Noah and Merlin.

I was responsible for the memorial portion of the dinner. I didn't want it to be heavy-handed, so I made poster boards with photographs of Scott at every stage of his short life. I made Genna a board too. It was impossible to know how big a part she may have played in the accident that caused Scott's death, but I'd known her almost as long as I'd known him. They were both good people, inextricably woven into the fabric of my life.

I sorted through hundreds of photos in the big storage bins where Morgana had stored them. Many of the pictures included other people who were also dear to me—Bronwen, Morgana, Tilly, and their once upon a time husbands, including my father. A teenage Elise had made it into a few of them as she was my babysitter way back when.

Every couple of hours, Travis offered his help, but I declined it. The work was cathartic for me. I laughed and cried and said my private goodbyes, before climbing into bed at two thirty in the morning. The next day I set the poster boards on easels in the living room. If anyone wanted to look at them, they could, but there was no requirement to do so.

When we were gathered around the table, there was enough warmth and laughter to make us forget the dismal weather outside. Merlin immediately helped himself to the stew before passing it on to Noah. According to my aunt, he tried to sneak a taste when it was cooking and received a few hearty swats with a spatula for his efforts.

"When do we get to hear about the case?" Noah asked, adding under his breath that he couldn't believe Jake was going to miss this one. The boys had enjoyed learning the whys and wherefores of each case, along with the kind of personal details Travis and I could provide that often didn't make it into the news, even when Travis was the reporter. Some details were better kept in the family.

"Any minute," I said, waiting for the talking and clanging of platters and utensils to die down. When I opened the floor for questions, Tilly's hand shot up.

"Why didn't Lillian ever tell Scott he had an identical twin?"

"Because she didn't know either, until Brett showed up at her door after Scott's funeral. The biological mother, Susan, had just lost her husband in Afghanistan when she found out she was pregnant with twins. She already had two young children and felt she couldn't care for *two* more babies on her own, so she put one up for adoption."

Travis picked up the story to give me a chance to eat. "Lillian had suffered two miscarriages after having Charlie. She nearly lost her life with the last one. So when she and her husband heard about the baby, they thought their prayers had been answered. Susan never told them the child had a twin. As a condition of the adoption, they had to sign an agreement to move out of town. Susan never told Brett he had a twin brother either. She supposedly wanted to avoid the complications of that much honesty. Of course it's all come back to bite her now."

Elise put down her fork. "I can't imagine what a shock it must have been for Brett when he saw Scott's photo in the obituary."

"Finding out more about Scott became his mission," I said. "He wore his mother down until she told him where Lillian lived. When Lillian first opened the door and saw him, she thought he was Scott's ghost. Brett introduced himself and as they talked, she started to see the little differences sometimes only a mother can see. Their shared grief forged an instant bond between them."

"You know what?" Noah said, "I bet when Lillian thought Brett was Scott's ghost, he got the idea to pretend to be."

Travis helped himself to a large square of veggie lasagna. "Exactly right. He wanted to terrify the people who were at the lake that night as punishment. He believes that every person who was there bears responsibility for not trying to stop the binge drinking and for not calling the police, until it was too late."

"Tilly, this stew is the best I've ever eaten," Jerry said, ladling out a second portion.

"Thank you. I'm glad you're enjoying it. Some people just stuff their faces without a word to the chef." She sent Merlin a pointed glance.

He lifted his chin indignantly. "*Stuffing my face,* as you put it, is the highest compliment."

"How did Lillian decide Genna and Tony were to blame when the police couldn't figure it out?" Elise asked, refilling her water glass from the pitcher on the table.

"You could say she didn't require the same level of evidence as the courts," I replied.

Noah frowned. "But what about *reasonable doubt*?"

"I'm pretty sure she didn't have any."

Merlin sighed loudly enough to get everyone's attention. "Can we move on to the important part? I want to know who's going to fry for hiring the hit man. They never talked about it on the news."

"Someone's been watching too many old gangster movies," Jerry said, laughing. "Sorry to disappoint you, Merlin, but the reason you didn't hear about it on the news is because no one is going to *fry.* New York hasn't had the electric chair in over fifty years."

"New York doesn't even have capital punishment anymore," Noah added.

"In that case, somebody please pass the stew."

On my left, Tilly pushed away her plate, her food half eaten. "I'm having a hard time believing Lillian hired a hit man to kill Genna and Tony. Yes, she's always been strong-willed and independent, but arranging to have people murdered—well that's…that's…I'm at a loss for words."

I put my hand over hers. "Aunt Tilly you have to remember, ten years had passed with no justice for her son. She must have felt as if his death had been quietly swept under the rug, while everyone else went on with their lives. She became obsessed with getting justice for him. Her growing certainty that Genna and Tony were responsible for Scott's death must have convinced the others too.

Brett was tortured by the loss of a twin brother he would never have a chance to know. They commiserated with Lillian, piling their heartache on top of hers. They wanted her to know they shared her misery. They didn't understand how adversely it affected her. When they realized what she was up to, they insisted on helping to pay for it. Charlie had a young family to support and Ashley's bakery had only begun to show a profit, but they offered her what they could. Lillian refused, knowing it would make them parties to the crime."

Travis looked at me and raised his eyebrows. I knew what he was asking. We'd gone back and forth about telling the group the last bit of the story. I shook my head. In my heart I believed everyone at the table would promise not to ever tell another soul, but time passes and promises fade. More importantly, it wasn't my decision to make. With Lillian's permission, I had told Travis, because we were partners in the investigation. According to her, Charlie, Ashley and Brett did help pay for the hit man. It was always in cash, small amounts over the months and years, so they couldn't easily be accused as accomplices.

"What about Tony?" Noah asked. "Is he going to prison for shooting Brett?"

"A temporary insanity plea got him out of serving time," Travis replied. "But he has to see a therapist to work through his issues."

Merlin burped loudly. "Now how about some dessert?" Everyone groaned about being too full, but half an hour later, we managed to scarf down far too much cake, pie and ice cream.

By the time my guests were ready to leave, the rain had stopped and the sun was winking through a slit in the clouds like someone peering between venetian blinds. I was surprised by how low in the sky the sun was for the hour. It wouldn't be long before we'd be setting the clocks back to Eastern Standard, bringing night on even earlier.

After everyone left, Travis helped with the last of the cleanup, while I fed the cats. "I forgot to tell you. I bumped into Courtney and the kids in the Glen the other day," he said. "They're doing well and they're crazy grateful for our help in solving the case."

I laughed. "News is your business. How can you forget important stuff like that?"

"I know, it's indefensible. I'll be lucky not to be fired!"

I hit him with the dishtowel. "Well I for one am very glad to hear good news like that." I glanced around the kitchen. Everything was neat and shiny. "Now, did you remember to keep the fire going?"

"You'll have to come see for yourself," he said, taking my hand. Sashkatu, who would normally have been curled up somewhere for a post dinner nap like his brethren, followed us into the living room.

As promised the flames were still dancing among the logs. I plunked myself down on the floor to enjoy the warmth. Sashki, a fan of warmth in any form, joined me. Travis was busy rummaging in one of his pants pockets, then the other.

"Did you lose something?" I asked.

"My memory it seems. I forgot where I put this." He pulled his hand free of the pocket, a small red velvet box balanced between his thumb and forefinger. He knelt on one knee beside me as he opened it. "Kailyn Wilde," he intoned, "sorceress beyond compare, descendent of the great and awful Merlin, will you deign to marry a mere commoner such as I?"

Later Travis would tell friends and family that my mouth hung open for a good minute and a half. He said it was impressive that I didn't drool. "Are you okay?" he asked finally, worry creasing his brow.

"Yes, I'm okay," I blurted out once I got my tongue to work. "But before I give you my answer, I have a few questions for you."

"Fair enough." He sat down next to me.

"Have you given enough thought to what life with me would be like? I must have at least one daughter, if my line is to continue. I have no idea what kind of magickal abilities she might possess. There's also a good chance that at some point I will try to take Merlin back to his proper time and place. I'll need to continue experimenting with time travel in any event. And have you considered how your parents may react when they learn the truth about me and my family?"

"Believe me, I've thought a great deal about all of those things and more. And what I came up with every single time is that I love you and I will make it work no matter what it takes."

"Those are lovely, but very easy words. You—" Travis kissed me, effectively shutting me up.

He tilted his head away for a moment. "Kailyn—Just. Say. *Yes!*"

"Yes. Yes. Yes!" I cried, kissing him again. He took the ring out of the box and placed it on my left hand. It was a beautiful round diamond solitaire, surrounded by blood red rubies.

Two energy clouds appeared in the far corner of the room as if they'd been waiting in the wings for their cue. Morgana and Bronwen were aglow with happiness, bouncing up and down like celestial yo-yos, unable to contain their glee. In less than a minute, they winked out again, for once careful not to overstay their welcome. Sashki heaved what sounded like a sigh of relief.

He turned in our direction to give us an approving bob of his head, after which he took his steps up to his perch on the couch and promptly fell asleep.

Acknowledgments

Huge thanks to my daughter for being the most conscientious beta reader and for driving us to New Jersey at 2 in the morning in the pouring rain.

In case you missed the first delightful Abracadabra mystery, keep reading to enjoy a sample excerpt of the series launch…

MAGICK & MAYHEM

Available from Lyrical Underground, an imprint of Kensington Publishing Corp.

Chapter 1

"You need to summon a familiar of your own," my grandmother Bronwen said. Her voice was easy to recognize, despite the fact that it emanated from a small, amorphous cloud of energy hovering above my new computer. Both she and my mother had been steadfast in their refusal to buy into the technology age, so when she popped out of the ether that morning, I expected a tirade against the computer that now occupied the desk behind the counter. It took me a few seconds to realize that my recent purchase wasn't the subject of her visit. I briefly considered telling her the computer was my familiar, but I didn't think she would see the humor in it.

"Hand-me-downs never work properly," she went on. "Surely we've taught you better."

"Besides," my mother chimed in, from a second cloud that appeared beside Bronwen's, "my Sashkatu is ancient, and the five others aren't worth the cost of their kibble."

"Morgana!" my grandmother scolded, "you mustn't write them off that way. You summoned them and they came. They're our responsibility now. I mean Kailyn's," she muttered. "I keep forgetting that we're dead. In any case, it's entirely possible the problem was more yours than theirs anyway."

I held my breath, hoping my mother might finally realize that arguing about such things was pointless. I'd thought death would mellow the two of them, but so far they'd proven me wrong. Maybe the sudden, unexpected nature of their passing had left their souls on edge, and once they adjusted to their new circumstances they'd put their earthbound bickering behind them. Then again, maybe not. I'd always suspected they enjoyed the verbal sparring far too much to give it up.

"What exactly do you mean it's my fault?" my mother asked indignantly, dashing my hopes. "You didn't have any better success at restoring our mojo than the cats or I did."

"I'd been semi-retired for three years," Bronwen sputtered. "You'd taken the reins of the business!" The chimes over the front door jangled like a bell ending a boxing round.

"Hey, we have company," I hissed at them. "Make yourselves scarce!" They vanished without a second to spare as a middle-aged couple ambled up to the counter. I was grateful I didn't have to explain the presence of clouds in my store.

The woman's eyes were flitting around the shop with anticipation, but her companion looked like a child who'd been dragged to the dentist. I made a mental note to buy a comfortable chair for the men who were coerced into making the trip.

"Welcome to Abracadabra," I greeted them, trying to shake off the negative energy my family had left in their wake. "Take your time browsing. If you have any questions, I'll be happy to answer them. There are some baskets at the far end of the counter to make shopping easier." I'd talked my mother and grandmother into buying lovely wicker baskets instead of the ubiquitous plastic ones available in all the grocery and drugstore chains. They cost more, but they were more fitting for our shop.

The woman thanked me and went to take one, her husband grumbling, "How much do you plan on buying here?"

"Well, I'm sure you don't want to drive up here again anytime soon," she said sweetly as she started down the first of the four narrow aisles. I'd heard the warning in her undertone, but I doubted that he had. Back in my early teens, I'd realized there were certain subtleties of mood in women's speech that often eluded men.

I sat down behind the computer to finish setting up my online banking account. Although the shop wasn't large, it took most people half an hour or more to browse through all the lotions, potions, unguents, and creams with intriguing names and mystical purposes. Until about fifty years ago, the inventory had been smaller, meant specifically for those who were practiced in the arts of sorcery and witchcraft, but that was before tourists discovered our quaint little town of New Camel, New York. My enterprising grandmother had seized the opportunity to add a line of the health and beauty products our family had been whipping up for our own use as far back as anyone could remember. It didn't take long before word of mouth brought a steady stream of customers to our door. The other merchants in the town prospered as well. A couple of bed and breakfasts opened to accommodate visitors who wanted to spend the night. One local resident was able to drum up enough financial support to open a small ski resort nearby. Snow is never in short supply around here in winter.

When the couple returned to the counter, the woman was beaming with success. Her husband was carrying the basket, now piled high with our most popular products. He looked as close to dying of boredom as anyone I'd ever seen. He yawned widely, without bothering to cover his mouth.

"You ought to have a website so people could order your products online," he groused as I rang up his wife's purchases. "You're way out here in the boonies, no public transportation, hard to get to from everywhere. It's a miracle you have any customers at all."

Not a miracle, I wanted to say, just a little magic. But that was one secret ingredient we never talked too much about. "Thanks for the advice," I said instead. "I'll definitely look into it." I had considered going ahead with a website after I inherited the shop, but although Morgana and Bronwen were deceased, they hadn't totally passed on. The thought of arguing with them about it on a daily, if not hourly, basis quickly shut down my enthusiasm for the project. Besides, I was still euphoric about finally having a computer on the premises.

"My friends all swear by your products," the woman said with a smile. "So I had to try them for myself. I told Robert here that we'd make the trip into a bit of a vacation, but for him if there's no golf, it's not a vacation." She sighed and searched my face for some empathy. I nodded and smiled back, though I was finding it hard to relate to her problem. She could have left Robert home and driven here alone or with friends. Maybe it was simply the difference between her generation and mine. Had it been me, I would have preferred to make the trip alone. But then, I've had strong, self-sufficient women as role models all my life. My father left when I was five, and my grandfather, years before my birth. Morgana and Bronwen had carried on as if they'd never really expected their spouses to make the final cut.

Robert took the shopping bag I held out to them. "We should have been on the road fifteen minutes ago," he said to his wife, who was looking at a display of candles infused with healing oils.

"I love your shop," she said as he hooked his arm through hers and propelled her out the door. He pulled it shut behind them so hard that he startled Sashkatu, who'd been sleeping in the spill of sunlight on the windowsill behind me. The cat regarded me with regal contempt as if I'd been the source of the disturbance. Although he was fifteen, his black coat had kept its luster, and his emerald eyes were as sharp and bright as ever. If he pined for my mother, he kept it to himself and slept right through her visits from the other side. When he was done glowering at me, he sighed and laid his head down on the tufted goose-down cushion Morgana had made to ease his arthritic joints. Fortunately the five other cats didn't seem to mind being left back in the house during the workday. I didn't want to think about the destruction they could wreak on the shop's inventory with one high-energy game of chase. If I were to follow Bronwen's advice and summon my own familiar, there would be seven cats to deal with and a bigger bill for cat food and other feline necessities. I kicked that decision to an already-crowded back burner in my mind and prepared to close up for the night.

I was ready when my Aunt Tilly came through the connecting door from her shop, Tea and Empathy. She was my mother's younger sister and my one remaining relative, aside from a few distant cousins somewhere in the wilds of Pennsylvania. Although I loved Tilly dearly, she tended to be a bit scattered and eccentric. According to my grandmother, she was hands down the best psychic our family had ever produced.

She padded up to the counter in one of the frothy Hawaiian muumuus she'd taken to wearing after menopause settled in with some extra pounds. Her ballet flats dangled from her left fingertips and the turban she often wore at work was still perched on her head. She thought it lent her an air of mysticism. I thought it made her look like a Hawaiian swami with identity issues, but I would never tell her that.

"Did you want to wear the turban to see the attorney?" I asked, because I'd never seen her wear it outside the shop.

"Oh my," she said, plucking it off her short red hair and giggling. "Silly me—I forgot I had it on." I laughed too, because even as a child I'd thought of her as Silly Tilly. She plopped the turban onto the counter and finger-combed her curls. I beckoned my purse from the shelf behind the counter and was actually surprised when it popped up and floated into my hand. These days my magick was far from a certainty.

While I set the security code, Tilly slipped on her shoes. My little blue Prius was parked outside at the curb. Tilly climbed, or more accurately fell, into the passenger seat. I tucked in the edges of her dress and shut the door, before hopping behind the wheel.

Jim Harkens, who handled our family's legal matters, shared a small, one-story office building with the town's only dentist. It was less than a three-minute drive from our shops, hardly worth taking the car. But

Tilly had arthritis in her hips and corns on her feet. My mother had tried everything in her bag of tricks, but the ailments had proven impervious to her spells and potions. So we drove to our appointment.

When we pulled into the parking lot behind the building, Jim's big white SUV was the only vehicle there. I pulled into one of the diagonal spots and helped my aunt out of the car. Jim's office suite was off the short common hallway on the left. We opened his door and walked past Ronnie's unoccupied desk. She was Jim's receptionist, secretary, and paralegal all rolled into one. Since she only worked until four, we saw ourselves down to Jim's office. I knocked on the closed door. There was no response, but it wouldn't be the first time I'd found him asleep, his padded chair angled back and his feet propped up on his desk. Although he was on the brink of fifty, he'd confided to me recently that early retirement was beckoning with a Siren's call. I knocked again, then tried turning the knob. Since it was unlocked, I walked in, Tilly right on my heels. The room was dark, bits of sunlight creeping in around the edges of the closed blinds. When I stopped to let my eyes adjust, Tilly slammed into me and sent us both sprawling. If Jim had been awake to see our little vaudeville act, he would have enjoyed a good laugh. But he must have been sleeping soundly.

"Are you okay, Aunt Tilly?" I asked, doing a quick appraisal of my own condition. My left knee had taken the brunt of the fall, and although it hurt, I didn't think it was broken.

"I'm okay, dear. Just had the wind knocked out of me," Tilly said. "Guess I have more than enough padding these days."

Unfortunately she'd landed diagonally across my lower back and legs, softening her fall, but grinding me into the coarse, commercial-grade carpeting. As my eyes accommodated to the darkness, I could see that Jim's chair was empty. Maybe he'd gone to use the bathroom in the outer hallway. I was gathering myself to stand up, when I realized he hadn't gone anywhere. He was inches from where I lay, and even in the dim light I could see what looked like a dark bloody halo around his head.

About the Author

Sharon Pape launched her popular Abracadabra mystery series with *Magick and Mayhem* and followed up with *That Olde White Magick*, *Magick Run Amok*, and *Magickal Mystery Lore*. *This Magick Marmot* is the fifth book in the series.

Sharon started writing stories in first grade and never looked back. She studied French and Spanish literature in college and went on to teach both languages on the secondary level. After being diagnosed with and treated for breast cancer in 1992, she became a Reach to Recovery peer support volunteer for the American Cancer Society. She went on to become the coordinator of the program on Long Island. She and her surgeon created a nonprofit organization called Lean On Me to provide peer support and information to newly diagnosed women and men.

After turning her attention back to writing, she has shared her storytelling skills with thousands of fans. She's won widespread praise for her Portrait of Crime and Crystal Shop mysteries as well as the Abracadabra series. She lives with her husband on Long Island, New York, near her grown children. She loves reading, writing, and providing day care for her grand-dogs. Visit her at www.sharonpape.com.

SHARON PAPE

MAGICK & MAYHEM

An Abracadabra Mystery

SHARON PAPE

THAT OLDE WHITE MAGICK

An Abracadabra Mystery

Printed in the United States
by Baker & Taylor Publisher Services